THE CALL OF INDIAN SUMMER

Seasons of Change Series

Book one: Come Next Winter
Book two: The Promise of Spring
Book three: The Call of Indian Summer

The Call of Indian Summer

Seasons of Change Series: Book Three

**By
Linda Hanna
and Deborah Dulworth**

The Call of Indian Summer
Published by Mountain Brook Ink
White Salmon, WA U.S.A.

The website addresses recommended throughout this book are offered as a resource. These websites are not intended in any way to be or imply an endorsement on the part of Mountain Brook Ink, nor do we vouch for their content.

This story is a work of fiction. All characters and events are the product of the authors' imagination. References to real locations, places, or organizations are used in a fictional context. Any resemblance to any person, living or dead, is coincidental.

Scripture quotations are taken from the *Holy Bible, New King James Version®, NKJV®* Used by permission. All rights reserved worldwide.

ISBN 978-1-943959-66-2
© 2018 Linda Hanna and Deborah Dulworth

The Team: Miralee Ferrell, Nikki Wright, Cindy Jackson
Cover Design: Indie Cover Design, Lynnette Bonner Designer

Mountain Brook Ink is an inspirational publisher offering fiction you can believe in.

Printed in the U.S.A. 2018

Dedication

We dedicate this book to our Lord Jesus Christ. He daily supplies the grace and patience needed. Because of our intimate bond with Him, we want to share with our readers that they can have a close relationship with Him as well.

Thanks to my late husband, Ray Dulworth, for believing in me.
Love always, Deb

Acknowledgments

As always, we're grateful for our families. It takes a lot of love and understanding from them to put up with our unpredictable schedules and scattered minds.

We want to express gratitude to a number of people who made the publication of the Seasons of Change series possible. To the Mountain Brook Ink publisher and staff, Miralee Ferrell, Nikki Wright, and cover designer, Lynnette Bonner, thank you for your dedication and gently guiding us through the process. Your advice, input, and talent have been invaluable.

The people of our critique groups continually help us with their caring, inspiration, and humor. Thank you to: Barb Dixon, Crystal Miller, Darlene Clevenger, and Kim Vallance; and the Marion Writers' Group – Wenda Clement, James N. Watkins, Janice Miller, Dan Fuller, Marcia Gunnett Woodard, Winnie Shaffner, Judy Showalter, and Diana Klueh. Your gifts and talents keep us in awe. Special thanks to Cathy Shouse for her friendship and keen critiquing eye. Deep appreciation goes to our support system at Westview Wesleyan Church (Jonesboro, IN). Your loving prayers and backing continue to be a blessing.

CHAPTER ONE

AUGUST 15TH HAD FINALLY ARRIVED, AND the wedding reception at Powder Ridge Community Church was winding down. Sue North scooted her chair away from the table to get a better view of her only daughter throwing the bridal bouquet. The precious minutes left with Rikki ticked by unbelievably fast. She pushed the thought away as the bevy of beautiful single ladies clustered in front of the bride, their arms waving frantically to catch the posies of hope.

Powder Ridge, Vermont's least-likely-to-get-married woman, Alberta Gilbert, pushed up the sleeves on her polka-dot dress, licked her lips, and stood ready to block anyone in her way. The mere presence of the beefy high school gym teacher had a way of intimidating her former students. Coach Gilbert took the stance and clapped her hands over her head. "Pass it over here, North."

With a chuckle, Sue aimed her cell phone, ready to catch the play-by-play action on video. She heard Rikki call over her shoulder. "It's Mason, now, Coach. Get ready. Three . . . two . . . one!"

The bundle of blossoms flew across the room, ricocheted off someone's fingers and landed in Sue's lap. Alberta lunged for them. Sue fell from her seat, bumping the back of her head as she landed in a blue sequined heap on the floor.

"Sorry. Shake it off, you'll live." The coach lifted the now-frazzled bouquet over her head, did a victory dance in a shower of petals, and then disappeared into the crowd.

Masculine hands gently helped Sue to her feet and guided her to another chair. "Are you okay, Sue?" His comforting voice sounded familiar.

Sue blinked several times and peered into the man's eyes. "Stuart. Thank you." She patted his hand and smiled. "I'll be fine once the bells stop ringing."

Rikki and her new husband, Ethan, came to the table. She knelt and tucked a stray blonde curl behind her mother's ear. "You must have taken quite a hit from the coach. I had my back turned so I didn't see it happen."

"Neither did I." Sue shook her head. "I was focused on filming you. The last thing I remember, the bouquet landed on my knees."

"I'm sure Coach Gilbert didn't mean any harm." Ethan gave her a kiss on the forehead. "She's one determined woman on a mission to land Mr. Dinkus at Dinky Donuts. She's probably at his shop by now."

Ethan stepped aside making room for several friends and neighbors to gather around the table. They offered their congratulations and best wishes to the newlyweds as well as shared their concern for Sue.

After assuring everyone that nothing was hurt except her pride, Sue quietly excused herself and hurried to the powder room. She stood in front of the full-length mirror and checked for damage. No blown-out seams . . . check. Zipper intact . . . check. One earring . . . MIA.

Carol Mason-Bailey rushed in. "Sooze! Glad you're okay. I couldn't get to you any sooner." She gave her a hug and held out an earring. "I think this is yours. Uncle Stu found it on the floor."

"Thanks. I'm glad he helped me to my feet. I've never been so embarrassed." She took the jewelry from Carol, wiped the post, and fastened it to her waiting earlobe. "I couldn't believe Stuart made the long trip from Arizona for the wedding."

"Dad felt he should stay with Mom, and Uncle Stu decided to come in his place. He needed a break from the detailed paperwork and loose ends after Aunt Penny's death. Poor man's been overwhelmed." Carol's eyes softened. "Being widows, both of us remember the legal hoops you have to jump through when a spouse dies."

Sue added a touch of lipstick and looked at Carol's reflection in the mirror. "I'm glad he came. It's good to see him again."

"What a day! I'm whipped." She put a hand on Sue's shoulder. "Everyone's been sharing memories of Bob and how much he meant to them. Of course, they all wanted to meet my new husband." She shook her head. "Bless his heart. Frank's a good sport."

"You're the one who's a good sport. He only has one afternoon to be sized up, but you're under the microscope 24/7 at his church." Sue took one last glance in the mirror. "Are you ready to hit the reception scene again?"

Carol consulted her watch. "Absolutely. I don't know about you, girlfriend, but it's hard to wrap my mind around the fact our babies are married. In a couple of hours they'll be on their way to sunny Cape Cod for their honeymoon."

"And to think it all began when we were in college. God's timing is perfect. If my schooling hadn't been delayed for a couple of years, we'd never have been roommates." Sue nudged her, thankful for the longevity of their bond. "We've spent twenty-three years watching their relationship grow into true love."

"Ethan and Rikki are meant for each other. I'm proud of them for trusting in God's promises and following His will for their lives by working with the orphans at the reservation."

"I agree. That gives me peace in letting them go." Sue released a deep breath as they left the bathroom, linked arms, and walked across the reception hall.

"They'll love working at the Maverick Ranch." Carol gave her a little squeeze. "Those kids need a lot of TLC."

The two friends headed for the table where Frank and Stuart were laughing and drinking coffee.

Sue sat and scooted her chair close to Carol. "With the wedding over, I'm staring at an empty nest, and it has me thinking of my future."

"That's where our faith comes in."

"You're right, and the Lord's stretching my faith." Sue pushed the wayward lock of hair behind her ear and pointed. "The kids have changed clothes and are motioning for us to join them."

Frank jumped to his feet, took Carol's hands, and pulled her up. "Come on. If we want to see them off, we'd better make a mad dash."

"Let me be a gentleman, Sue." Stuart held her chair as she stood.

She grabbed Stuart's hand, and together, they took long strides to catch up to the others.

The women's heels clicked on the polished tile as the quartet headed for the door. Once outside, everyone blew a flurry of bubbles as the newlyweds passed.

Following hugs and kisses, Sue blinked back the tears of mixed emotions. Life was about to change once again. Rikki and her childhood sweetheart were married. Their eyes held the absolute purity of the love they shared, but it went beyond that. They were following the Lord's direction. She wiped her damp cheeks while she and Carol waved their final goodbyes.

After the decorated car drove off, Frank hugged his wife. "Most of the guests are leaving. If you ladies don't mind, Stu and I thought we'd stretch our legs for a while. Call my cell when you're ready to go."

Sue tossed her house keys to Frank. "You guys can go on to the house. Carol and I will take my car." Arm-in-arm, she and Carol returned to the table.

"Moving to Arizona worked out well for you, didn't it, Carol?"

"Sure did. Aunt Penny caused more than a few doubts, but Frank and I persevered." A good-humored grin appeared on Carol's face. "Since you're now an empty nester, why don't you think about moving out West?"

"I've been giving it a lot of serious thought lately. Vermont has always been my home, but with Rikki moving to the reservation, what's keeping me here?"

"Are you staying because of your bakery? You've only had the Pie Hole a couple of years."

"My main concern is Crystal Peak Resort is expanding. Again." Sue shrugged, trying to hide any evidence of the mounting stress. "They prefer working with one company, and my bakery isn't equipped to handle that much production. I don't want to get in over my head with building projects at this stage of my life, but without the resort's business, I'll go under."

"Why didn't you tell me earlier?"

"Sorry about that, but you've had a few things going on in your life too." The corners of Sue's mouth turned up in a smile. "However, the people at church surrounded me in prayer, and the Lord heard them. Last month the Lovin' Oven Bakery Company contacted me. They want to buy the Pie Hole facility."

A brief look of surprise crossed Carol's face. "Really? That's wonderful." She grabbed Sue's wrist. "Lovin' Oven is a huge national outfit."

"They were in a hurry to get the property because of

the location and growth potential of Crystal Peak Resort. I spoke with my realtor, and he suggested I hold out for a better offer."

"You had several upgrades to make when you bought the building from Jerome Harvey. You worked overtime to expand the business."

"Listen to this, the second price they quoted was double market value. They want a quick transaction. Can you believe it? All I have to do is sign on the dotted line and it's a done deal."

Carol squealed and clapped her hands. "How can you pass that up?"

"Who says I did? We close next week." She laughed and waved at the last two guests coming their way. "Hi, Elsie."

The older woman rubbed Sue's arm. "What a beautiful wedding. Rikki was the prettiest bride I've ever seen. Herb and I wish them all the best." Her silent husband nodded in agreement and shook their hands.

When they left, Sue lowered her voice. "I haven't told anyone else yet, but Lovin' Oven also put an offer on the house along with the furniture. The company says it's the most impressive home they've seen in the Powder Ridge resort area. They're buying it for the local head honcho."

"What an opportunity. It's a good thing you checked with your realtor."

"They quoted a more than generous offer." She tilted her head. "Actually, they asked me to take an administrative job, but I'm a baker, Carol, not executive material. Business stuff wears me down."

"Can't blame you there. You hit the half-century mark two months ago." She giggled. "Why take on extra stress in your golden years?"

"Golden years?" Sue's mouth curved into a grin as

she crossed her arms. "Why did you have to bring that up? Remember you're only three years behind me."

"Excuse me, three-and-a-half years."

"All right, then. Three and a half." Sue nibbled on her lower lip. "I can't wait to get out of that humongous house and leave all the bad memories of Grady behind. It'll be nice to have a place small enough to take care of on my own." Her thoughts wandered to a warm cottage with a picket fence, flowers, and a cobblestone walkway.

"We have condos in Apache Pointe with all the amenities you could ask for. I've heard the price is a little salty, but worth every penny. You're the widow of Powder Ridge's answer to Perry Mason, so I doubt cost is an issue."

"It's not the cozy cottage I pictured, but I promise to give it more thought." Sue rubbed the sore spot on the back of her head. "Grady did a lot of terrible things during our marriage, but at least he was a good provider. Rikki and I each inherited more than enough money to live on if we use it wisely."

"Sounds like the puzzle pieces are falling into place." Carol cocked her head and gave a teasing grin. "So, are you saying 'yes' to moving closer to your daughter, best friend, and future grandbabies?"

"Grandbabies? Talk about the ultimate trump card."

Carol giggled. "This is a decision you have to make on your own." She hesitated. "But come on, Sooze, Millie and I could use a third musketeer."

As she and Carol laughed together, the caterers swiped the azure coverings from the round tables. "Speaking of your cousin, how are she and Stuart doing since Penny died?"

"Millie loves being married. Lou's unconditional love is what she's needed all along." Carol fiddled with the button on her navy jacket. "You're not going to believe this, but Uncle Stu and Dad are thinking about retirement."

"Really? Now, that surprises me. They're both full of energy, and Stuart doesn't look a day over fifty-five. It's hard to think of them being ready to retire."

"Dad's sixty-five and Uncle Stu is sixty-four, so they're both old enough to consider it."

Sue shook her head. "Still hard to think of them slowing down. The last time I talked to Stuart, he mentioned interest in Native American Missions. Has he looked into it?"

"He's been working a little on the Maverick Ranch whenever possible." Carol wiggled her shoes on and stood. "I'd like for him to find new friends, but he doesn't see the need. He's fallen in love with all those kids, and they're pretty fond of him too. Rikki called him Poppy last summer, and most of them have picked up on it."

"How sweet." A warm sense of nostalgia engulfed Sue. "She used to call my dad Poppy. I bet Stuart eats it up."

Carol nodded. "He's this loveable guy who reads stories to the little ones and helps to rebuild trust in the older kids. This may not sound like a big deal, but he always brings gum as a treat and now they swarm around him like hummingbirds to nectar. These boys and girls desperately long to feel valued and respected. Uncle Stu has been teaching all of us how to meet their needs."

"You and I know how important it is to find a niche in your life after losing a spouse. I'm glad Stuart found his." Sue gathered their plates and cups from the table then glanced around the room. "Looks like the caterers are ready to clean up. I guess we'd better go."

Sue pulled her car into the drive-thru, rolled down her window, and ordered a large Coke. The tantalizing smell of onion rings made her mouth water. She reached into her purse for the ringing cell phone. "Hi, Carol. I haven't heard your cheery voice since the wedding two weeks ago. You called at a great time. I'm about to go crazy sitting in a long line at Jumpin' Jack's."

"Let me guess. The onion rings, right? Glad I can save your sanity. How are things going with the negotiations for selling Grady's law partnership?"

A yellow van behind Sue honked, and she inched her car forward. "Jillian Ingram is helping me, and things are going great. I honestly feel more comfortable with a lady lawyer. She takes a lot of pro bono cases, which tells me she's not in it for the money."

"It's good to finally have someone you can trust. Fortunately, not all lawyers are like Grady."

"It's difficult to remember when it's all you know." Sue tapped her fingernails on the steering wheel while the smell of deep-fried onions penetrated her nasal passages. "Jillian said the Lovin' Oven contracts went through. I have six weeks to vacate my home." She paused as her stomach growled. "The only thing left is to have Grady's law firm onioned . . . I mean, audited."

"Girl, get yourself something to eat."

Sue nodded as if Carol could see her. "I have more news. As of October first, Apache Pointe, Arizona will be my new home."

Carol screeched. "Do you mean it?"

"I do. Hang on a minute, the drive-thru line moved, and I'm next." Sue pulled up to the window, handed money to the cashier, then reached for the drink. "You know, Carol, the farther away I can get from Powder Ridge the better."

"That makes me happy. My best friend will be living close by just like the good ol' days."

"In a month my world will be a lot different, but I look forward to the change."

"Who knows? There might be a wonderful, compassionate hunk to escort you through your twilight years."

"Okay, knock it off. I'm going to hang up now. Talk to you later." Sue chuckled, turned onto the main drag, and took a sip of Coke. Where would the changes in this new life lead? Her marriage to Grady left many bitter regrets. Having a romantic relationship with any man, hunk or otherwise, made her stomach cringe.

She vowed never to go down that rocky road again.

CHAPTER TWO

IT WAS EARLY OCTOBER WHEN SUE stared out the passenger window of Carol's car as they headed to the Maverick Ranch for Children. Her only view for the last ten miles consisted of five cacti, a mesquite tree, and a few tumbleweeds wandering across the parched Sonoran Desert. From her side mirror, she saw a menacing wall of dust shadowing them.

"All this dirt we're kicking up is probably visible from a Russian satellite." She took a refreshing gulp of bottled water and wiped dribbles from her chin. "I'm still trying to wrap my head around all the stark changes of this past week. I've gone from the lush northeastern mountains to the dry, southwestern desert. Please tell me this move is the right thing."

Carol threw her a smile before turning down yet another rutted, dirt road. "I know it's overwhelming, Sooze, but if I can do it, you can too. Finding a place for you to settle permanently will help you acclimate to the area. That's our next priority."

"Meanwhile, the hotel I'm staying at is comfortable." Sue removed her sunglasses and blew the dust from the lenses. "I'm eager to get to the ranch. This will be the first time I've seen my daughter as a married woman."

"Rikki fits in well with this climate. She and Ethan are happy and thriving with all these children to love."

She scanned the bleak horizon. Desert living wasn't even on her radar two years ago. "This drive seems to be taking longer than the last time I came. When will we get there?"

"About another five minutes. We're on Maverick Ranch property." Carol pointed to the west. "See the tiny little dot on the horizon? That's the house."

"It's bigger than I remember." Sue laughed and Carol quickly joined her.

"Okay, smarty pants. I know you didn't have time to see everything on the ranch when you were here last winter."

Sue shrugged and recalled the ride with Carol's uncle. "You're right. I was disappointed that the house parents weren't there. Stuart and I missed out on the grand tour."

"It's actually a huge home with six dorms plus a room for Ethan and Rikki. Currently, they have a full house with thirty boys and girls. The cooks and ranch hands live separately in small cabins."

"Thirty-two people in one house? It better be big." Sue watched with fresh curiosity as they drove closer to the ranch. In her mind's eye, she pictured Rikki tending to scraped knees and wiping the dirty faces of so many little ones. Her daughter was amazing. Where did she learn to mother thirty children?

"There has to be plenty of space for beds, bathrooms, and a large dining area." Carol rubbed her neck. "They're running at capacity right now, so it's a tight squeeze, but somehow they get by."

Sue pulled a notepad from her purse and jotted down 'create more space' to her growing list of ranch needs. "I'm so proud of Rikki and Ethan. They're taking on a lot of responsibility."

"Don't forget they have help, both with the ranch and the house. The kids are learning to carry their share of the load too." An Australian Shepherd barked and ran to the car as Carol pulled into the circle drive close to the house. She lifted her sunglasses and winked. "That's Shep. Don't let him scare you. By the way, whatever you do, don't mention laundry or we'll be washing clothes all day. There will be plenty of opportunities to help later. Today we're here on business and don't need to be sidetracked."

"My lips are sealed, but I do want to see what's needed in that area." Reluctant to get out of Carol's air-conditioned car, Sue picked up her purse and notebook, then sighed. Searing heat smacked her in the face when she opened the door. She was used to sweet, tempting bakery aromas, and the pungent smells of a working ranch jarred her nasal receptors. Funny, she didn't remember the smells being this bad when she stopped by in February.

After stepping out of the car, Carol leaned in to peer at Sue. "Aren't you coming?"

The heat wasn't helping the barnyard smells. Sue covered her nose with a tissue, breathed through it, and wiped her tears. "It's only 8:30 in the morning and the car's thermometer said it's over a hundred degrees."

"But it's a dry heat." Carol laughed. "Or so I'm told."

"Like an oven." Her attention shifted to movement in the side mirror. Stuart came from the horse barn and headed their way. "Here comes your uncle."

"Hi, Carol." He walked to Sue's door and cleared his throat. "Hey there, Sue! Did you like your cross-country trip?" He took off his work glove and held out his hand to help her.

She took his offered hand. "Very nice, thanks." When she stepped from the car, he pulled her into a casual side hug. "It's good to see you again, Stuart." Sue felt a trickle of perspiration slip down her back. Would she ever get used to the heat?

"I'm glad you're finally here at the ranch, but I need

to get the kids busy on their chores." He pulled a red hanky from his rear pocket and wiped the sweat from his lightly creased brow. "Let's all get together for coffee soon."

"Iced coffee might hit the spot." Sue laughed. "We'll do it for sure."

He waved and headed to the barn.

Sue turned and frowned. 102 degrees outside and the man talked about coffee? She nearly melted in her shoes at the thought.

Carol nudged Sue's arm. "Your thoughts are showing. I know hot coffee in this kind of weather isn't appealing to us, but Uncle Stu and my dad have lived in this heat their entire lives. Unlike us, they're used to it."

"I remember a year ago, sitting on your porch on a day much like this. You were taking a cool bath while I drowned in perspiration."

"You'll never let me live it down, will you, Sooze?"

"Guess I deserved it for trying to surprise you. Let's get out of the heat. They do have air conditioning, right?"

"They have a few ancient window units that suffice for now."

Sue flipped her notebook open and jotted A/C.

The duo headed for the cracked sidewalk which led to the ranch house with two dormers looking out over the vast desert property. They climbed the steps of the wrap-around porch. Old blue ceramic planters filled with red firecracker plants bursting into bloom welcomed them at the entrance.

Rikki Mason came running out of the door, her long, blonde ponytail swaying with every step. "Mom! You're here." She threw her arms around Sue's neck, and they shared a tight hug.

"You'll never know how much I've missed you, Rikki. I didn't know what to do with myself in that big ol' house.

Let me look at you, married lady." She held her daughter at arm's length. "You're glowing."

"The proper term is sweating, Mom."

Sue pointed to the bright red plants. "I can see your special touches already. It's very colorful and inviting. You've done a good job with the flowers."

"The six-and-seven-year-olds love helping me in the flower garden. They have fun getting into the dirt and hosing off later." Rikki turned and gave her mother-in-law a hug. "I didn't mean to leave you out, Carol. Thanks for bringing Mom to the ranch. Ethan will be here in a few minutes. He's in the corral teaching the little ones to lasso."

"My boy's learned how to lasso since the last time I visited?"

"He picked it up pretty quick." Rikki pointed to a couple of men sauntering their way. "Mom, this is Martin Rush and one of the ranch hands, Jack Wolf." She placed her hand on Sue's shoulder. "This is my mother, Sue North, and you both remember my mother-in-law, Carol."

The man with the plaid shirt, red bandana, and sandy-colored sideburns shook their hands. "Howdy."

Rikki smiled. "The kids like to call this guy Flapjack because of his insatiable love of pancakes."

The ranch hand nodded. "Excuse me, ladies, I gotta git back ta work." In the true spirit of Old West courtesy, he touched the brim of his straw hat and moseyed in the direction of the corral.

Martin stepped forward and tipped his Stetson. "Pleased to meet ya, Mrs. North. Everyone calls me Marty." The older man was dressed in blue jeans, a western stitched shirt, and a bolo tie. His dark chestnut eyes danced with friendliness.

"Hi, Marty." Sue's attention settled on his striking

Native American features, the chiseled cheekbones, prominent nose, and firm jawline. As she reached out, he covered her hand with both of his before releasing it.

"Marty is a tremendous help to all of us at the orphanage." Rikki gestured his way. "He's the liaison between the missionaries and the tribal leaders. He also helps with adoptions."

A smile came to Sue's lips. "How long have you worked here?"

"I was born on the reservation, but I've been here working for the Lord for the last twenty-five years." He took off his wire-rimmed glasses, huffed on a lens, and wiped it. "It's been a good life, and I've enjoyed ever' bit of it." As he turned his head to Carol, his steel-gray ponytail came into view. "Nice to see ya again, ma'am."

Carol touched Marty's arm. "Sue and I want to thank you for taking our kids under your wing. It's good to know they're in capable hands."

"It's my pleasure. They're a great addition to the ministry and dedicated to the Lord." He took Sue's elbow and pointed to the large house. "It's gonna be a scorcher today. Maybe we should go inside and get out of the heat."

As they entered the air-conditioned ranch house, Rikki headed for the kitchen.

Marty stepped to his right where a middle-aged man had joined them. "Sue and Carol, this is my nephew, Brian Campton. He lives in Phoenix but comes out here to help in my office once or twice a week."

Sue noticed Brian's tan complexion wasn't as dark or weathered as Marty's. Light crinkles around his eyes suggested he had to be at least fifty. He was every bit as handsome as his uncle, but closer to her age. She straightened the collar on her red-checked shirt and averted her eyes, not wanting to appear interested.

Carol pushed her sunglasses to the top of her head, then reached out and shook his hand. "I'm Carol Bailey. Nice to meet you."

"Happy to meet you too, Mrs. Bailey."

Sue eyeballed the man's salt and pepper hair pulled into a ponytail and secured at the nape of his neck like Marty's.

Brian offered his hand. "Then, you're Sue?"

She smiled and shook his outstretched hand. "I'm pleased to meet you."

"Glad you're both able to join us. I look forward to knowing you better, Miss Sue." Brian's dark eyes gleamed as he firmly held the tips of her fingers.

A hint of aftershave drifted her way, and Sue felt strangely flattered by the warmth of his grip which indicated a sincere welcome . . . and then some. She freed her hand from his, and quickly focused on the old upright piano, trying to regain nonchalance. Granted both men were attractive, but Brian's obvious flirtations made her nervous.

Rikki came from the kitchen and spoke to the men. "These wonderful ladies are here to make a list of things to purchase for the ranch. I need to show them around. Ethan should be here in a few minutes to go over those papers with you and Mom. While you're waiting, help yourselves to the donuts and coffee on the counter."

"Don't mind if we do." Marty rubbed his belly and headed for the kitchen. "Come on, Brian."

Rikki grabbed her mom's arm, pulled her toward the stairway, and motioned for Carol to follow. "Let's go, we have a lot of work ahead of us."

"Once again, nice meeting you, Brian." Carol hurried to join Rikki.

Sue stopped at the bottom of the stairs and sneaked one last glance at Brian. He watched her and gave a subtle nod. As soon as their eyes met, unsettling thoughts raced through her mind. Forget it, girl. You don't need another ride down the bumpy road.

CHAPTER THREE

DURING THE THIRD WEEK OF OCTOBER, Sue eagerly started
the shopping expedition for the ranch. The electricians
had finished rewiring last week and the plumbers
promised to be done in two days. Today she and Carol
would try to make a dent in their extensive list of needed
appliances.

She turned the corner and parked in front of Floral
Scent-sations flower shop. How had her first three weeks
in Arizona gone by so fast? With one final check of her
hair in the visor mirror, she hurried from the car and
headed for the entrance. Hopefully, Carol had finished
her work and was ready to go.

Sue poked her head inside the front door. "Yoo-hoo!
Carol, are you ready?"

"You bet I am." Carol unbuttoned her pink smock as
she came from behind the glass counter. "Give me five
minutes to freshen up and then let the gallivanting
begin."

"This is like the good ol' days. I've sure missed them."
While waiting for her friend, Sue wandered around the
store and stopped at a display of crystal knick-knacks.
She picked up a delicate hummingbird, mesmerized by
the reflecting light.

Stuart came from the workroom, placed a floral
arrangement in the refrigerator case, and hurried to greet
her. "Hi there, Sue!" He cleared his throat, leaned
forward, and gave her a quick hug.

"We meet again, Stuart." She loved how his warm,

kind voice and friendly display of affection made her feel at ease.

"Carol says you're going appliance shopping today. Make sure to tell them you're buying for the Maverick Ranch for Children. They'll probably give you a big discount."

"Great suggestion. Is there any way you could go with us? We have a list of what we want from our online research, but we want to make sure local dealers will follow up on a decent maintenance plan before we buy. We could use your man-brain to ask the right questions and help get the best price."

Stuart glanced at the wall clock. "I can probably get off an hour and a half at lunch time. Would that help?"

"It would help a lot." Sue patted his shoulder. "We'll give you a list of the ones we want, and you can finalize the deal and set up the delivery dates."

"Boy, it's gonna be a hot one today." Stuart whipped out his hanky and wiped his hairline. "By the way, I'm on a mailing list for a seniors-without-partners group. It's called Singled-Out. They're having a meeting the first week in November. I don't want to go alone." He gave a nervous cough. "Carol suggested that since you're fifty and single, you might consider going with me."

Old enough or not, was she ready to attend a senior's gathering? She shuddered as the feeling of obligation roosted on her shoulder; after all, Stuart just agreed to do her a favor. "What kind of meeting is it?"

"I really don't know. The flier said to bring our questions. They probably get a group together to go to the Phoenix Suns games and things like that."

"Sounds interesting." According to Carol, her uncle needed to get out of the house more. This group would be a good way for him to mingle casually and without commitment. Hopefully, this wasn't a ruse to find a single man for her.

"Millie thinks I should find a hobby to keep myself busy. My goal is to make a few new bowling friends and maybe join a league." His hesitation turned into a lopsided smile. "I'd like someone to go with me for the first time. I don't want to come across like a pathetic Elmer Fudd hunting babes."

"Hunting babes?" Sue covered her mouth unable to control a burst of giggles at his joking remark.

"C'mon, Suzie. It might not look right if I ask a man to go with me."

The pleading in his eyes led her to cave to the strange request. "I suppose I can go. Let me know the date and time of your babe hunt."

"Now, wait a second. I only want guy friends. Dealing with gals on the hunt is what I need you for." He wiped his beaded brow again and laughed. "Thanks, glad you're going. I'll feel safer with you as my personal bouncer."

After a busy morning on their feet, Sue and Carol stopped for lunch at The Desert Flower Cafe.

Sue scooted her chair to the table and picked up the menu. "Stuart said he'd meet us here, but to go ahead and order if he's late. He knows we're going to check out condos and houses while he's haggling over appliances."

"I know Uncle Stu comes across as meek and mild, but let me tell you, under his handsome exterior lays a world class haggler."

"Speaking of a handsome exterior, Stuart looks a lot happier and more relaxed than the first time I met him."

"You're right. Aunt Penny's aggressiveness took a toll on the poor guy. In the short time she's been gone, we've noticed the stress in his face beginning to ease."

Sue rearranged her silverware. "When Grady died, I stopped being as inflexible and learned to like myself all over again. It'll take him a while, but he'll eventually get there."

"It's great to watch him heal. If anyone deserves to be happy, it's Uncle Stu." Carol cocked her head to one side. "Meanwhile, I'm starving. Are you ready to order?"

"The spiral ham sandwich platter looks pretty good."

Carol pointed to a picture in the menu. "The Bison Burger is Uncle Stu's favorite. I'm going to get the same thing." She turned and motioned for the waitress who tugged a pencil from her carrot-colored up-do as she walked toward the table.

They recited their three meal choices and the young woman hurried off.

Out of the corner of her eye, Sue noticed Brian Campton coming into the dining area. She looked away, hoping he wouldn't notice her.

Footsteps approached their table. "Hi, Sue." He leaned on her chair. "I thought I saw you."

She rested her forearms on the table and forced a smile. "Brian." Something about the man made her tense. He reminded her of—that's silly, he's not Grady. Furthermore, he's been a trusted member of the ranch board for years. She'd only met him once, hardly enough time to judge him.

"Mrs. Bailey." He flashed a smile at Carol, then returned his attention to Sue. "You've been in Apache Pointe a few weeks now. Are you settling in yet?"

"It's been a hectic time, but I'm working on it. Carol and I are having a great time shopping and catching up on the latest."

"Good for you." Brian straightened his shoulders. "I'm supposed to meet a client--guess I'd better get to our table. Enjoy your lunch, ladies." He began to walk away, then returned to their table, and smiled at Sue. "I was just thinking would you consider going out to dinner with me some evening? I'd like to show you around Phoenix."

Sue glanced at Carol who nudged her foot. In spite of her slight misgivings, she nodded, hoping the shock didn't register on her face. "Sounds nice. Thank you."

"I'll call you later this week and set a time." He handed her a business card and pulled a gold pen from his pocket. "Why don't you write your number on here?"

In the middle of scrawling her number on the card, she stopped and closed her eyes. Giving him her number seemed like a commitment and she wasn't ready. "Would it be all right if I keep your card and call you?"

"That's fine. I understand." Brian nodded and slipped the pen back into the breast pocket of his shirt.

Sue watched him walk away, aware of his broad, athletic shoulders filling the expensive suit jacket. "He seems nice enough."

Carol winked. "And he's handsome too."

"I'm not going to dignify that remark. Finding a man is not on my to-do list, remember?" Sue leaned closer. "But, for curiosity's sake, what else do you know about him?"

"Okay, Miss I'm-Not-Interested. I only know what Ethan and Rikki have told me. He's Marty's nephew and Native American Missions is one of his clients. I think he's on the mission's board of trustees too."

Sue squinted and tapped her chin. "I keep hearing the word client bandied about. Exactly what is his vocation?" She noticed the greeter leading Stuart to their table. "Your uncle's here."

Taking his seat, Stuart flashed his ready grin which accentuated his rugged jawline. "I finally found my girls.

Have you ordered yet?"

Carol nodded. "I ordered gourmet bison burgers for you and me."

"I haven't lived in the wild and wooly West long enough to try bison." Sue unfolded her napkin and put it in her lap. "I decided to stick with the ham sandwich platter."

"They're both excellent choices." Stuart scooted closer to the table. "So, do you have a list of appliances you want me to purchase for the ranch?"

Sue reached for her purse, pulled out her notes, and handed them to Stuart. "Here's a list of all the model numbers. One manager suggested we contact a manufacturer directly for the larger pieces like the refrigerators, washers, and dryers. He said they're very generous to charitable organizations."

"Sounds good." Stuart waved one of the papers. "Do you want me to order the smaller appliances listed here from the store instead of the manufacturer?"

"Right." Carol sipped her water. "I bragged to Sue that you're a world class haggler, so please don't let me down."

"We appreciate you doing all this for us. Let me give you the credit card I use for the ranch." Sue put her hands in her lap, allowing the server to place her platter on the table.

Following Stuart's prayer, Carol squirted ketchup beside her fries. "The manager said they can bundle a deal for us if we're interested. That would save us a ton of money. We'll talk to Rikki and the kitchen and laundry crew to see which day works best for delivery."

"The ranch has been saddled with hand-me-downs for years. It will be great to see them with new, top-of-the-line appliances." Stuart lifted the bun on his bison burger. "This smells good."

"Don't look now, Sooze." Carol flicked a hurried glance in Brian's direction. "But your admirer keeps staring at you."

"Well, stop gawking at him." Sue lowered her voice even more. "And by the way, you never did tell me what he does for a living."

"There's no easy way to say this, my friend." Carol put her hand to the side of her mouth and whispered, "Now promise me you'll keep an open mind."

Stuart pointed to the ketchup. "Pass the Heinz, please."

After handing the bottle to him, Sue took off the top of her bun, and munched on the pickle chip. "Please stop hem-hawing and get to the point." She stared at Carol. "There's something wrong or you wouldn't be acting like this. He's a medical examiner, isn't he?"

"No, silly." Carol licked her lips. "This probably isn't something you want to hear, but from what Ethan and Rikki say, Brian's a nice guy who . . . happens to be . . . an attorney."

Sue couldn't conceal her disgust. "You're kidding, right? You sat there and almost let me accept a date from a lawyer?"

"I couldn't stop that train wreck. Didn't you feel me nudging your foot? Then I remembered you said you weren't interested in him, ergo it shouldn't have made a difference. He's simply a debonair guy who wants to show you around Phoenix. You've worked hard all your life, now it's time to find a little pleasure in it." She laid her French fry down in a pool of ketchup. "You took his card. Are you going to call him?"

Sue shrugged, closed her eyes, and huffed. A lawyer. It all clicked into place now. Marty had mentioned Brian worked with him once or twice a week. "Don't tell me Marty is one of those too."

Carol nodded. "Afraid so. But since he retired, he's been working as legal counsel for the missionaries."

"What's wrong with being a lawyer?" Stuart wiped buffalo juice from his chin. "It's an honorable profession." He took another bite of his burger.

"Let's merely say I have trust issues." Sue's mouth twisted into a smirk. "I've not had the best experience with lawyers."

Stuart tilted his head. "Maybe so, but remember, one wormy apple doesn't spoil the whole tree."

"Okay, Johnny Appleseed." Sue looked from one to the other. "I didn't move all the way to Arizona to find a man. Especially another lawyer."

He pointed his French fry in Brian's general direction. "I don't want you to cross anyone off your list too soon."

"Read my lips, people!" Sue smacked the table and firmly whispered. "I have no list. However, if I did, a lawyer would go under the guy who scraped flat armadillos off the road." She forced a lock of hair behind her ear and looked at Carol. "Understand?"

Carol held up an index finger as she swallowed a bite of her sandwich. "I'm sorry. We won't discuss any possible dates unless you bring it up first."

A gentle expression came to Stuart's face. "Sorry." He patted her hand and then gave a mischievous grin. "Does this mean you don't want to be my date to the seniors group?"

Sue's amusement and embarrassment escalated. "You're making it hard for me, but yes, I'll still go to the meeting with you."

"Wait a minute." Carol's eyes popped as she set her burger on the plate. "You two are going out on a date? Together?"

He waved both hands. "It was your idea for me to ask

her, Carol."

"I'm going to protect him from the onslaught of overzealous man hunters." Sue pushed her half-eaten lunch away and wiped at her smile with a napkin.

"Don't laugh, girls. I'm now an eligible bachelor with a pristine reputation to uphold. Marisol Clayborne from church is already giving me the hairy eye." He shook his head and gulped. "I get the willies just thinkin' about it."

Sue frowned as Carol pulled a phone from her purse. "Who are you calling, Carol?"

"I'm calling Millie, of course. She'll want to know her dad is going out on a date, and it's with you."

Sue grabbed the phone. "Give me that. It's not a real date."

Playfulness radiated from Stuart's grin. "The more I think about it, maybe it is a real date. Stranger things have happened." He quirked an eyebrow.

Sue held her head with both hands. "Et tu, Stu?"

CHAPTER FOUR

Sue had waited nearly two weeks before deciding to contact Brian. So what if he was a lawyer? It wasn't fair of her to judge the man on his choice of career. Plus, she was tired of hotel food. It might be fun to have a night out on the town.

Lively Greek music greeted Sue and Brian as they entered the elaborate restaurant foyer. The delightful aroma of garlic, basil, and oregano made her mouth water.

She smoothed the hem of her coral silk blouse as they passed the small gurgling fountains. "I love this place, Brian."

"Good. I was sure you'd appreciate it." He gently grasped her elbow and directed her to the podium where a cheerful hostess stood.

"Hello." The brunette offered a wide smile. "Welcome to the Pegasi. Do we have a reservation this evening?"

Brian nodded. "Campton."

Her finger ran down the roster. "Yes, here we are. Campton, party of two. Follow me." She gathered a couple of menus and led them between white Corinthian columns. Voices murmured and water-filled goblets clinked with ice as they slowly weaved their way through the maze of hungry diners. The hostess stopped at a secluded corner table. "Your server will be with you shortly."

Brian's manners shone as he held Sue's chair. He softly whispered in her ear. "You're stunning tonight, sweetheart. I'm the luckiest man in the room."

"Thank you." Turning to her date, she found his face so near that she could see the hairs in his nose. She leaned back slightly to refocus on his dark eyes.

He took his seat across the table, adjusted the slide on his bolo tie, and then began to peruse the menu.

Sue gnawed the inside of her cheek as she considered the unfamiliar Greek delicacies, hoping to find something without figs and grape leaves. "You've been here before. What do you recommend?"

"My favorite is the Plaka Plate." He pointed to the menu entry. "It's gyro meat over rice and served with pita bread."

She moistened her lips. Sounded safe enough. "I'd like to try that."

The young server, dressed in a bright red and yellow embroidered vest stood next to her. His hand was poised to write. "My name is Eli. May I start you off with a drink?"

Brian laid his hand on hers. "What would you like, Sue? They have an impressive wine selection."

Her eyes went to the waiter. "I'd like a glass of raspberry tea, please."

With a defeated shrug, her date closed the wine list. "That's fine, make it two."

Eli quickly wrote it down on his order pad. "Are you ready to place your order or do you need a few more minutes?"

"I believe we're ready." Brian cleared his throat. "For the appetizer, we'll have Falafel and hummus."

"And your main course, sir?"

"The lady and I would each like the Plaka Plate."

"Very good. I'll get your order in right away." He picked up the menus. "I'll check back to see if you need anything else."

Sue's gaze went to the older couple arguing at the table next to them.

"Why did you tell the waitress all we could afford was the soup, Henry?" The woman tapped her fingernail on the edge of her ceramic bowl. "Never in my sixty-seven years have I been so embarrassed." She paused. "Are you listening to me, Henry?"

With a napkin neatly tucked beneath his chin, Henry slurped his soup before offering a non-committal "Yes, dear." He was a slight man sporting a curly Salvador Dali mustache. He added a handful of unbroken crackers to his soup, then noisily crushed them with his spoon.

Sue chuckled to herself. Was Henry purposely trying to vex his wife or was he used to tuning her out?

Leaning toward her, Brian spoke softly. "I wish people would mind their manners in an upscale restaurant." He gazed into her eyes. "You're one sophisticated lady, Sue. I can't imagine you'd ever display the same crude behavior. I appreciate that."

"Everyone has an off day once in a while." She sipped her water. "How often do you come to the Pegasi?"

"I bring new clients here once in a while. They seem to enjoy the atmosphere."

"I can see why." She moved her iced tea glass as the waiter placed their appetizer on the table. Each hot falafel ball held a toothpick and sat on top of hummus, garnished with chopped parsley and twists of lemon.

Brian motioned to the platter. "Help yourself, Sue."

After she took her portion, he served himself and waited for her to take the first bite. Although hummus wasn't on her list of top ten favorites, she had an adventurous palate. She popped a falafel ball into her mouth. Not bad.

Finishing her serving, she settled back and enjoyed the large panoramic mural of Greece's brilliant blue

Mediterranean waters. Beyond that, bright colored lights focused on the nearly eight-foot Pegasus fountain centered at the far end of the open courtyard.

"It takes a special lady to handle someone like me." He touched her fingers. "And I think you're pretty special."

Handling him? Sue pulled her hand away, relieved when a man dressed in colorful Greek garb and playing a mandolin came into the dining area from a side entrance. The traditional music grew in volume and tempo as he strolled through the maze of tables and headed to the large patio. Three women stood clapping in front of the fountain. Three men with hands on each other's shoulders danced in time with the music.

Whoops and hollers came from the patrons at the tables.

The dancers' kicks and turns grew as the music swelled. Their lively performance ended with a hearty stomp of their feet and the tallest dancer yelling, "Opa!" The enthusiastic crowd clapped and returned the cheer in unison.

As Sue applauded, a broad, athletic man wearing a western-cut suit approached their table.

He gave Brian a few hard pats on the shoulder. "Haven't seen you around the gym for a while, buddy. Have a big case going on?"

"One right after the other, but now I'm hoping to spend more time with this pretty lady. Dew, this gorgeous creature is Sue North." His face reflected pride. "Sue, this is Dewey Eckert, my favorite sparring partner."

"Hello." Sue reached to shake his hand. Interesting. Brian liked to physically spar at the gym and verbally spar in the courtroom.

The tall man squatted and took her hand. "It's a pleasure to meet the knockout who sucker punched our boy.”

Brian put up his hands. “Okay, okay. Don’t you have someplace to be?”

The man rubbed his square jaw. “Just be careful little lady, the FBI registered those perfectly manicured fists as lethal weapons.”

“Stop it, Dewey. Are you trying to scare her away?” Brian laughed. “He’s quite the kidder.”

“Yeah, I like giving him a hard time. The waiter’s coming with your food.” Dewey sidestepped the server. “I’d better get back to Doris. Enjoy.”

Steam rose from the meals placed on the table in front of them.

The tantalizing aroma of the Plaka Plates surprised Sue. However, disappointment set in when Brian picked up his fork and scooped a bite of meat. He wasn’t going to pray before the meal? She bowed her head and silently prayed.

“Do you know another thing I admire about you? Your commitment to your faith. Here we are in a packed restaurant and you pray anyway.” He picked up his pita bread. “You’ve opened my eyes and that’s a good thing. I need to make a point of doing that. See, you’re already making me a better man.”

“I feel it’s important to give the Lord thanks wherever I am.”

“My mother taught me the same thing. As a boy, I’d sit at her feet while she read the Bible and prayed with me.” He sniffed. “Those were wonderful times.”

Aww, how sweet. Brian’s mother laid a spiritual foundation for him. Was it time to give him the benefit of the doubt? She nervously traced the Greek key design on the rim of her dinner plate. Stuart and Carol were right. Not all lawyers were like Grady.

CHAPTER FIVE

SUE PULLED HER SEATBELT AWAY FROM her neck and glanced at Carol behind the wheel. "Is it normal for the final days of October to be chilly in the evening? I needed a sweater the other night."

"During this time of year, our temperatures tend to be in the comfortable range. Maybe you'll find being a desert dweller won't be so bad after all." Carol switched lanes. "Speaking of the other night, how did your romantic rendezvous with Brian go?"

"Knock it off. I think he tried to impress me. He took me to the Pegasi Restaurant in Phoenix."

Carol flipped on the turn signal at the stoplight. "Really? I've never been there, but heard it's expensive. Did you like it?"

"It was gorgeous." Sue closed her eyes and pictured the ornate restaurant. "Large white columns and lively Greek music gave it a great ambiance. One mural had a lovely panoramic view of the Mediterranean."

Carol looked her way. "You haven't mentioned the Greek food. Did you like it?"

"I can't remember the name of the dish, but it had gyro meat with rice and pita bread. We also had falafel as an appetizer."

"How did you get along with Brian?"

Sue shrugged. "I may have to rethink my opinion about lawyers. Brian behaved like a gentleman all evening and didn't talk about habeas corpus or other over-my-head topics. He wants to take me out again after

I get settled."

"I'm happy for you. Think you'll go?"

"Probably. It was nice to investigate a new place." Sue released a deep breath. "The best part was that Brian didn't push for a goodnight kiss or anything."

Within a few minutes, Carol pulled into Gabby Blythe's drive. "We're here. What do you think of the complex?"

"It's beautiful and well-kept." Sue followed her up the curved walkway, thankful the teasing had stopped. "I'm excited to finally meet Millie's mother-in-law. Everyone has talked highly of her."

"Gabby is one amazing woman. Even with a double doctorate, she's still down-to-earth and approachable." Carol grinned. "Your multi-tasking skills have always been off the charts, but this gal is unbelievable. She leaves me exhausted."

"Hold on, should I be jealous?"

"Not at all." They stepped onto the white-railed porch and Carol rang the doorbell. "Think of what you two dynamos can accomplish together."

"I like this complex." Sue glanced around the well-kept cul-de-sac. "It has a feeling of community, not as formal as the one we saw earlier."

"Mom and Dad live over on the west end." Carol nodded to her left. "They still like to visit with their neighbors as much as possible."

"Good to hear. Your folks are wonderful. Maybe I can tag along the next time you go to see them."

The door opened and a silver-haired woman in a light green skort and matching top greeted them. "Glad to have visitors. Come on in."

As the two ladies stepped inside, Sue immediately caught the faint, lingering aroma of peanut butter.

"Would you like iced tea?"

"Sounds good, Gabby, but first, let me introduce my friend, Sue North."

"I'm happy to finally meet you." Gabby shook Sue's hand. "Carol tells me you're searching for a condo in this complex."

"That's right. She took me to a few other places across town, but they weren't quite what I had in mind. The units here are impressive."

"Finding the right place isn't an easy task, is it?" Gabby pointed to the dining room. "Why don't you gals have a seat? I'll bring the tea, and then we can talk more about it. After we're done, I'll give you a tour of my place."

Carol stood by the table and hung her tan purse on a chair. "It's nice of you to have us over."

"I've been looking forward to it," Gabby called from the kitchen. "Make yourselves at home." Within a few minutes, she returned balancing three filled glasses, a plate of peanut butter fudge, and napkins on a silver tray. "I finally unpacked my mother's silver and crystal. Since none of my boys want to inherit it, I've decided to put it to use."

Sue reached for an ornate goblet. "They're beautiful. Did your mother entertain a lot?"

"Both she and my grandmother frequently held formal dinner parties because my grandfather happened to be a college president, and my dad conducted a symphony."

"Must have been an interesting life." Sue wiped the condensation gathering on her drink. "How long have you lived in your condo, Gabby?"

"A little over nine months, and I've enjoyed every minute of it. If there are any problems, maintenance is quick to respond. There are no solicitors allowed, and I feel extremely protected being in a gated community."

"Always good to know." Sue pointed across the room. "What about the shared wall? Do you hear your neighbors?"

"I haven't heard a peep from my neighbors, but then, they've been in Europe for an extended stay." Her infectious grin turned into a lighthearted laugh.

Sue glanced at Carol and smiled at the older woman's carefree spirit.

Gabby took a drink of tea. "The only fussbudget around here is Phoebe Ferguson. Some call her Sarge because she's a retired WAC and proud of it. You can't miss her place. It's the one with a Hummer parked out front."

After swallowing the bite of fudge melting in her mouth, Sue wiped her fingers on a napkin. "Hope she doesn't play reveille every morning."

"Fortunately, the complex manager outranked her and straightened her out on bugle regulations. Anyway, she complains about everything, including the smell of her own shoe inserts." Gabby grinned. "It is pretty pungent. I make it a point to only visit when she's outside sweeping her porch."

The doorbell rang and Gabby hurried to answer it.

Sue turned to Carol. "She's the bubbliest person I've ever met. It would be a blast to have her as a neighbor."

"I knew the two of you would make a connection." Carol drained her glass. "Are these condos a contender?"

"I like the outside, and what I've seen in here is great." Sue gestured around the room. "Even without a full tour of the available unit, I'm ready to move in."

The booming bay of a hound came from the hall, quickly followed by the click-click-click of toenails wandering into the dining room. A basset waddled across the room to Sue, put his long-eared head on her lap, and blinked at her soulfully.

Millie soon came in after him. "Hi, girls. Mom Blythe said you might come today. If Farfel is bothering you, go ahead and push him away, Sue. His daddy tried to teach him about personal space, but he's a slow learner."

"Farfel's no bother, are you, boy?" Sue patted the little knot on top of his head while his tail thumped against the chair next to her.

"I brought him over because Grandma is going to puppy-sit for a few days." She grinned and lowered her voice. "I won't mention any names, but a certain someone spoils him rotten."

"That's a grandma's prerogative." Gabby gave him a Farfel-sized dog biscuit.

Carol's eyes widened with mock surprise. "Oh, yeah! This is the week you and Lou are going to Texas, isn't it, Millie?"

"Sure is. I've been so excited. The Warble-Heirs are going to cut a new CD in Lubbock." She lowered her voice. "Lou and I are going to make it a second honeymoon too."

A dare-devil spark lit Gabby's eyes. "Va-va-voom, Millie!"

"Sounds like romance is alive and well from Apache Pointe to Lubbock, Texas." Sue winced as the words fell from her mouth. Had she spoken out of turn? She hadn't known Millie long.

Millie laughed. "Speaking of romance, I heard through the grapevine that Brian Campton asked you out."

Sue squinted at Carol. "Must you share everything, Miss Grapevine?"

"I promise," Carol raised her right hand, "it wasn't me who tattled. Mills and I haven't talked in a couple of days."

A giggle erupted from Millie's throat. "My dad

happened to be the leak this time. He also said you weren't too happy about Brian being a lawyer."

Sue frowned at the comment. "What else did Mr. Jabberjaws have to say?"

"Only that the two of you have made definite plans to attend a Singled-Out meeting next week."

"Hold on. Back up the gossip train." Gabby's eyes nearly popped out of their sockets as she scooted to the edge of her seat. "Stu Drake asked you out on a date?"

"Not an official *date* date. We're going to broaden our horizons and find out more information for singles. This isn't a big deal."

Carol chuckled. "I beg to differ. He said he has a pristine reputation to uphold and chose Sue as his shield."

"I'm practicing my Miss Piggy karate chops now." Sue wildly chopped the air.

"Thanks for getting Dad out of the house." Millie stood as her phone beeped with a text. "It's Lou reminding me to get home soon." She smiled at Sue. "I hope you take one of these condos. Mom Blythe really likes it here."

"I'll talk to the manager tomorrow and walk through the vacant apartment with my checklist." She turned to Gabby. "Would you mind having me as a neighbor?"

"This cul-de-sac is sadly in need of another fun person. I'm getting tired of being the lone voice of jocularity around here."

Carol threw an arm over her friend's shoulder. "Take it from one who knows; Sue North is the perfect addition to your neighborhood."

Three days following Sue's purchase of the empty condominium in Gabby's cul-de-sac, she stood in front of it and blew a long sigh of contentment. Her new home. One she'd picked out herself, not something Grady chose for appearance's sake.

The stately house she'd left in Vermont less than two months ago loomed in her memory. This light and airy condo represented more of her taste than the dark mausoleum where they once lived. Fortunately, the few things she'd treasured most were waiting in storage.

The day began with one of those golden October sunrises. Sue watched the empty U-Haul pull away from the cul-de-sac. Striking out on her own was daunting, but she'd never been happier.

She breathed in the cool, crisp air as Gabby approached. "Welcome to my new abode, neighbor. Come on inside, pull up a box, and sit for a spell." She held the door open so the woman could go inside.

Gabby's gaze wandered over the anemic apartment. "I love what you've done to the place. The monochromatic color scheme tells me a lot about your psyche."

Wiping her hands on a paper towel, Sue nodded. "It's called Corrugated Modern. As you can see, I'm not one to think outside the box."

"Good one." The older woman gave her a thumbs up and then sniffed the air. "Do I smell fresh brewed coffee? I sure wouldn't turn down a cup, should it be offered."

"Sorry, the movers beat you to it. I'll make more." Sue put coffee grounds in the filter, added water, then pointed to the counter. "I have ooey-gooey cinnamon rolls up for grabs, in case you're interested. They're still warm from the oven."

"In case I'm interested?" Gabby reached to help herself to a pastry. "One more reason to be thankful you live across from me."

Sue placed her fist on her hip. "Before I dole out my baked goods, you are here to help, right?"

"I can be bought with an extra cinnamon roll." Gabby sent her an innocent look and crossed her heart. "I promise to work between bites."

The doorbell chimed and Sue hurried to answer it.

A short tank of a woman with dark curls pushed her way inside. "The name's Sergeant Phoebe Ferguson. You'll find my quarters two doors down from Mrs. Blythe." Loud clomps from her steel-toed shoes echoed on the Spanish tile in the foyer.

"Hi, Ms. Ferguson. Glad to meet you." Sue forced a smile as the assertive neighbor sidestepped her and headed for the living room. Gabby had described her military presence to a T. She fought the urge to stand at attention. "I'm Sue North."

"I've heard." The sarge made a sweeping assessment of the room. "Where's Blythe? I observed her coming to your door at 0800."

Gabby stood at the kitchen door holding a Styrofoam cup. "Here I am, Phoebe. You're limping today. Did you hurt yourself?"

"Talk about vexation to the nth degree. I put new industrial strength Reek Eaters in my shoes, and they brought on a chemical reaction with my medicinal orthotics." She frowned. "That's what happens when you wear civilian shoes. Glad I keep these military issues for backup."

Gabby shook her head. "Bless your heart. You need to go to the Army Surplus Store and get another pair, then you can trade off once in a while."

"Might splurge and get two pair." Phoebe raised her head and sniffed the air. "Exactly what I thought, cinnamon."

Sue offered a sympathetic smile. "I'm not being very

polite. Would you like a cinnamon roll and a cup of coffee?"

"Roger that. A cup o' Joe sounds good. I'll take a couple o' them rolls too before heading home." She reached for the cup Sue offered. "Thanks. Give a shout if you need help with the spit and polish detail. Otherwise, looks like things are squared away here."

"Thanks for stopping by." Sue gave her the cinnamon rolls in a bag. "I hope you enjoy these. I'll walk you to the foyer."

Sue shut the door and eyeballed Gabby. "I think I've been drafted."

CHAPTER SIX

AN EARLY NOVEMBER RAIN DRIZZLED DOWN the windshield. Sue reached for the umbrella on the floor by her feet while Stuart pulled into the parking lot of Apache Pointe Senior Center.

She popped a Sassy Lassie breath mint into her mouth. "Do you have your list of questions ready?"

"Yeah, I've got a few on retirement." Stuart patted his pocket, then turned off the windshield wipers and ignition. "Let me be a gentleman and get the door for you, Suzie."

"Okay." In all the years of marriage to Grady, the man had never opened any doors for her. She could get used to this. What a handsome gent Stuart was. As he helped her out of the car, she smiled at him. "I'm not used to such chivalry. Thanks, Stuart."

"You betcha, m'dear."

As they walked to the senior center entrance, three women dressed to the nines approached. The tallest wore a red-and-white hat which bobbed as she dodged a large puddle. Stuart pasted a smile on his face, took a sweeping bow, and gallantly held the door for them.

Sue stepped aside and let the trio go ahead. "Looks like you've become the official doorman for the night, Stuart." She lifted her hand for a high five.

"Enough of the chivalry." He grabbed her hand and pulled her into the building behind him. "Did you see the way the hat woman looked at me?" He cleared his throat. Twice.

"I couldn't help but see it. The cat in the hat checked you out, you silver hunk."

Stuart held his breath and stared at her for a second before bursting out in laughter. His undiluted glee ended with a substantial nasal snort.

"Mighty attractive, Stuart." She giggled. "We'll have to work on your mating call."

He bent over, shoulders shaking as he chuckled and pinched his nose. "Stop making me laugh."

She took his arm and led him to the registration table. They both took a card and began to fill it out. Sue finished first and handed it to the man behind the table.

"Here's your nametag, and that'll be a ten dollar membership fee for each of you, please."

Sue glanced at Stuart who mumbled about his email address. She had no desire to join this group, but it seemed important to Stuart. She placed a twenty-dollar bill on the table and pointed to her befuddled escort. "This is for both of us."

Stuart shook his head. "Does this look like my email address?"

"Who knows? I've never emailed you. We'll call it close enough." She waved her hand. "Turn your card in. There are people behind us."

Stuart released a soft cough, placed the card on the table, and joined Sue. "Great. Now we're going to get swamped with junk mail."

She laughed. "Let's get inside and find a seat in the rear. As my first official act as your bouncer, I suggest you find a seat on the end of the row, then the hat lady can't sit next to you." She grinned and nudged his arm. "You were right about the babes."

"I know. There has to be a ratio of four to one." He frowned, wiped his brow yet again, and lowered his voice. "Those aren't good odds to come up with a bowling team, and I'm not going anywhere with a busload of jabbering women."

Once inside the main room, Sue and Stuart were shocked to find individual tables, each with two chairs.

A slight man dressed in a tan suit and cowboy boots came and greeted them. "Put on your nametags. One man, one woman at a table, please."

Stuart instantly grabbed Sue's arm, dragged her to the closest table, and pulled out a chair for her. "You're my date for the evening and don't forget it."

Glancing around the room, Sue sat on the offered chair. "This has to be the strangest set up for a meeting I've ever seen."

"Maybe they're going to feed us."

A buzzer sounded. "Find your seats, ladies and gentlemen. We want to welcome our newest members this evening. As you all know, we have eight minutes to ask our questions before the buzzer sounds."

Stuart nodded to Sue and pulled the list from his pocket. "See, I told ya."

"Once you hear the buzzer, the men move on to the next table."

Stuart's eyes glazed over.

"When you find a possible match, jot their name down on your little notepad. The questions are a particularly important part of finding the love of your life. On the count of three, start asking your questions to the person with you at the table. Ready? One . . . two . . . three."

He stared at Sue, his eyes wide and fearful, like a deer in the headlights. "What in the world?"

Embarrassment heated her face. "Stuart, you nut! You brought us to a speed dating event." Why hadn't she Googled the Singled-Out group prior to coming?

His brows drew together in a puzzled expression. "A

speed what?"

"We're supposed to ask these people personal questions to see if we want to date them."

Stuart gasped. "Date? This is a setup. I guarantee there wasn't one word about dating on the flyer."

"We're in it now. Let's make the best of it." Sue rolled her eyes. "Who knows, we might find our true loves tonight."

"What do I say?" He wiped his hands on his pants. "I don't want to know about these people."

"Then I guess you'll have to answer their questions, Stuart."

He moaned and his eyes filled with panic. "Let's get out of here!"

The buzzer sounded. "Gentlemen, please move to the next table."

Metal chairs scraped across the tile floor. Stuart submissively stood. "Ahem." He threw one final pleading look at Sue.

"Go ahead." Sue waved Stuart on and watched him sit down with his hands pressed between his knees. The silver-haired woman with dark streaks looked to be in her late fifties. She wore a zebra print outfit from head to toe.

When Sue turned around, a man with a mustache and goatee had already planted himself at her table. Definite hunger welled in his eyes.

"Let's get started." He rubbed his pudgy hands together. "I'm Curtis Hunter, owner of Hunter's Gun Shop. You might remember me from my commercials." He puffed up his chest. "I don't wanna get rich, I just love to sell guns. Heh-heh-heh!"

His nasal voice was as irritating as a swarm of Vermont mosquitos. Sue bit her lip and sunk in her chair. She would never tease Stuart about the overzealous man hunters again. "I'm sorry. I'm new to the area and haven't seen your commercials." She jotted his name down and drew a gun next to it.

"Okay, then. I'll start with the questions. Do you like to shoot?"

"I wish I had a gun right now." She didn't know if she'd use it on herself, on this man, or maybe Stuart for dragging her here. Someone definitely would be losing toes, for sure.

Curtis rested his beefy elbow on the table. "So, do you have a question for me?"

She couldn't look him in the eye. "If you were a wild animal, what would you be and why?"

"Uhh, I've never been asked that before."

While Curtis busily drummed his fingers on the table, Sue glanced at a red-faced Stuart sitting with his head in hand. The zebra woman chattered non-stop. Served him right. Boy, was he ever going to hear about this on the way home.

The buzzer sounded again. Curtis gave her a limp handshake and moved on.

She looked for Stuart, but lost him in the sea of dating hopefuls. Then, from across the room, she heard Stuart's resounding, "Ahem."

"Pardon me."

Sue turned toward the soft voice. This new man happened to be a definite step up from the happy gunman. She peered at his chin dimple. No, make it three steps up. Not even on the same staircase.

His smile seemed genuine. "Me name be Cameron Brewster, and I be a driver for Dolly McElf snacks."

The unexpected Scottish burr made her sit up straight. His rolling Rs came too fast. She'd have to pay close attention to his sentences. "Hi, Cameron. My name is Sue, and I'm new to the area." She wasn't going to give anyone her last name.

He nodded. "Where be ye from, lass?"

"Born and raised in Vermont." Oh crud. That information nugget slipped out. Hopefully he didn't write it down.

"Aye, Vermont. How do ye like Arizona living?"

"I've only been here a few weeks. To be truthful, it feels like living on the smokestack of Hades." That statement made her sound as obnoxious as the gun seller. "I shouldn't have put down the great state of Arizona. Sorry. It's a lovely place." She relaxed a bit and pretended to check a list of questions.

He chuckled. "Aye, ye be right the first time, lass. 'Tis a dreadfully hot place, fer certain. I may be usin' that sayin'."

"Where are you from . . ." She paused and glanced at his nametag. "Cameron?"

"Me birthplace be Loch Ness, Scotland, with a wee bit o' time away for university." He scooted his chair closer. "Do ye think yer cup be half empty or be it half full?"

"Right now, I'm thankful the cup can be refilled." Sue clamped her lips for a moment and took in his neat appearance. He might be hard on the ears, but he certainly wasn't bad on the eyes. "Would you mind telling me how old you are, Cameron?"

"Not at all. I be fifty-five in January." He glanced at his list of questions. "Have ye e'er been married, lass?"

Sue nodded. "For twenty-six years." A pang of bitterness clenched her stomach. Would the resentment of Grady ever fade enough for her to find another man? Did she want someone else?

"That be a long time. So . . . yer divorced, then?" His eyes slightly narrowed as he asked the question.

Sue shook her head. "I'm widowed and have one daughter. Have you been married?"

"Unfortunately, the right lass ne'er turned up on me doorstep. I be determined to keep waiting fer Miss Right instead of settling for Miss-Stake."

The buzzer finally sounded again. Cameron stood, gave a slight bow, and shook her hand.

An hour and six painful interviews later, Sue reconnected with Stuart. Perspiration soaked his unbuttoned shirt collar.

"Let's get out of here, pronto. My knees are shaking." He guided her into the hall and handed her the car keys. "Will you drive?"

"Was it really that bad?"

A groan emerged from his gut as they stepped outside into the cool evening air. "Remember the cat in the hat woman?" His eyes grew large and wild. "She wants me, Suzie-Q."

Sue laughed. "Hey, this fiasco was your idea, buster, so own it. Even your lady can't be worse than the guy who loves to sell guns." She looked into Stuart's terror-filled eyes and added, "Heh-heh-heh."

"At least he's not stalking you. And she's not my lady." Stuart shivered. "I think we need a caffeine fix. Let's go to Perky's on the bypass."

"Poor Stuart's traumatized. Let me open the car door for you."

"I'd 'preciate it." He sank into the passenger seat and looked up at her. "If I ever have another lunkhead idea like this one, you have my permission to smack me upside the head."

She slid behind the steering wheel, turned on the ignition, and sat staring out the windshield.

"What are you waiting for?" His voice pled in genuine concern. "Step on the gas, girl."

"Since I don't know how to get to the bypass, you'll have to give me directions. Which way do I turn?"

"Turn east at the stop sign."

Sue looked at Stuart. "East? You've got to be kidding." She shrugged and flipped on the left signal.

Stuart took a deep breath. "Try the other east."

Ten minutes later, he had directed her to Perky's Coffee Shop. They stepped inside and found a corner booth.

"What would you suggest I order, Stuart?"

He wiped his brow one more time. "I don't know about you, but this ol' boy needs a double shot of espresso."

"And it's a definite no for this ol' gal. I don't want to have nightmares about Curtis Hunter selling me guns." She peeked at him and grinned. "But if you want to dream about the cat in the hat using you as a scratching post, you go right ahead."

Stuart's mouth pulled into a sour twist. "Point taken."

The waitress came to the booth and set two glasses of water on the table. "Hi, Stu."

"Hi, Pickles. I'd like to introduce you to our family friend, Sue North. She and my niece, Carol, have been buddies for years." He glanced at Sue. "This is Juanita Dilley. Everyone calls her Pickles. She's Perky's sister, and they both go to our church."

Sue held out her hand. "It's nice to meet you, Pickles."

"Likewise, I'm sure." The waitress looked from Sue to Stuart. She sent a sly wink to him and drew a pencil and notepad from her apron pocket. "Okay, lover boy, what's it gonna be?"

"Don't be thinkin' what I think you're thinkin', Pickles. It isn't like that." He coughed into his fist. "Now, how's your day been?"

Pickles rested a hand on the table. "We've had a busy

one. Thankfully, my shift's almost over. The two of you are my last customers."

"We'll try not to take too long, then." Sue looked into the woman's weary blue-gray eyes. Did Pickles seriously wonder if they were a couple?

"That's okay, honey. Have you made your choice of drink? We have both hot and cold coffees plus assorted teas."

Sue held up the menu and pointed to her order. "I'd like to try a half-caf, double grande," she paused and placed her fingers on the words, "Whipped Coco-Loco-Mocho."

"Sounds good." Stuart nodded. "Make it two, along with a large piece of cherry pie with lots of whipped cream." He picked up his water glass.

Pickles winked at Sue. "Do you want your own piece of pie or would you rather have two forks?"

Stuart bent forward, choking on his water.

Pickles chuckled. Her chubby hand pounded the middle of his back. "Don't worry, Stu. Your secret rendezvous is safe with me."

"No, no." Sue brought a hand up to stifle her giggles. "He had his rendezvous earlier this evening, didn't you, Stuart?"

"Oh, really?" Pickles leaned forward. "I'm all ears. Tell me more."

"Sue!" His face had turned a bright red. "I'll have you know there was not a hint of rendezvousing, Pickles."

"If you say so." She turned to Sue, her mouth quirking with humor. "What have you decided about the pie, dear?"

"I wasn't going to have any, but suddenly cherry pie sounds delicious. I'll have a small piece, without whipped cream, and my own fork, please."

The giggling waitress nodded and left with their

order.

"I'm sorry about teasing you, Stuart. You've had a lot of stress this evening."

"Let's not mention Cat Lady ever again." Stuart offered a weak smile. "So, tell me about your interviews. Did you meet anyone you're interested in?"

"One guy wasn't too bad compared to the others. His name is Cameron, never married, and he's a truck driver for Dolly McElf."

"You and the Pillsbury Doughboy have baked goods in common. Sounds promising. Tell me about the others. Anyone else catch your eye?"

"I've already mentioned the Hunter gun guy, but another one stood out."

Stuart shifted in his seat. "Do tell."

"While I concentrated on writing Cameron's name on my one-person list, this guy came to my table dressed in a suit jacket. He had a flower in his lapel and a silk tie. The large tie tack had a capital D engraved on it."

"Sounds pretty spiffy . . . for the nineteen-sixties." Stuart chuckled. "Did you like Lord Fauntleroy?"

"Wait, there's more. He had matching cufflinks too." She crossed her eyes. "However, when the buzzer sounded, he stood. Dapper Dan wore plaid Bermuda shorts with black garters holding up his red socks. Talk about stunned. I don't remember a word he said."

Stuart guffawed and smacked the table. "He'd be a good match for my feline stalker. Did you write his name down?"

"No, only Cameron's. He seemed nice enough. What about you? Did you make any connections?"

"I saw one good-looking gal. Toni Phelps."

"The one wearing the zebra print clothes, right?" She tried to envision Stuart draping his arm around the lady who had silver hair with coal black streaks.

Stuart nodded, placed both elbows on the table, and twisted the corner of his napkin. "She's a retired algebra and trigonometry teacher. She might be a little over my head, but as long as she doesn't test me on equations, I should be okay."

"So, will you ask her out?"

Concentrating on his napkin, Stuart mumbled. "Thinking about it. At least her name's on my list. I'm not sure about the whole dating thing. Solitude is nice." He looked up and raised his hands. "I only wanted to join a bowling league. Ball games sounded good too."

CHAPTER SEVEN

SOFT MUSIC, TOGETHER WITH THE HIGH ceilings and crystal chandeliers, created a pleasurable ambiance at the Grand Oasis Inn. "I'll have what he's having. Thank you." Sue handed her black and gold menu to the waiter.

Brian checked his cell phone then pocketed it. "You look beautiful tonight. Those sapphire earrings make your blue eyes sparkle."

"Thank you." Leaning into her curved back seat, she sent him a Mona Lisa smile. "Brian, I'd like to ask you a legal question."

"Sure, go ahead. It'll even be free of charge." The ice cubes in his glass rattled as he took a drink of water.

"You're too kind. My husband's financial advisor finally sent the documents I've been waiting on to update my will. This should be the last of the paperwork I need amended. Who would you recommend to help me?"

Brian raised his eyebrows. "Wouldn't you rather keep the original attorney?"

She hoped he wouldn't ask questions. "No, and let's leave it at that." The last thing she wanted was to have Grady's old law partner involved in any more of her legal work. She didn't trust him any more than she'd trusted her late husband.

"Rewriting a will is an easy job. I can do it for you like this." He snapped his fingers and threw her a confident grin.

Queasiness briefly fluttered in Sue's middle. Her past experience with lawyers told her not to mix business with friendships. She glanced away. What bothered her most? His title of attorney, or the fact he was a man?

"You seem to be hesitating, Sue. I assure you, my twenty-five years in the most prestigious law firm in Phoenix makes me highly qualified."

What should she say to prevent hurting his feelings? She adjusted her position at the table and bit her lip. "Thanks for the generous offer, Brian, but in all honesty, I'd feel more comfortable keeping friendship and business matters separate. If you could just recommend someone."

Even in the dim restaurant light, she knew instinctively his inner lawyer ego had already formed a closing argument.

He leaned forward, took her hand, and rubbed her knuckles with his thumb. "Think of it this way, wouldn't it be better to have someone who genuinely cares about protecting your assets and your future?"

She slowly drew her hand free from his grip, her mind devoid of any rational excuse. "I see what you mean, but—"

"Okay. Call my secretary Monday morning, and she'll make an appointment for you." Brian propped his elbows on the table and steepled his fingers. "We'll get it taken care of in no time."

Her mind registered something akin to déjà vu. Brian seemed to be exhibiting the same controlling style as Grady. How would she get out of this? Sue squirmed. "Thanks for your advice. I'll be sure to think about it."

"I'm here to help you get through the process with the least amount of hassle." He offered her a quick smile and then glanced away. "If you want my assistance, come to my office."

Sue licked her dry lips and took a sip of water. She wanted to kick herself for bringing up the topic in the first place.

"I like helping my friends." Brian reached over and held her hand again. "And, I think we're going to be very good friends."

Ignoring the last remark, Sue carefully withdrew her hand and focused on the server as he placed their meals on the table in front of them. She unfolded her napkin and spread it on her lap. "What do you do for fun, Brian?"

"As you know, I enjoy going to the gym three times a week. I actually picked up boxing in college and find it's still a great stress reliever." He drummed his fingers on the table. "I also like to visit Hunter's Gun Shop for target practice. He has one of the busiest firing ranges in the area."

Her smile faded. "I've heard about the place. That's where the owner doesn't want to make money, he just likes to sell guns."

"You've seen those creepy commercials." He laid his fork down and gave an exaggerated shudder. "I have to mute the television every time it comes on, but I do like to hang out there."

At least the man had good commercial discernment. Sue shrugged. "You must have a love for guns. Interesting. Other than being a lawyer, what's one job you'd love to have?" She carefully watched for a reaction.

"Don't have to give it a second thought. My ultimate goal is to be a judge. And I will be one day." Brian wiped the corners of his mouth, then offered a grin. "I have influential friends who are supporting me."

Sue's stomach did a catawampus somersault. "Very ambitious." She wondered if he craved power like Grady, or to be a hero and restore decorum to the judicial system. Either way, the truth would eventually come out. It didn't matter right now since she only wanted a casual friendship with him.

"So, you've been in Apache Pointe for about a month now, Sue. Are you retired, or will you be looking for a job?"

"Haven't decided about retirement yet, but, for now, I want to take time off to settle in and learn my way around. Spending time with my daughter and helping her at the ranch are extremely important to me."

"That's good." Brian toyed with his linen napkin. "When the Native American Missions board studied your daughter's resume, I noticed your family lived in Powder Ridge, Vermont. Quite a contrast from Arizona. Do you mind my asking what kind of job you had there?"

Sue set her glass down. "I worked in a bakery for several years." *Better be careful not to say too much. He didn't need to know she owned the business.*

"Sounds like a sweet job for a sweet lady." Brian chuckled at his joke. "No wonder you knew what kind of appliances they needed at the ranch kitchen."

"Cooking and baking for a crowd every day requires reliable, heavy-duty equipment. Buying the cheapest is never the cheapest."

Brian nodded. "I'm impressed you have the means to supply their needs. It's awfully generous of you." He used his knife to cut the chicken breast and held the bite mid-air. "Would you like to return to that line of work?"

"I might consider it, but maybe in a different capacity." Sue spread butter on her baked potato. *She liked how Brian seemed interested, but his slick way of getting personal information bothered her. Maybe she was being paranoid.* "I enjoy the challenge of decorating wedding cakes the most."

"Was that your full-time position at the bakery?"

Sue returned the crystal peppershaker to the table. *Why was it so important to him? Time to be careful and* vague. "I only filled in whenever the orders piled up. Usually I baked cookies."

"From what I've seen and tasted at the ranch, you have a wide range of baking abilities." He patted her hand. "Your cookies and sweet smile have definitely won me over."

The following Sunday morning, Stuart made his way to the sanctuary of Apache Pointe Community Church, relieved to get away from Myrtle Faye Dunlap and Veda Smith. The two widow ladies had pestered him all through Sunday school with their continual offers of breath mints, chewing gum, and Butterscotch Life Savers. Their undivided attention fed his social anxiety.

Visitors filled the row where he usually sat with Millie and Lou. After greeting all five guests, he settled comfortably into the seat behind them, and glanced at his bulletin. Today was the all church carry-in dinner. How could he have forgotten?

Sticking the paper in his Bible, Stuart stretched his arms across the top of the pew, and kept an eye out for his daughter's arrival.

Without warning, heavyset Veda with her salt-and-pepper hair, plopped down on his left. Their closeness gave the appearance of his arm around her. As he scooted away and attempted to remove his arm, Myrtle Faye slid in on his right. She smoothed out her blue geometric print dress, smiled demurely, and batted her doe eyes. The soundtrack from Jaws rang in his head.

There he sat, sandwiched between the hungry competitors with no place to go. Sweat beaded in his thinning hairline. He anxiously searched the room for

Millie and Lou. Of all the Sundays for them to be late for service.

The congregation stood for opening prayer. The overpowering aroma of Parisian Midnight wafted his way as Veda sidestepped closer. Stuart automatically hedged her approach and bumped into Myrtle Faye. He felt Veda nudging against him . . . again.

Soft giggles came from the pew behind him. When he peeked over his shoulder, Carol and Sue straightened their faces. He rarely rolled his eyes in disgust, but this definitely turned out to be one of those eye-rolling situations. *Please Lord, don't let this be one of Pastor Frank's long-winded Sundays.*

By now, Myrtle Faye and Veda were closing in like a bench vise. His claustrophobic senses piqued. It was fight or flight, but he didn't have room to spread his wings.

Music welled around the sanctuary. Apparently, he had missed the pastor's amen.

The music director held up a mic. "Let's welcome each other while we sing, "The Family of God." Altogether now." He lifted his baritone voice to the familiar words. "I'm so glad I'm a part of the family . . ."

Veda immediately grabbed Stuart's hand and shook it vigorously. "We can sit together at the carry-in."

Myrtle Faye clutched the pew in front of her and leaned forward. Her pitchfork glare sent a primitive, non-verbal message to Veda.

Not to be outdone, Veda's venomous whisper took on a serpent-like hiss. "I saw Stu first." She narrowed her eyes at the adversary, hooked a beefy arm through Stuart's, and tossed her a self-satisfied smirk. "He's sitting with me at dinner."

That did it! The duo of dueling dowagers had crossed the line.

The congregation sat. Not wanting to sit cheek-to-cheek-to-cheek, Stuart tripped over Myrtle Faye's size ten-and-a-half orthopedic clodhoppers as he climbed out of the pew. Head bowed, face red, he scurried down the center aisle, trying not to let his panic show.

The corners of the usher's mouth quirked upward as he held the door open in anticipation of Stuart's brisk exit. His voice was barely audible. "Run, Stu, run!"

Sue shook her head as the sanctuary doors closed behind Stuart. She couldn't believe how quickly the amusing scene got out of hand. The prospect of snagging an eligible bachelor seemed to egg on the cutthroat assertiveness between the two brazen widows.

"Poor Uncle Stu." Carol laid her Bible on the pew. "I need to talk to him. I'll be back in a minute."

Sue's first reaction to follow Carol tempted her. She reached for her purse and then had second thoughts. Stuart wouldn't mind his niece being there, but he didn't need a non-family member interfering.

She closed her eyes. *Heavenly Father, please calm Stuart and don't let him grow bitter.*

CHAPTER EIGHT

AFTER A LONG DAY AT THE ranch, Sue and Stuart made their typical stop at Perky's Coffee Shop. They'd been there so many times, it had become "their place". As he held the door open for her, the immediate aroma of fresh, hot coffee and cinnamon baked goods made Sue's mouth water. She couldn't help but smile when Stuart's stomach growled.

When the waitress came into view, Stuart raised his hand and called out, "We'll have our usual, Pickles."

A cheesy smile spread across the server's face as she nodded. "I'll get it to you in two shakes, hon."

Sue's eyes darted from one diner to another as she and Stuart headed for their favorite corner booth.

"Look who's here: Wanda and Fred Singleton." Stuart motioned to Sue. "Have you both met Carol's friend, Sue North?"

Wanda's lilting laugh filled the air. "We sure have, she's been coming to our Sunday school class. Hi, Sue." She grinned and looked at her watch. "It's late. What are you two doing here together?"

Sue felt compelled to explain, but Stuart spoke first. "We go out to Maverick Ranch a couple of times a week. Her daughter and my nephew, Ethan, are married and manage the place."

Patting his arm, Sue interrupted him. "Stuart volunteers out there, and he's kind enough to take me along so I don't have to drive alone at night."

"What a gallant gesture." Wanda winked at Sue. "I

can see the headlines now. Knight in shining armor helps damsel in distress."

Her husband gave a thumbs up. "Way to go, Sir Stu."

"Come on, Fred, it's not like that." Stuart's face flushed while he grabbed the man's shoulder. "Please don't start any rumors. Poor Sue could do a whole lot better than a grizzly, goofball like me."

Sue lightly tugged on his arm. "Nice to see you, Fred and Wanda. Come on, goofball, let's go sit down. I'm ready for coffee and pie."

The thick whirr of a frothing machine came from behind the counter as the two slid into their leather seats across from each other. Sue set her purse beside her, then looked up and noticed Stuart's forehead glistening with sweat.

"This teasing stuff is getting mighty old." He took a quick swipe at his brow with his paper napkin.

"I'm sorry, Stuart." Sue reached over and gave his fingers a gentle squeeze. "The little encounter with the Singletons got kind of rough, didn't it?"

"Why do I always have to be the nice guy and stop to speak to everyone I know?" Stuart laid his denim-clad arms on the table and shook his head. "I could've waved to them without having an embarrassing exchange."

"Think about it like this—the Singletons would've noticed us and wondered about our situation anyway. Now, they know the truth, so we'll simply enjoy our coffee and pie and not worry about it."

The waitress arrived with their orders. "Here you go, folks. Is there anything else I can get for you?"

"I think we're good." Stuart picked up his napkin-wrapped fork. "Thanks. My mouth's been watering for your cherry pie all day."

"It's our top seller and a great way to start a new week. Enjoy." Pickles headed for another table.

Sue looked at Stuart over her cappuccino cup. "I don't know about you, but I think the weekend went by a little too fast."

"Parts of Sunday morning seemed to drag for me." Stuart took a long sip of his black coffee. "What, no witticisms from the pew behind?"

"I wasn't going to say a word, but since you brought it up, Veda Smith sure is a hands-on person, isn't she?"

"This has me stumped. I've never encouraged either of them." He glanced away, then looked back at her. "Okay, I do remember holding the door open for them at church once, but in my defense, it was raining outside."

Overcome by the memory of Sunday's tug o' war over Stuart, her attempt to hold off a giggle failed. She cleared her throat and tried to be serious. "That's all it would take. To be honest, a true gentleman is hard to come by these days. I'm afraid it makes you a prime mark, my friend." She covered a smile with her hand. If Stuart had an inkling of how good-looking and irresistible he was, he'd go into hiding.

"Speaking of gentlemen, did you ever go out with Brian? I seem to recall he asked you for a date when we had lunch at the Desert Flower."

She set her cup down and used the napkin to dab cappuccino foam from her lips. "We went out a couple of days ago. He's nice enough, but I can't forget his occupation."

Stuart placed his elbows on the table and slowly shook his head. "That's still bugging you, isn't it?"

"I can't seem to let it go." She shrugged and tapped her finger on the table. "Being a lawyer, my husband had a way of manipulating everyone, especially me. Maybe I'm being overly cautious, but once in a while I detect a hint of the same flaw in Brian."

"Give the guy another chance." Stuart's dark eyes

softened. "I'd hate to see you miss the possibility of a good relationship."

After taking a sip of cappuccino, she licked her lips, and looked directly at him. "Once you've lived with oppression, you want to avoid it at all cost, which is why I have no desire to seriously date right now . . . if ever."

Stuart ran his finger down the side of his water glass. "I probably understand that better than anyone. If I got into another relationship, it would be like me to misread the signs and end up with another Penny. Or worse." He glanced at her and shook his head.

"I'm sorry, Stuart." She offered a weak smile. "It's hard to maintain a good attitude when you've lived with a negative spouse, isn't it?"

"The Lord helped me to survive my marriage to Penny for forty-three years. Every time I think of the situation, it feels like I'm suffocating all over again." He swallowed hard. "She even tried to ruin Frank and Carol's relationship as well as Millie and Lou's. The woman didn't have a single good word for anyone until the last month of her life." He exhaled and his shoulders drooped.

"Like you said, with the Lord's help, you survived." His ongoing pain brought compassion to her heart, and she wanted to hug him. Instead, she sent him the warmest smile she could muster. "In spite of everything, you and Millie have such sweet dispositions."

"I can say the same about you."

Her face heated as she pushed her empty coffee cup aside. "Would you mind my asking why you stayed in the marriage?"

Instant silence filled their booth as a small group of high school students walked past. Stuart took a deep breath and fiddled with his little red stir stick. "Mostly because of my daughter, and I wanted to honor my vows.

I always thought life would get better after Millie was born, our finances improved, and so forth." He looked deep into her eyes. "What about you?"

"Unfortunately, my reasons weren't as lofty." She sighed as a veil of lament descended over her. "Grady was all about appearances. He wanted everyone to think he had the perfect life, however, behind the scenes it was anything but. Being a bully and habitually unfaithful throughout our marriage took care of that pretense."

"I'm sorry." Stuart tilted his head and frowned at the noisy teens clamoring into a nearby booth.

Sue wiped a coffee ring from the table and forced her tone to remain calm. "This is difficult to share. Our marriage had nothing to do with love, only his control. I knew to take him seriously."

Anger rose in Stuart's eyes as he shoved a napkin into his empty cup. "He never knew what a treasure he had."

"Thank you." Feeling secure in his acceptance, she repositioned herself in the seat. "He not only promised to write us both out of his will but also threatened to close down my bakery, which would have been my only means of support." She grabbed his hand. "Please don't tell anyone. Rikki doesn't know anything about it, and I intend to keep it that way."

Stuart's strong fingers closed around hers. "I promise to keep it to myself. I'll be praying for you as you deal with your past."

"I appreciate it." Sue looked away as a comforting warmness eased up her arm. Trying not to let him see how the gesture had affected her, she slowly removed her hand and settled into the booth. "Now you understand why I hesitate to go out with Brian."

"Only you can decide if dating him is the right thing for you." He patted his heart. "You'll know in here."

For over twenty-six years, she'd floundered in a whirlpool of misery, but time with Stuart allowed her to see glimpses of peace and camaraderie.

The cell phone hummed next to her hand. "Sorry, Stuart. It's Rikki. I have to take this. I'll make it quick." She turned in her seat, answered the call, and pulled a notepad from her purse.

Stuart jutted his chin and formed a fist thinking of all the torment Sue had endured. How could any man be so cruel?

Having been down the same road with Penny, he understood Sue's reason to avoid another relationship. His mind searched for ways to heal and protect her from the hurt, but with his romantic track record, how could he give advice to the lovelorn?

He longed to get closer to her, but for now, knowing they shared a similar history seemed enough.

With a voice sounding as if nothing from the past bothered her, Sue casually spoke to her daughter on the phone. He saw joy return to her eyes when she glanced his way. The thought of this strong woman withstanding such stress to shield her child from evil tugged at his heart.

Sue jotted something down in her notepad, then covered her free ear as rowdiness from the teenagers continued to escalate, punctuated by their raucous laughter. "Would you mind if I call you back later, Rikki?" She pocketed her phone and turned to watch the unruly young customers.

Perky, the café's owner, firmly set his jaw as he stomped to the teens' table. He pointed his stubby finger to the mess they created. "Okay, enough's enough. I want every one of you kids to take the noise outside before I have to call the cops."

Stuart gave his frustrated friend a thumbs up as the teens scrambled from the café. "Good job, Perk."

The owner looked at Sue. "Sorry for the disruption, ma'am. I know some of these kids, and for the most part, they're a good group. I hate to break up their fun, but look at the spilled drinks not to mention the pie on the seats and floor." He wiped his hands on his apron. "Someone has to teach them respect for others."

"You don't need to apologize, Perky." Sue spoke softly. "You did the right thing and handled the situation well."

Sue's gentleness calmed Perky. Stuart smiled. She had the knack of putting everyone at ease. His eyes focused on the long, gold earrings barely touching her tanned neck. Swallowing a hard gulp, he removed his glasses, carefully wiped the foggy lenses, and rubbed his eyes.

His new feelings were growing for the sweet lady, and it flustered him. At this point, he couldn't let her become too important in his life. After all, neither of them wanted a relationship, especially with the age difference blocking their way. A knot formed in his stomach.

He rested his chin on his fist. Pull yourself together, Drake. Time to focus on tomorrow's first date with Toni Phelps. Was his heart really into it?

CHAPTER NINE

THROUGHOUT THEIR DINNER AT THE MACTAVISH Pub and Grille, Sue delighted in Cameron Brewster's Scottish accent and happy countenance. However, she couldn't say as much for her meal of bangers and mash with a side of haggis.

She silently burped into her napkin, and then wiped her mouth. "Don't think I can eat another bite." After checking her dark green pantsuit for crumbs, she pushed the barely touched plate aside. "Is it time to leave for the movie yet?"

Cameron pushed up the sleeve of his argyle sweater and checked his watch. "Aye, and we best be goin'." He scooted his chair back, then stood and helped her from the table.

Outside, she took a deep breath of haggis-free air. "You haven't told me which movie we're going to see."

"I wanted it to be a bit of a surprise." He smiled and opened the car door. "The movie hoose is having a revival of Brigadoon. 'Twas a favorite of me sainted Granny Brewster."

She settled into the front seat. "I love those old movies and Gene Kelly is so cute."

Cameron slid behind the wheel and smiled at her. "Granny raised me an' insisted I take dancin' lessons as a lad." He started the car. "She fancied me the next Gene Kelly. Bless her soul."

"Is she still living?"

"Nae. She passed a few years back." He sniffed and

wiped his eye. "Her lungs gave way."

Sue rubbed his arm. Why did she have to ask about his grandmother? "I'm sorry. Losing her must have been very hard on you."

"Indeed. Gran was me second mum. The lady was as sweet as honey, like ye be." He made a left-hand turn into the theater parking lot, found an empty space, and took a deep breath. "Might wanna be grabbin' yer sweater." He opened the passenger door and took her arm.

Once inside the theater, the buttery smell of fresh popped corn made Sue's mouth water. She was close to starving after picking at the haggis, bangers and mash.

Cameron grumbled under his breath about the high cost of movie tickets as they headed for the concession stand. He glanced at the prices, then retrieved his coin purse.

Sue half expected to see a moth fly out when he opened it. "Listen, Cameron. You paid for our dinner and the tickets. Please let me buy the snacks. What kind of soft drink would you like with the popcorn?"

"What a winsome lass, thank ye." The dimple in his chin surfaced. "I'll be havin' a Coke, please."

While ordering, Sue's eyes caught a glimpse of the Jujube display. Stuart's favorite. She pointed to the candy. "I want a box of those as well."

Elevator music welcomed them into the theater. She snitched a few kernels of hot popcorn as Cameron led her up carpeted steps to a higher vantage point.

"Yer hands be full. Let me hold the seat down so ye can sit."

"Thank you, Cameron. You're sweet." She lowered herself into the cushioned seat.

The tall, nice-looking Scotsman sat next to her. "'Tis a tad bit nippy in here. Will ye be warm enough, lass?"

With a sparkle in his eyes, the cute dimple returned above his plaid bow tie. "Or, might ye be needin' me strappin' arm about ye?"

Covering her mouth, she giggled at the description of his physique. "Thanks for the generous offer. I'll keep you posted should the need arise." It took a few minutes before she regained her composure. What would it be like to have that strong arm around her? She shook her head, not wanting to entertain any thoughts that hinted of commitment. *Guard yourself, girl.*

"Don' be forgettin', lass." He sent a wink and crossed an ankle over his knee.

Sue noticed his argyle sock and couldn't help but smile. It matched his sweater.

A string of people came in and took seats around them. She was surprised to see so many interested in a 1954 musical. Her jaw dropped when the zebra lady, Toni Phelps, strutted in with Stuart holding her arm. The woman's glistening silver hair with black streaks made her easy for Sue's eyes to follow. They sat three rows directly ahead where Sue could see every move.

As the houselights dimmed, voices dropped to a whisper. Sue tried to focus on the previews instead of the silhouettes of Toni feeding Stuart popcorn. How could she not watch that?

For the next hour and a half, she eyeballed the zebra lady as she flirted unashamedly with poor Stuart. When he leaned away, Toni's arm draped across his shoulder and reeled him back. The man was too attractive and easygoing for his own good. No wonder assertive women strove to dominate him.

Sue returned her gaze to the alluring dairymaid speaking on the movie screen.

"I'm highly attracted to ye," Meg Brockie said. "Why, when I look at ye, I feel wee tadpoles jumpin' in me spine."

A hearty laugh came from the audience, but she didn't feel inclined to join in the merriment. Throughout the remainder of the film, her attention continued to ping-pong from Stuart to the Brigadoon characters.

When the theater lights came on, Sue realized she'd missed most of the movie.

Cameron stood at the end of the aisle and took her hand. As they headed for the busy lobby, his 'strappin' arm' went tightly around her shoulders.

Red flags and warning bells brought out her fears and nightmares of Grady's control. Was this Cameron's initial attempt at taking ownership?

He leaned down and placed a light kiss on her temple.

Sue stopped dead in her tracks as her mood veered from uneasiness to vexation. "Let's not go there."

"I didnae think ye'd mind." He lowered his arms to his side and wore a perplexed look on his face. "I be truly sorry."

She nodded. "No harm done, but listen, I've had a weary day. Do you think you could take me home now?" She walked to the glass door and saw Stuart in the parking lot helping his date into the car.

Sue tried to keep her lip from curling. For some reason, seeing Stuart with the likes of Toni Phelps soured her stomach. Or was it the haggis?

The silent twenty-minute drive back to her condo seemed to take an hour. She chastised herself for taking her frustration out on Cameron. He wasn't trying to control her as Grady had, and the smooch on the temple was sweet and unassuming. And it wasn't his fault that Stuart was out with the zebra. She needed to rectify her harsh response.

Cameron pulled to the curb in front of her condo and

put the car into park. "I want to be apologizin' for me actions earlier." He continued in a hushed tone. "I thought we be havin' a joinin' o' the hearts. Appears it be me wishful thinkin'."

Sue reached for her tan purse. "I'm sorry too. I'm still trying to get over my late husband. It's just not the right time for me to get serious with anyone."

"Aye. Our next date I'll be keepin' me hands to meself." He reached into the backseat of the car and pulled out a box. "Will ye be acceptin' a peace offerin', then?"

A box of Dolly McElf Twinkle Cakes? "Thank you, Cameron. Honestly, with the holidays coming up, I won't have any time to go out. My family comes first." She started to open the car door and then had a second thought. "May I pray for you before I leave?"

He threw her a look of bewilderment. "Aye."

She bowed her head. "Dear Heavenly Father, I ask for Your guidance in Cameron Brewster's life. Please help him understand that his life is precious and give peace as he searches for the woman You have for him. Give this kind man traveling mercies as he returns home. In Christ's name, amen."

"Ye be an angel, Sue North." He cleared his throat. "Thank ye fer the prayer."

She nodded and stepped from the car. "Keep looking, Cameron. Your Miss Right is still out there."

CHAPTER TEN

AFTER SEARCHING THROUGH HER RECIPE BOX for Thanksgiving desserts, Sue collected the needed mixing bowls, ingredients, and baking pans. She looked at the clock on the stove. Six-thirty. Gabby would be there any minute for their baking marathon.

She pulled the seal from a new can of coffee. The tantalizing aroma of fresh coffee grounds reminded her of being with Stuart at Perky's two days ago. She smiled. He got flustered trying to protect her and still answer Fred and Wanda's questions, which only confused the matter. After giving it some thought, his boyish awkwardness gave him an endearing quality. She shrugged the notion away. Best not allow her mind to entertain the charming side of Stuart Drake.

With the coffee brewing, she retrieved two mugs from the cupboard. A single knock on the door told her Gabby had arrived right on time. "Good morning, Gabby."

"Hello dear friend. It smells good in here." She removed her light jacket and placed it on the dining room chair, then washed her hands at the kitchen sink.

Sue offered her an apron. "I'm glad you could help me get these Thanksgiving desserts cranked out for the ranch board of trustees' dinner."

"Happy to do it. It's more enjoyable to tackle big jobs with a friend." She put the loop of the apron around her neck and turned around. "Would you help me tie this? I can't reach it with my arthritis."

"Sure." A small cloud of white dust rose from the

flour bag as Sue set it on the counter. She secured Gabby's apron strings in a bow. "Do you think we should make the cookies, pies, or brownies first?"

"I vote for the brownies. While they're baking we can get started on peeling apples for the pies." The older woman covered a couple of cake pans with non-stick spray and began to assemble the brownie ingredients.

Tap-tap-tap.

Gabby jumped, and her red silicone spatula fell to the floor. "That's Phoebe Ferguson. I'd know her military tap anywhere." She grumbled and bent down to retrieve the utensil. "Mind if I hide in your pantry?"

"I think it's too late, my friend." Sue laughed and tossed Gabby a hand towel. "I'll bite the bullet and answer the door. Get prepared to salute." As she approached the entryway, the front door popped open.

Phoebe marched into the kitchen and scoped the surroundings. "Neighborhood scuttlebutt has it you and Blythe have Operation Thanksgiving underway. I'm here to get my boots on the ground."

Gabby chuckled. "We classified Operation Thanksgiving as top secret. Do you have security clearance, Ferguson?"

"Always a comedian in the ranks." Phoebe's brow formed a V as she checked the pre-heating oven. "Looks clean, no ash build-up." She returned to the counter and scribbled on her clipboard. "It's been a while since I've had KP duty. What are my orders?"

Sue nodded in the direction of the stainless-steel refrigerator. "Why don't you get a dozen eggs for us?"

"On it." Sergeant Ferguson opened the fridge door, grabbed a carton, and dropped it on the counter a bit too hard. Yellow ooze dribbled from the container and down the cabinet. "Oops, sorry about that. It slipped from my fingers."

"Get the paper towels!" Sue sprang to action. How would they get G.I. Jane out of the kitchen?

Phoebe's mouth twisted to one side. "As you can tell, KP was never my bailiwick. Sorry to leave you gals in a lurch, but I need to get back to my lookout post. Carry on, ladies."

With a stiff salute, Gabby clicked her heels and watched the sergeant leave. "This is the first time I've seen Phoebe embarrass herself. You have to feel sorry for her. Beneath her abrasive façade is a lonely person looking for friends."

"I'm willing to be her friend, as long as she lets me do the cooking." Sue finished swabbing her slimed cabinets. "That woman brings new meaning to the term 'mess hall'."

"Speaking of friends, how did your date go with Brian last week?" She reached over and pushed the egg carton away from the edge of the counter.

Sue washed and dried her hands. "He seems like a nice man." She carefully measured a half-cup of oil and poured it into the mixing bowl. "We had a pleasant conversation for the most part. Thank you for asking." She added the cocoa powder hoping the topic had ended.

"Nice try, but you can't fool Momma Blythe." Gabby tweaked Sue's cheek. "I've been curious to find out where he took you."

"We went to the Grand Oasis Inn." Sue grinned and put her wooden spoon on the counter. "And before you ask, the dining area was beautifully decorated with crystal chandeliers, giving it a great atmosphere. I ordered a medium rare steak and a fully loaded baked potato, with a side of asparagus."

"Sounds delicious." Gabby peered at Sue over her glasses, then scraped the side of her bowl with the spatula and tapped it on the side. "For having such a nice time, you don't sound too enthused. What's wrong, girl?"

"I made the mistake of asking him to give me a name of a lawyer to help with my will. He quickly offered to do it for me." She slowly stirred flour into her fudgy mixture, then added chocolate chips and walnuts. "Maybe I'm crazy, but like I told him, I'd rather keep business and friendships separate."

"Of course you're not crazy, honey. If a personal relationship fails, you don't want said individual to be in charge of your legal issues." Gabby popped a few chocolate chips into her mouth, then wiped the counter. "Makes perfect sense to me."

"I want to trust Brian, but for some reason I tend to judge every lawyer as if he was a Grady clone." She moved the mixture to a prepared pan. "Why can't I break through that barrier?"

Gabby looked into Sue's eyes. "Your husband did serious damage to your life. Over twenty-five years is a long time to be under constant tension. It'll take a while to overcome the trauma he put you through." She scraped her chocolate batter into the other cake pan, put both of them into the oven, and set the timer. "From what I can see, you've handled it very well over the years because Grady wasn't able to destroy either you or Rikki. In my book, you're quite a woman."

"Thank you." Sue gave the wise woman a strong hug. "Your words of encouragement mean a lot to me."

"Let me offer one more observation. There's no urgency to update your will. Wait until you know Brian better, or find another lawyer. Without his direction."

Sue breathed out slowly. "You're right. There's no need to be in a hurry. Thanks, Gabby. Let's peel those apples."

The bell over the front door of Floral Scent-sations jingled as the realtor left. Stuart turned off the lights, joined his brother in the work room, and heaved a deep breath. "Did you see how much work we have to get done before we can put this place up for sale?"

Max hiked up his gray work pants. "We'd better roll up our sleeves and get busy since we only have a month. Let's try not to let the work overwhelm us. At least there are two of us to share the load."

"I'm sure Millie and Carol will be able to give us a hand with the inventory. Those gals have helped us a lot and know more about where things are stored than we do."

"Fortunately, we have Harry Reitenoffer to guide us through the process of selling the flower shop." Max rubbed his forehead. "We've talked about retiring for a whole year. I can't believe we're actually going through with it."

Stuart examined his brother's face for a reaction. "Don't tell me you're getting cold feet already?"

"Of course not. Sylvia and I have been looking forward to spending more time together while she can still get out." He picked up the papers Reitenoffer left for them. "Maybe reality is setting in. Can you imagine not coming to the flower shop every day? Floral Scent-sations has been a part of our lives since we were kids."

"Dad had us sweeping floors and lugging things around after school and on Saturdays." Stuart took the coffee cups to the sink and emptied the coffeemaker. He narrowed his eyes. "Funny how I always seemed to get stuck unloading those heavy fertilizer bags."

"You'll never know how sorry I am."

"That's probably because you aren't the least bit remorseful, you rat." He gave Max's arm a solid nudge.

"Suckering you into the smelliest job was a challenge as you grew up and got wiser." He huffed on his fingernails and buffed them on his shirt. "I counted it as a bonus perk of being the older brother."

Stuart threw his head back and laughed, then grew serious. "You know, Max, even though we've remodeled and added on since Dad passed, I still see his presence all around the shop." He glanced away. That would be the hardest part of selling the business.

Pulling up a stool next to Stuart, Max sat and leaned an elbow on the work counter. "When do you think we should tell the family we've finally decided to retire?"

"They've known we've been thinking about it for a while, so this shouldn't come as any big shock." Stuart felt his brother's firm grip on his shoulder. "Everyone will be at my house for Thanksgiving tomorrow."

"Great. Let's tell them then. Maybe we can get a couple extra volunteers for inventory."

Stuart nodded. "Good idea. Gabby and Sue might be willing to spend a little time helping us out." He tried to tone down his excitement at the thought of working side-by-side with Sue.

His smile quickly faded. Would his retirement coming to fruition make him appear less desirable in her eyes?

CHAPTER ELEVEN

SUE ARRIVED AT STUART'S HOUSE. WITH HER arms loaded with dinner rolls and desserts, she rang the doorbell with her elbow. Millie answered the door with the ever-faithful basset hound by her side.

"Happy Thanksgiving, Millie. Gabby and I came together. She's gathering her things from the car."

Millie pulled Farfel out of the way as Sue stepped inside. "You ladies were only supposed to bring the dinner rolls and one dessert. What else did you whip up?"

"I have a couple of the cherry pies your dad is partial to, and a pumpkin pie. Then, in this bag I have Double Chocolate pinwheel cookies." Sue's eyes twinkled. "And I'm not taking this stuff home with me."

"Let me help you." Millie removed one of the pie carriers from Sue's grip and accidently bumped into Farfel. The dog's resounding yelp followed as he moved to an uninhabited corner. "I'm sorry, boy. You have to stay out of Mommy's way."

Gabby bumped the car door closed and hobbled up the driveway. "Don't shut the door! I'm coming, honey."

Taking a step back, Millie kissed her mother-in-law's cheek. "I'm thrilled you're here with us for the holidays."

"Thank you, dear. I've looked forward to this since I moved here last year." Gabby opened a bag to expose a pan of brownies. "Sue and I had a blast baking and testing all these goodies. I love living so close to a baker."

Millie nodded toward the dining room. "Come on in

and set them on the sideboard."

"The desserts aren't only for us today." Sue lifted her index finger and winked. "We made extra for Rikki and Ethan to take home to the ranch. Those kids deserve a lot of sweets for the holidays."

The tender aroma of spices and roasting meat filled the air.

"My, my, my. Smell the turkey. It's making my mouth water. I can't wait to sink my dentures into it." Gabby giggled. "However, we're here to work first, what do you want us to do?"

"My sweet dad peeled ten pounds of potatoes last night, thankfully, that job is done." Millie pointed to the dining room. "The table still needs to be set, if you don't mind. You'll find fresh tablecloths in the buffet."

After taking off her jacket, Gabby glanced around the room. "Speaking of your dad, where is he? I'd like to say hi."

Sue merely nodded, not wanting to appear overly eager to see him. She needed to keep her cool where their host was concerned. She mentally grimaced. Far too many people were reading something into their platonic friendship.

"Dad remembers the stress from past holidays. I want this season to be fun-filled and joyful. Lou took him to prep turkey dinners at the Bradford Homeless Shelter this morning to keep his mind off negative things. They'll be back around noon." Millie headed for the kitchen. "I'll be in here while you're working on the table."

Sue chuckled and removed the mauve centerpiece. "Carol wasn't exaggerating about her aunt's love of the bubblegum color. Penny must have used every shade of pink she could lay her hands on."

"You're telling me. Let's get rid of this old pink tablecloth. I brought something to improve the atmosphere." Gabby's sly grin widened as she drew a replacement from a box.

Sue helped her unfold the cream-colored cloth with gold threads running through it. Together, the two ladies centered the fabric on the Victorian-style table and smoothed it out. They set an orange candle in the middle and surrounded it with acorns and pinecones. They covered the paper Thanksgiving plates with clear disposable ones at each setting.

"My plan is to eat the turkey dinner on the clear plates and then toss them." Gabby held up the holiday plate. "We'll have dessert on these."

Millie came into the room and gasped. "What have you done?"

"Did I overstep my mother-in-law bounds?" Gabby put her arm on Millie's shoulder. "We can always put the pink cloth back on."

"Don't you dare!" She walked around the table admiring their work. "I'm speechless. The room has never looked so welcoming. Wait until Dad sees this."

Gabby's eyes gravitated to Millie as she added silverware to each setting. "I know it's a little late to be asking this, but is having the dinner here too much for Stu?"

"No. I would've said something when you brought it up. Dad mentioned this house was the best place for family get-togethers. He'll perk up once we're seated around this beautiful table and enjoying each other."

"And what about you, honey?" Gabby offered a concerned look. "How are you handling the day?"

"I have mixed emotions, but I try not to dwell on what was and what could have been." Millie wiped her eyes and hurried to the kitchen with Farfel trotting close behind.

Sue sighed. "Maybe we should have gone to a

restaurant.”

Shaking her silver head, Gabby leaned on the chair. “Her mother didn’t make life easy for Stuart or Millie. Facing past struggles in this house is an important step for both of them.”

“I can sympathize with the need for self-preservation.” Sue remembered the sick feeling, the dark hesitation that overcame her, every time the need arose to go into Grady’s office. His inner sanctum.

“Sometimes it’s necessary to force ourselves to move ahead in order to heal and find our future.” Gabby rubbed Sue’s shoulder. “I know you’re going through the same thing.”

Sue nodded. “True enough. Come on, our work here is done. Let’s go help Millie in the kitchen.” She led the way. She certainly didn’t want to stir up any additional thoughts of her late husband.

Carol entered the house. “Happy Thanksgiving, ladies.” She walked into Sue’s open arms for a hug. “I’m glad you’re here to celebrate with us, Sooze.”

“One of the best decisions I ever made.” Sue held her tight.

Carol’s husband, Frank, and her son, Andy, were the next to come through the front door carrying grocery bags.

Andy handed a large container to Millie. “We stopped at the deli to buy Uncle Stu’s favorite fruit salad.” He nodded toward the living room and lowered his voice. “Can me and Frank watch the pre-game on TV?”

“Sure. We’ll call when it’s time to eat.”

“I expect you and Frank to keep your feet off the furniture.” Carol’s face shone with pride as her son scurried away.

Sue stood beside Carol and gave her a hip-bump. “His impish smile makes him look younger than seventeen."

"He's still my little boy." Carol spoke in a hushed tone, then giggled. "But don't tell him I said that."

The doorbell rang. "Go on to the kitchen. I'll get it." Sue opened the door and came face-to-face with Stuart, leaning on the doorframe. Lou stood directly behind him.

"Hi, Sue. Happy Thanksgiving." A sheepish grin appeared on Stuart's face. He slowly pushed his sunglasses on top of his head. "I seem to have forgotten to take my house keys this morning." He stepped inside and his gaze locked on hers.

Sue's heart skipped a beat. Maybe two. Shocked by her cardiac response, she crumpled the idea of touching him, and promptly tossed it into her mental trashcan.

Clearing her throat, she stepped aside, allowing the men to enter. "Frank and Andy are watching a game on TV." Why did her voice quiver? She nervously cleared her throat again. "Dinner should be ready soon."

"I can hardly wait." Stuart rubbed his hands together and headed for the living room.

Joining them, Millie kissed her dad, and went to Lou standing behind a chair. She wrapped her arms around her husband's waist. "The turkey will be ready to carve in about fifteen minutes. Meanwhile, Dad and Lou, you might want to see the dining room before you wash up and change clothes."

Sue, Carol, and Gabby gawked at each other as they waited for Stuart's reaction to the table makeover. Would he like it or not?

He whistled. "Would you get a load of that?" Stuart stood next to Millie, his brown eyes twinkling. "I haven't seen this room look so good in . . . forever."

Watching his face brighten, Sue breathed a sigh of relief. "I'm glad you like it. We didn't overdo things?"

"Are you kidding? Absolutely not." He looked at the

other women and then pulled Millie into a tight embrace. "It's great. Right, Princess?"

She laid her head on his shoulder. "It's beautiful, Dad."

For a moment, stillness filled the room while everyone, with the exception of Sue and Stuart, admired the decorations. Their eyes locked once again and lingered, as they seemed to hover on the brink of romantic recognition. The enchanting spell ended when he dropped his gaze.

"I've wanted to make changes for years, but Penny wouldn't hear of it." Stuart rubbed his neck. "Funny, but now that the opportunity is here, the only things I've managed to toss are a few pink doilies, knick-knacks, and fringy throw pillows, but it's like spitting in the Dead Sea."

"Dad wants to sell the house and get something smaller." Millie patted his back.

Avoiding Sue's eyes, he shrugged. "I've even been to a realtor, but he said, and I quote, 'the unfortunate décor brings down the value of the house.' I need to make the rest of the place look this nice."

"We can all help." Gabby took a step toward Sue. "I had a brainstorm. This can be our project for the new year. It would be fun to de-pink and update the house. It will sell sooner."

Would being close to Stuart be fun or downright dangerous? Sue stared at his rugged profile. Why was she drawn to him?

Carol rubbed her hands together. "And declutter, de-fringe, and de-wallpaper."

A whistle came from Andy's direction. "I get first dibs on yanking up the nasty pink Barbie Doll carpet."

"You have your work cut out for you, boy." Stuart laughed. "Penny put pink carpet in every room."

"Believe me, I noticed." The teen nodded. "Let me rip the plastic wrap off the couch too."

"Have at it, Andy." Stuart laughed. "I'm taking that overstuffed puppy to the Salvation Army first chance I get."

Gabby clapped her hands. "We'll get this place whipped into shape in no time. You'd better get ready to move, Stuart."

The doorbell rang and Andy sprinted to answer it. "It's Grandma and Grandpa Drake."

Carol hurried to greet her parents. "Glad you're here. Watch your step, Mom." She held her hand out to steady her mother as she stepped inside.

"Welcome. Come on in." Sue watched as Sylvia gingerly moved her walker across the floor. What a blessing to have her still with them after suffering a stroke last Thanksgiving.

The love Max and Sylvia demonstrated provided a great example of what God intended marriage to be. Sue thought of her miserable life with Grady. How easy it would be to become jealous of the Drakes' relationship. She swallowed and forced the thought from her mind as she embraced the older couple. "Hi, Max and Syl. How great to see you both."

Sylvia answered by giving Sue's cheek a frail pat. Her mouth formed a crooked smile and a pool of tears gathered in her chocolate-brown eyes. "Good."

With a hand on his wife's waist, Max guided her to the dining room. He pulled out a chair and held her hands as she lowered herself to the seat.

The older woman ran her hand over the festive fabric. "P-pretty table."

"Thanks, Aunt Syl." Millie kissed her forehead. "The ladies did a wonderful job with it. Excuse me, I hear my timer." She called over her shoulder and headed for the kitchen. "Who's going to help me get the food on the table?"

Andy called from the living room. "Ethan and Rikki are here. Let's eat."

The other women hurried to help Millie fill the table with the mouth-watering Thanksgiving cuisine.

Within minutes of Rikki and Ethan's arrival, the family took their places around the well-supplied table.

"Before we pray, Max and I want to tell you about our recent decision. We're finally selling the flower shop." Applause filled the room and Stuart waited for everyone to quiet down. "As you know, Max longs to have more quality time with his lady love."

"I wish we had done it sooner." Max kissed the top of Sylvia's head.

Stuart nudged his brother's arm. "My recent devotion to the ranch has influenced my incentive to sell."

"It'll be the end of an era," Max wiped his eyes, "And the beginning of a new chapter for my little brother."

Millie and Lou stood, his arm draped on her shoulder. "We don't want to horn in on your big surprise, but Lou and I have exciting news to share as well. We'd like to announce that . . ." She looked at her beaming husband. "Baby Blythe will be joining our family in April."

A celebration of excited hugs and well wishes exploded around the room as Lou popped his knuckles. The grandparents-to-be, Stuart and Gabby, embraced.

Stuart stood, his eyes filled with tears as he kissed his daughter's forehead and shook Lou's hand. He sat down and looked across the table. "God has showered us with His grace this past year. Frank, would you return thanks for our many blessings?"

"I'd be honored. Let's bow our heads." Frank stood and began a heartfelt prayer of thanks and blessing over their feast.

Mashed potatoes, dressing, and the all-important green bean casserole made the rounds as hungry guests filled their plates to the brim.

"I love this tablecloth. It gives the room a completely new character." Millie smoothed her hand over the off-white table covering. "With all the up-and-coming house renovations you've been talking about, I'm looking forward to seeing the end result."

Chatter about Stuart's impending house renovation brought on many suggestions.

Sue sat rigidly in her chair unable to join in on the conversation. Her mind drifted to the last time she and Stuart were together at Perky's. Two weeks later, his gaze and the warmth from his touch still affected her.

Her main fear had been romantic entanglement, and today she encountered those emotions infiltrating her well-guarded soul once more. Under the pretense of blending in, Sue forced a smile, determined no one would enter that sacred place in her heart again.

CHAPTER TWELVE

SUE POURED MORE COFFEE INTO PHOEBE'S Go Army mug and peered at the clock. "I'm glad you stopped by this morning, but Gabby and I have to leave in a few minutes."

Pulling out a dining room chair, Phoebe turned it around, and straddled it. "What's the hurry? Black Friday Shoppin'?"

"Not on our list this time. We promised to help someone at nine o'clock."

"If you need extra muscle, my workout's done, and I'm rarin' to go." The stocky woman proudly flexed her biceps.

Remembering Phoebe's klutziness in the kitchen a few days before, Sue let the unsolicited offer hang in the air for a moment. However, Ol' Sarge did have the strength they needed for ripping up carpet. The job would get finished a lot quicker. They'd still have to supervise because one wrong blow with her beefy biceps, and Stuart's house might end up as a pile of pink wreckage.

Gabby poked her head in the front door. "Sorry I'm a little late. Stuart's probably chomping at the bit to get started on Operation De-pink. Are you ready to go?"

"What? Operation De-pink?" Phoebe sat up straight. "Sounds like a full-fledged battle plan."

"Phoebe, is that you?" Walking into the kitchen, Gabby's eyes widened. "Hi there. I didn't know you were here this morning."

"Yes, ma'am. Been here since 0800 on the dot." She hoisted her large mug. "Best cuppa Joe outside the Army. Sure hits the spot after morning calisthenics. My offer for demolition duty still holds. I got a couple o' hours to spare."

Gulping, Sue sent a questioning glance Gabby's way. "I thought Phoebe could help Andy rip up carpet."

"Sure you don't mind some hard work?"

"I live for hard work." Phoebe, stood, blew on her hands, and rubbed them together. "The harder the better."

"That settles it." Gabby shook her keys and headed for the door. "Let's get crackin'. My car's out front."

"Don't you wanna go in my Hummer H1? It's a sweet ride."

Gabby's cringe morphed into a half-smile. "As tempting as it sounds, I already loaded our gear in my car. Why don't you follow us there? You'll be able to leave when you want. We need to go now, we're running late."

When the trio reached Stuart's house, they unloaded buckets, cans of paint, and other supplies.

Andy joined them on the porch. "I'll take the stuff inside."

Without hesitation, Phoebe stepped forward and introduced herself to the teen. "The name's Sergeant Ferguson." She offered her hand. "Phoebe Ferguson."

"Phoebe." Sue took one step forward. "This is my friend Carol's son, Andy Mason. He's excited to tear up the carpet."

"I'm on carpet detail with you, soldier. Guess that makes us comrades in arms."

"Yes, ma'am." Andy gave her a weak salute and nearly bumped into Stuart who stepped onto the porch. "Better salute, Uncle Stu."

He lifted his right hand to his brow.

With arms behind her back, Phoebe gave Stuart a detailed inspection. Her voice deepened. "Who's this hot new recruit?"

A few seconds passed as Stuart's eyeballs moved from side-to-side as if searching for the new soldier. Recognition hit and a slight frown creased his forehead. "Ma'am, Stuart Drake, ma'am."

"At ease, private." She walked behind Stuart and continued to assess his relaxed stance. "Good man."

Bless his heart. Stuart didn't need another bossy woman right now. Sue put her hand on Phoebe's arm and pointed to her friend. "This is Carol Bailey. She's eager to seek and destroy like the rest of us."

"S & D. I like it." A pause followed and her focus returned to Stuart. "Troop's lookin' good." She pivoted and marched into the house, while the others paraded behind.

Gabby grabbed Sue's arm. "Want to go AWOL?"

"Don't tempt me." Sue stared at her. "What have we unleashed?"

Hands clasped behind her, Phoebe surveyed the main floor. "Shoot me now." She spun around and shook her head at Stuart. "Stars and stripes, Drake. You allowed this pink hooey to happen? Let's chuck a grenade and call it a day."

"Woo-hoo!" Andy cheered. "I'll be the chucker."

"Settle down, private." Phoebe put two fingers in her mouth and released a jarring whistle. "Attention! Listen up, people. Here's our plan of attack. Drake, you clear walls and gather the dust-catching gee-gaws. Toss 'em or box 'em, your call."

"On it, Sarge."

A slight grin broke surface as Phoebe took in the surroundings. "North, Blythe, Bailey, prep the wallpaper for removal. Mason, you're with me on carpet detail."

Standing erect and firm, she peered at the squad. "Got that?"

The platoon silently nodded with wide eyes and sagging jaws.

"We'll assemble here at 1200 hours and assess our progress." She smacked her hands. "Move it. Move it. Move it."

Three hours later, light streamed through the window and exposed dust particles floating in the air. Sue sneezed and her eyes watered as she carefully scraped the last small piece of outdated wallpaper in the living room. "It's much brighter in here now."

"Doesn't look like the same room." Gabby rested her arm on a ladder. "Millie will be shocked when she sees this transformation."

After setting her scoring tool down, Carol stretched. "You ladies don't realize how oppressive this dark house became for her and Uncle Stu."

"Did I hear my name?" Stuart dragged an overflowing trash bag from the kitchen. He removed his glasses, mopped his sweat-soaked forehead with a sleeve, and settled into an easy chair in the middle of the room. "This is the third bag of knick-knacks I've found. No wonder my bank account remained anemic all these years."

A shrill whistle rattled the windows. "Inspection." The sarge made haste to the living room. "Much better without wallpaper. Never liked the stuff." She pumped her fist in the air. "Good job with gee-gaw detail, Drake."

"Thank you. The pleasure was all mine."

"You've been a great troop." Phoebe motioned to Andy. "I promised the boy a ride in my Hummer. We'll grab some chow. Be back in an hour, tops. Got your license, Mason?"

Andy's eyes popped as he patted his pocket. "Sure do. You're gonna let me drive that fine piece of machinery? Let's go, Sarge."

"You worked hard today and proved yourself to be a man of honor." She clapped him on the shoulder as they walked out the door. "Uncle Sam could sure use a recruit like you."

Carol grabbed Sue's arm as the unlikely duo exited the room.

"Don't worry, Carol." Sue laughed. "He's not going to sign any enlistment papers yet." She quickly changed the subject. "Millie invited me to the family Christmas dinner this year."

Gabby nodded. "This will be the first time she'll be the hostess in her own home. She also had a great idea. The churches came through with a ton of gifts for the ranch kids; we need to have a gift-wrapping party."

"I love your idea." Carol lifted an arm and cheered. "Yay! That will be fun."

"Perfect. I'll provide gift bags and tissue paper." Sue made a mental note to buy the holiday supplies.

"I'm all thumbs when it comes to wrapping presents." Stuart rubbed the stubble on his chin. "Penny and Millie always took care of it."

Sue grinned. "You're not going to get out of it so easy. I'll help you."

"Sounds like a plan to me." Gabby pulled paper from her pocket and scribbled a note. "I like to stay organized."

"I'm glad someone's organized." Picking up a lamp, Sue looked at Stuart. "What do you want me to do with these filigree lamps?"

"Toss 'em." Stuart unplugged the nearest one and

placed it in the trash pile on the floor.

Shaking her head, Gabby retrieved the light. "You don't want to do that. Let the Salvation Army pick up all this stuff."

Sue lifted a ceramic Victorian dancing figurine. "I wonder how much Curtis Hunter would give you to use this thing as a target in his shooting gallery."

"Why don't you ask him on your next date?" Stuart's lips twitched into a broad smile.

"What's this?" Carol's eyes widened. "Next date? Have you been holding out on me?"

Sue crossed her arms. "I never went out with the man. I marked him off my list, thank you very much."

"Date--list? What am I missing?" Gabby peered at Carol. "I guess we're out of the loop. Spill it, you two."

Sue put her hand on his shoulder. "Good ol' Stuart told me about a singles support group, and he wasn't brave enough to go by himself." She grinned at him. "Shall I go on?"

"They don't need to know everything." He grabbed a Walmart bag. "Do you think Millie might want her mother's doilies?"

Gabby's hands went to her hips. "Don't go changing the subject. This sounds like a good story."

"Sue, we've always been honest with each other. If you're dating, I should know about it." Carol released a deep breath. "Do we have to twist your arm?"

"It's like this. Stuart thought Singled-Out was a support group for single mature adults. He figured they'd have a bowling league and go to Phoenix Suns games together."

Stuart chuckled. "They sent a flyer saying to bring our questions. What would you think?"

"Probably the same thing." Gabby laughed with him. "What kind of meeting did it turn out to be?"

His face flamed as he kicked a ruffled throw pillow across the room.

"Allow me, Stuart." Sue placed her fingers on her chest. "After I paid our membership fee to get in, we discovered we'd joined a speed dating service."

"Wait a minute." He held his hand up and frowned. "I don't remember a membership fee."

"Ten dollars each. I took care of it because you were busy grumbling and filling out your questionnaire."

"So I owe you twenty bucks?"

"You don't owe me a thing. Watching you with the cat in the hat lady was worth every penny." Sue giggled. "You should've seen her. This woman stood every bit as tall as Stuart and wore a red and white striped hat."

"The entire time she asked questions, I shook in my boots."

"At least Stuart introduced me to Perky's Coffee Shop after the bizarre event."

He winked and threw her a teasing smile. "And I did get you a slice of cherry pie for your trouble."

"You sure did." Her eyes met his in a split second of spontaneous camaraderie.

Gabby looked at her watch. "This juicy conversation reminds me, it's time for lunch."

"Is it that late?" Carol's face grew serious. "Millie has a prenatal appointment this afternoon and I have to relieve her at the flower shop. 'Bye." She turned and ran out the door.

With his arms loaded with old romance novels, Stuart stopped at the bottom of the stairs near the dining room. Muffled voices caught his attention.

"I'm sorry, Sue." Gabby's voice remained soft and soothing. "And nobody knew? I can't believe your husband would do that to you."

"Please don't tell anyone, Gabby. It's too embarrassing. Even my best friend, Carol, only knew a fraction of the problem." Sue's voice cracked. "I want to get on with my life without having to explain my past and seeing pity in their eyes."

"Your story is safe with me. I wouldn't dream of adding to your pain."

"Thanks. It feels good to vent."

Stuart held his breath and backed away from their private conversation. The thought of Sue's husband harming her set his teeth on edge. His sudden urge to protect her came as a surprise. Not knowing the details would keep him awake tonight, but for now, he had to be careful or his raw emotions would give him away.

Sue had become one beautiful mystery to him, and he wanted to know more. Maybe she'd feel free enough to share with him some day. There may be more cherry pie in their future.

CHAPTER THIRTEEN

THE VISION OF CHILDREN'S SMILING FACES appeared in Sue's mind as she and Stuart sipped their second cup of coffee at Perky's Coffee Shop.

"We only have ten days before Christmas." She added more cream to her hot drink, then pulled her dessert plate closer. "The ranch kids really enjoyed decorating the cookies tonight, didn't they, Stuart?"

"They had a ball. JJ Lopez wore more frosting than the cookies did. That kid cracks me up." A glimmer came to his eyes. "I have a hard time not hugging him."

"Why don't you?"

"They have rules at the ranch. Men aren't to touch children because a few people perceive it as sensual. They can touch us, but we can't initiate it." He shook his head. "It's sad."

"These kids lack the love of a father. I remember my dad giving me the biggest hugs. It made me feel wanted and safe."

"Max and I grew up in a family of huggers, Penny didn't. After our wedding, we had little show of affection. I made sure Millie received the kind of parental devotion she needed."

"Grady was like Penny in that regard, but in public he doted on both of us." She broke a piece of crust from her pie. "You can tell their pie crusts are homemade. They have a good baker."

"I like a lot of their bakery items, but their pies are my favorite." Stuart licked the cherry goo from his finger.

"Speaking of baked goods, what happened on your date with the Dolly McElf guy?"

"It wasn't particularly exciting, although Cameron was nice. I had to concentrate on understanding his Scottish accent all evening, and I had to taste sheep entrails. But I did get a box of Twinkle Cakes out of it. Would you like a few packages?" Sue scooped a bite of pie on her fork. "Did you enjoy your date with, umm, Toni what's-her-name?" She pictured the uninhibited woman flaunting her zebra-inspired ensemble while feeding poor Stuart popcorn like peeled grapes.

"That's right. Toni Phelps." His grin widened. "What can I say, she was a very attentive date, and I didn't have to eat animal guts."

"I'm happy for you." Sue felt a twinge of something but wasn't sure what it was. A sudden awareness nearly blocked her air passages. *Please, Lord. Don't let it be jealousy.* She coughed. "Are you going out with her again?"

"She wants to take me roller skating. I haven't been on skates since grade school." He planted his elbows on the table. "If memory serves, falling hurts."

"Wrap your backside in a few layers of bubble wrap, and you'll be okay." Sue giggled.

"Yeah, thanks for the suggestion. I'll let you know how it goes." A frown creased Stuart's brow as his fork poked a cherry in the pie.

"You're quiet. Is anything bothering you?"

For a moment, Stuart seemed uneasy as he dragged his hand across his mouth. "Look, Suzie-Q, I'm sorry, but I overheard you talking to Gabby about your husband a couple of weeks ago."

"I see." Sue's face warmed.

"If you'd rather not discuss it, we don't have to go there." He stared at his napkin. "I can identify with what you went through because of my personal experience. I'm here if you ever want to talk."

Sue noticed the tenderness in his expression. She could trust him. "I don't know how much you overheard, but my marriage was filled with fear and tension. Grady didn't start out as a mean person, but money, power, and lust changed him. His domineering personality eventually came out at home, then at work, and later with friends."

"What a shame." He shook his head and fixed his gaze on the window behind her. "My wife behaved the same way. She interfered with everyone's life for years. It's almost impossible to live with that type of person. Fortunately, the Lord changed her a few weeks before she died."

"How wonderful. I wish my husband had done the same."

The buzz of conversation around them lessened as customers finished their coffee and left the cafe.

She looked into his deep-brown eyes. "Let me ask you this, how did you hold it together for all those years?"

"If it hadn't been for the Lord's strength, I might've left Penny early in our marriage. Then Millie came along. She became the brightest spot in my life. How could I leave her?" He rubbed the back of his neck. "One day I found Millie watching soap operas with her mother. I made a point to take my little girl with me to the flower shop whenever possible. Max would bring Carol, and the two kids played Here Comes the Bride."

"How sweet. I can envision little Carol with her long, blonde hair wanting to play the bride." Sue sipped her coffee and returned the cup to the saucer. "Grady's law practice had him working long hours, especially the week before a case went to trial. He kept an odd schedule and many times didn't bother to come home. Like I mentioned before, he felt he had a right to –" She waved off her comment and looked away. "You know."

"Say no more. I understand." Stuart lightly patted her hand.

His warm smile reflected compassion which made him more appealing. Sue quickly drew her eyes away from his and studied the spoon in her hand. "To be honest, a part of me didn't care, but another part of me was crushed." She took a deep breath and released it slowly. "I could never be enough for him."

"I felt the same way about Penny's romance novels. Those perfect fictional heroes were too much competition for me."

"Grady only stayed with me because he wanted people to think he had a perfect family life. It made him appear wholesome and trustworthy to his clientele. He said our façade made him appear like a family man, and would aid him for a future in politics."

"It took a lot of courage to stay." He leaned back in the leather booth.

"I had to for my daughter, the same as you." Her eyes saddened. "Rikki doesn't know this, but he threatened to have me declared an unfit mother and take her away from me if I even thought of leaving. He worked hard to build a following of powerful individuals to support him. I knew it wasn't an idle threat."

"It took a lot of gall and selfishness for him to exploit someone as sweet as you." Stuart leaned over the table, his voice grew raspy. "No one deserves to be treated like that."

"Thank you." Sue managed a half-hearted smile. "I'm glad the horrible time of my life is over, but I still struggle with my feelings toward him."

A look of disbelief came over his face. "Do you mean

you still love him after all he's done?"

"Of course not." Her eyes narrowed. "Quite the opposite. My husband has been gone for a year and a half, and I still struggle with despising the man."

The sound of a crying toddler from across the restaurant broke into their conversation. The mother gave him a sippy cup and a handful of snacks as the waitress came with a booster seat.

Sue drew her attention to Stuart who washed down the last of his pie with a gulp of black coffee.

"I found out the hard way that hate gets you nowhere." Stuart wiped his mouth with a napkin and sat up straight. "1 John 4:20 hit me between the eyes. 'If someone says "I love God" and hates his brother, he is a liar; for he who does not love his brother whom he has seen, how can he love God whom he has not seen?'"

She sat frozen, left elbow on the table, and chin resting on her palm. So, how did God expect her to get over the contempt for so many years of being trapped with Grady's intimidation, threats, and unfaithfulness?

"Hatred is a strong emotion. My struggles dragged on for years. Finally, the realization came. My refusal to forgive Penny kept me chained to the past. One memory led to another until it owned me. If I wanted to be free, I had to let go of the pain daily in order to have a future. The chain of pain had to be unlocked by God, Who holds the keys." Stuart touched her hand. "We must choose between slavery and freedom."

"You're such an easy-going person. I can't picture you hating anyone."

"My wife was the only one to bring the animosity out of me. But you know what? The more I learned of her abusive childhood, it gave me an understanding of what she lacked."

"Grady didn't have that excuse, he had a great

upbringing. Actually, he came across as Prince Charming in college. Later, the more successful his law practice became, the more greed and lust took over his heart."

Sue's hand felt warm. She looked down, shocked to see her fingers entwined with Stuart's. Did she reach first or did he? Her skin prickled at the realization. Their friendship might've turned the corner. She couldn't let that happen.

Their eyes met. Heat crept up his neck as both jerked their hand away.

This couldn't be happening. Stuart rubbed his clammy palm on his pant leg. His attraction to Sue North had become downright embarrassing. She was too young, for crying in a bucket. Way too young.

He didn't want Millie and Carol to think of him as a dirty old man. He cringed. Was he? Right now, he felt like one. He'd have to shy away from Suzie—from Sue until his inappropriate fondness for her died.

"It's getting late, we'd better go." He cleared his throat. "I think Perky wants to lock up."

CHAPTER FOURTEEN

On her way to Christmas dinner, the mild sixty-five-degree temperature amazed Sue. Compared to the frigid winters of her former Vermont home, the weather seemed downright balmy. This year she'd miss the cozy snuggling in a down comforter in front of the fireplace. Even though snowy northern winters were prettier, the frigid arctic air had attacked her lungs like slivers of glass.

She looked forward to a family Christmas at Millie and Lou's. This was the first time they were hosting a family get-together at their house. It promised to be a full day with wrapping gifts for the ranch kids followed by an outdoor Christmas dinner.

After parking her car in front of the modest, neatly kept house, she gathered her basket of baked goodies and shopping bag of gifts. Her agenda for the day was to have fun and keep her mind from dwelling on Stuart.

Lou opened the front door and gave her a hug. "Hi, Sue. Glad you could make it." He took the basket, led her through the house, and to the back door. "Stu's out on the patio with Farfel. Grab a cup of hot apple cider, and then the two of you can chat until the others come."

So much for her plan to keep from thinking about the man. An uneasy expression flitted across Stuart's face as she headed for the circle of lawn chairs where he sat by the burning fire pit. Farfel ran to greet her.

Repositioning his Santa hat, Stuart smiled and casually nodded her way. "Afternoon, Sue."

She took a deep breath. "Santa." An unexpected sting of disappointment pricked at her. He called her Sue? What happened to Suzie? He generally called her that when they were alone. Maybe she should offer a slight wave. She sent him the innocent gesture and buzzed to the drink table near the house where Gabby and Millie were adding ice to a large pitcher.

"Have Yourself a Merry Little Christmas" played softly from the cell phone Gabby placed on the table. "Music will get this party up and running."

After drying her hands on a towel, Millie approached Sue with open arms. "Thanks for coming. Those pecan pie bars you brought for dessert are wonderful. The baby and I already enjoyed one." She pointed to the far end of the patio where gift-wrapping necessities lay in the center of a long folding table. "Seven of us have sixty gifts to wrap. Frank and Carol will be here any minute, but in order to get done before breakfast, we'd better start now."

"I'm ready." Sue eagerly rubbed her hands together. She could focus on the task rather than let her mind fixate on holding hands with a certain someone.

Gabby pulled Stuart to the table and sat him in the chair next to Sue while "I Saw Mommy Kissing Santa Claus" played in the background. "If I remember correctly, Sue promised to help you wrap presents for the ranch kids."

A distinct barb of discomfort threatened to unravel Sue's calm demeanor. She took a deep breath. Thanks to her prior marriage, she'd learned to go through the motions without revealing her true feelings. *Please Lord, don't let anyone suspect my growing interest in Stuart.*

She had to catch her breath when he glanced at her. Faking nonchalance might be a little harder than anticipated.

Gabby brought out a large box filled with stuffed

animals. "Okay, Stuart and Sue, here's your box of gifts to wrap."

"Remember ladies, I'm not too good at wrapping stuff." Stuart's mouth quirked. "But I'll do my best."

"We've made this as simple as possible so we can finish quickly." Gabby's voice softened. "Think of it this way, Lark will get one of these animals."

"Nuff said." He grinned. "Hand me a roll of wrapping paper and the tape."

Sue held up a sack. "No wrapping. We have bags and tissue paper. You'll see. It'll be a snap." Without benefit of personal eye contact, she set a small Teddy bear in front of him. "You put the bear in the bag and add tissue. Ta-dah. You're done."

Sue looked up as Frank and Carol came from the house with their carton of gifts. She pointed to the chairs across from her. "Merry Christmas. Are you ready to join Santa's workshop?"

Frank donned his green and white striped elf hat with jingle bells. "I think this official North Pole fedora speaks for itself." He plopped into a chair across from Stuart.

"You know, if I had one of those elf hats, my hands would work a lot faster." Stuart laughed as he stuffed a purple hippopotamus into a glossy bag.

Carol nudged her husband. "Why don't you trade hats with Uncle Stu?"

Bells jingled as Frank whipped off the pointy hat and tossed it to Stuart. "There, that should keep your noggin toasty. Now, get to work, Glitter Toes. I want to see those fingers flying."

Sue continued to maintain a safe distance from Stuart as they worked together. They instinctively took turns pulling animals from the carton and reaching for gift bags. It had been a full week since the handholding incident at Perky's, and she didn't want either of them to experience the same discomfort again.

After setting aside another filled bag, Sue felt a heavy weight on her feet. She peeked under the table where Farfel happily gnawed on a stuffed pig with blue pants. "Aww, Farfel. Where did you get the piggy?"

The dog's tail thumped on the ground. She reached for the stuffed animal and the keep-away game was on. He ran from under the table and waited for action with his rear in the air and excitement in his big, brown eyes.

"Come on, Stu." Frank sprang from his chair. "I'll get him from this side, and you grab him from there."

With ears flapping, Farfel took off across the yard with Santa and Glitter Toes in hot pursuit. The basset managed to dodge between them at every turn. A muffled woof came from his stuffed mouth.

Gabby stood and kissed the air. "Here, Farfel." Kiss-kiss. "Want a yummy?" Kiss-kiss. "Come to Grandma." She turned to Sue and Carol at the table. "I'm glad we bought a few extra toys."

A loud whistle came from outside the door and Farfel headed for his daddy. "You little rascal. You're always getting into mischief. Go lay down."

The dog's ears lay flat as he circled his blanket and flopped down, the dripping toy still clenched between his teeth.

Lou called to Gabby. "You don't want this nasty thing back, do you, Mom?"

She shook her silvery curls. "Nope. Merry Christmas, Farfel."

After brushing grass from his knees, Frank caught up with Stuart, and they headed to the table.

Lou had his arm around Millie as they came from the house and joined the happy wrappers. He helped her into a chair beside Sue.

The display of tenderness pulled at Sue's heart. She wondered how life would've been different had Grady been as caring. Leaning close to Millie, she lowered her voice. "I love how attentive Lou is to you."

"He's enamored with the baby. I'm glad I married a man as affectionate as my dad." Millie handed Carol another gift bag.

"Thanks again for including me in your family circus, I mean, Christmas." She smiled at the mother-to-be. "This has been a lot of fun."

"You've been in Apache Pointe for almost three months, and I feel bad we haven't been able to connect."

"Time flies, doesn't it? I'd love nothing better than to get to know you." Sue squeezed Millie's hand and then reached for another animal. "Let's make a goal to fix that situation after the holidays."

Millie rubbed her stomach. "The morning sickness is finally over, and I'm game for anything now." She placed a bow on the small gift.

"Let's sing some Christmas carols." Frank's voice broke into a rousing rendition of "Deck the Halls." and the others quickly joined in.

For the next thirty-five minutes, the singing group continued to fill Christmas bags and stockings.

Stuart stood. "Attention. I want you all to witness me filling my last bag." He shoved a fuzzy, pastel unicorn horn-first into the sack then stuffed the bag with tissue. "Ta-dah!"

Gabby applauded first. "And you didn't think you could do it."

He scooted his chair under the table. "If any of you he-men want to join me, I'm heading to the fire pit."

"I'll be with you shortly." Lou patiently stuffed the snowflake patterned tissue paper into the small sack.

Sue's eyes followed Stuart, standing alone in the

glow of the fire pit, immersed in his own thoughts. Did he feel the same sense of confusion about their feelings for each other? Her hand touched her throat. Or, had she disappointed him with the admission of her contempt for Grady?

"Hey, Carol." Frank smiled across the table to his wife. "I think Stu needs company. You can finish here, right?"

Carol waved her hand. "Go ahead."

"Poor Dad seems lost." Millie nodded in Stuart's direction. "I don't know what's happened, but he's been moping around for the last few days."

Sue's interest was piqued, but she fought the urge to glance his way again.

"If you ask me, it's a simple case of being lonely." Gabby didn't look up from the name tag she was filling out.

Concern showed on Carol's face. "Bless his heart. I hate that he's unhappy. It would be nice if he could find someone to go out with once in a while."

Sue's chest tightened at the thought of Stuart dating other women. She decided to suggest someone less threatening than her silver nemesis, Toni Phelps. "How about those two church ladies who sat close to him during the service?" She kept her voice low. "They seem awfully interested."

"You mean Veda Smith and Myrtle Faye Dunlap?" Carol pressed her fingers to her lips covering a grin. "I've noticed they didn't give him any wiggle-room in the pew."

Millie reacted with open-mouthed shock. "They're both after my dad?" She placed her fists on her hips. "I wonder if that's why Myrtle Faye asked me what kind of insurance he had."

Carol's hearty laugh echoed across the lawn. "Could be. Now, Veda's less picky. Your dad's single, drop-dead gorgeous, and breathing, which is the trifecta of availability in her book. The bonus is the man can still drive."

"Well, this is awkward. Poor Dad." Millie shook her head. "Veda Smith?"

Farfel interrupted the pensive moment as he begged for a treat.

"Get used to it, Mills." Carol tossed a cracker to the dog. "Once the word is out that Uncle Stu's ready to date, the she-sharks will be circling."

Sue schooled her emotions to remain calm. She still hadn't put a name to her feelings for Stuart but knew it had to be more than a mere friendship. Her mind swirled in confusion. Did she dare reveal her obscure interest in him to Carol or Gabby?

A hefty bump against her leg caused Sue to jump and pulled her from the conundrum. "Hi, Farfel." She scratched the dog's long ears. "Well, ladies. I think we're all finished with the wrapping. Let's clean up."

Gathering the leftover bags and tissue paper, Gabby tossed them into a small box.

Carol stepped closer to Sue and lowered her voice. "I've been dying to ask if you're still dating Brian."

"We've gone out a few times." Sue shrugged.

"Didn't you hit it off?"

"Yes and no. My only problem with him is, he acts a little too eager to check into my finances. It makes me uncomfortable." She tilted her head. "Who knows? Maybe I'm being too picky, or I'm not ready to date. Either way, I'm giving him the benefit of the doubt."

"She'll know when the right man comes along." Millie patted Sue's shoulder then pointed to the house. "Since the table's cleared, you ladies want to help me get the food ready?"

Gabby called to the men. "Would you take the gifts to

the church van before Farfel helps himself? Please be careful not to tear the bags." She opened the door and called to them again. "When you're finished, watch for Max and Sylvia. They may need your help getting her to the backyard."

The women followed Millie into the kitchen. The room was warm and inviting with its pale yellow walls and white trim. Matching café curtains hung at the window, separating pine cabinets.

"I have a holiday tablecloth on the counter by the fridge. Mom Blythe, would you mind spreading it on the table outside?"

Carol gathered the paper plates. "I'll take these out." She turned her head. "I hear Frank hollering for me. I better see what he wants."

"I'll get the ham and scalloped potatoes out of the oven and put the dinner rolls in." Millie sat the roasting pan on the counter and handed a meat platter to Sue. "Would you slice the ham and put it on here, please? The knife is on the counter."

Sue reached for the carving knife. "I'd be happy to. Everything smells delicious, Millie. Carol said you were a great cook." Within a few minutes, overlapping slices of ham filled the large plate.

The door slammed and Carol rushed into the kitchen. "Frank's the Chaplain On-Call at the hospital tonight and got an emergency call. I'm sorry, we need to say goodbye to everyone." She hugged Millie. "Please tell Mom and Dad I'll call them later. Merry Christmas!"

"Wish you didn't have to go." Sue put an arm around Carol's waist and followed her to the car. "You're still going to the ranch tomorrow for family time, aren't you?"

"That's the plan. We wouldn't want to miss it. However, Frank and I won't be at the New Year's Eve party." She opened the car door, wiggled her eyebrows, and lowered her voice. "It's our first anniversary."

"I don't need to tell you to have fun." Before Sue closed the door for Carol, she leaned down to talk to the man behind the wheel. "Bye, Frank. We'll be praying your hospital visit goes well."

Heading for the house, she noticed Stuart peering out the front window. His face grew solemn as he turned away.

He acted different tonight. His no-nonsense attitude toward her seemed inconsistent with the warm man she had coffee with only a week ago.

Following supper, Stuart added another log to the fire pit. His eyes searched for Sue. Where did she go? He sat on the lawn chair, crossed his arms, and stared at the growing flames. Did the intense need to pursue her come from plain ol' sympathy because her husband had been such a brute? He raked his fingers through his hair and exhaled into the night. If anyone understood the turmoil she'd lived through, he did.

Gabby and Lou settled next to the fire with their stringed instruments and played "O, Christmas Tree." Everyone's voices blended in beautiful harmony on the first verse. When no one remembered the words to the next stanza, they laughed and switched to "Jingle Bells."

Hearing Sue's alto voice in the background reminded Stuart of the chasm between them. There hadn't been an argument, so nothing needed mended or healed. Time was the only enemy. The empty space between their years prevented them from the loving relationship they both needed.

Lou strummed a few chords. "This song always reminds me of my dad. "I'll Be Home for Christmas." You want to sing it for us, Momma?"

"Sure." Gabby gave a little cough. "I'll be home for Christmas, you can count on me . . .'"

Stuart twisted in his chair and watched the glowing embers of the fire. He saw himself as a nineteen-year-old army private returning from Vietnam. Other than his mother and brother, Penny had been his only contact from home. She wanted to get married, and he, eager to get his life back to some kind of normalcy, agreed.

His family warned him not to marry Penny right away, but her insistence coupled with his stubbornness won out. That one irresponsible act of rebellion saddled him with an explosive wife which he wasn't equipped to handle.

Max sat in the lawn chair beside him. "Looks like you've got some things on your mind, little brother. Wanna share it with me?"

With his hands folded across his middle, Stuart continued to stare at the flame. "Thanks, but not right now."

"When you're ready to talk, remember I'm only a phone call away."

Nodding, Stuart stood and went into the house. He sank down in a living room chair and lowered his head to his hands as the image of Sue's sweet face loomed in his mind. He admired her gentle smile, compassionate spirit, and steadfast courage. Suddenly, he became aware of the inability to stop the momentum of his feelings for her.

Who do you think you are, Drake? Forty-six years wasted in a loveless marriage. You had your chance at romance and blew it. Now, it's too late.

Stuart wiped his eyes as the thoughts continued to jab at his heart. The only fair thing to do would be to shield Sue from this 'old man crush'. He needed to encourage her to date men closer to her age. He cringed. Someone like . . . Brian Campton.

CHAPTER FIFTEEN

The day after Christmas brought bright and sunny skies. Sue climbed into the seat behind Carol while Frank loaded the cargo area of the church van with additional Christmas gifts for the ranch staff.

She adjusted her seatbelt. "I appreciate you and Frank giving me a ride, Carol. I wasn't thrilled about driving in the desert by myself."

"I wouldn't want you to do that. We're glad to have your company."

"Rikki says the kids are excited for their first real Christmas." Sue leaned forward. "I forgot to tell you, the people from our church in Powder Ridge are planning to send a work team down next summer."

"What a blessing. The ranch needs a lot of work, and the more hands, the better." Carol brushed the wrinkles from her lightweight coat and readjusted the seatbelt.

Frank got behind the wheel and shut the door. "We're all set, ladies. I heard a rumor that Santa might make an appearance today." He turned on the ignition and a Christmas CD began to play as they pulled out of the drive.

"You heard right." Sue chuckled. "I hope you brought your elf hat. We still need a Santa's helper."

"That rascal, Stu, never returned it to me." Frank glanced in the rearview mirror. "He'll have to fill the position."

"We might need two elves. The congregation in Vermont joined your Angel Basket ministry for the kids.

It must have been a big hit considering the number of shoeboxes we received."

Carol shifted in her seat. "I'm as giddy as the kids are. It's going to be fun watching their faces as they open their presents. I hope you have your camera, Sooze."

She pulled out her phone and waved it. "Sure do, and I'm ready to take lots of pictures."

"Wonderful. Ethan's going to update the website soon, and I'm sure he'll want to add some of your pics to it."

Sue looked out the side window. Sand and cactus were visible as far as she could see. After spending her life in the snowy mountains of Vermont, she struggled to adjust to a warm, dry holiday season. However, it was a small price to pay to be near her daughter and the mission. And then she thought of Stuart.

Thank You, Father for using Stuart to remind me of the importance of letting go of my hate for Grady. I'm making a promise to You and driving a stake into the ground, determined to follow Your ways. Please help Stuart and me to resume our friendship as You would have it.

For the next half hour, they listened to Christmas music and shared chocolate-covered pretzels. Frank finally made the turn onto the road which led to Maverick Ranch.

Rikki and Ethan met them at the front door, surrounded by children with eager brown faces. Some were already running amuck on the porch, a few were jumping up and down, and one lone girl hid behind Rikki.

The mouth-watering aroma of fried chicken filtered through the large house as they stepped inside with their arms filled with baskets of food.

"I'm happy you came. Let me help with those things."

Rikki held out her arms. "The kids have been watching for you all morning."

Frank stepped over the threshold with an armload of brightly decorated packages for the staff and took them to the Christmas tree standing in the corner. Cheerful multi-colored lights and homemade ornaments adorned the Fraser fir. Once Frank put the last gift down, he called to Ethan. "We have a few more things in the van. Want to help me?"

"You betcha. Let me get my shoes on." Ethan put his hand on a young boy's shoulder. "JJ, you need to calm down and stay out of the way."

The boy with a cowlick wrinkled his nose. "But I wanna help." He stomped his foot.

Ethan held JJ's chin firmly. "Look at my eyes and listen. We need you to stand at the window and watch for Poppy. You tell us when he's here."

A short time later, the mound of presents grew as the older kids got them from Frank and Ethan and placed them under the tree.

Sue, Carol, and Rikki took side dishes and desserts into the kitchen. Happy, hungry youngsters surrounded the food table and eyeballed the Rice Krispie treats, cupcakes, and fudge. The ranch cooks, brandishing wooden spoons, hustled all of them into the great room.

Sue laughed. "This is going to be more fun than I thought."

The screen door squeaked open as Millie and Gabby came into the house. Lou brought up the rear carrying a guitar case and a banjo. A couple of the older boys added folding chairs to the living area.

Ethan took Millie's hand and led her to an upholstered loveseat. "We saved this spot especially for you, little mommy. It's the best seat in the house." He motioned for Gabby to sit beside her.

No sooner had Sue and Carol gotten comfortable on the sagging green couch than the five smallest children climbed into their laps and began to chatter nonstop.

"What's your name, sweetie?" Sue adjusted the bow on the girl's braid.

"My name is Sandy and I gots a loose toof. Wanna see?" The little girl held her head back, opened her mouth, and pointed to the dangling incisor.

"Look at that." She touched Sandy's chin. "Are you going to let Miss Rikki pull it?"

A great hush came over the room and five sets of chocolate-brown eyes grew wide as they stared at Sue.

Sandy clamped a shaking hand over her mouth and slid from Sue's lap. The youngster's braid wiggled as she vigorously shook her head.

"I'm sorry, sweetie." Sue held out both hands. "If I promise not to touch your tooth would you give me a hug?"

The six-year-old nodded, inched her way to the couch, and put her pudgy hands on Sue's knees. Within seconds, the two embraced.

"Miss Rikki, Miss Rikki!" JJ ran from the window. "Poppy's here! Can we see if he has gum in his pockets?"

"Yay!" The children raced to the door.

Rikki clapped her hands. "Settle down, kiddos. Wait until he gets inside. Be careful and don't knock him down this time." Her voice grew louder. "JJ, I'm talking to you."

Sue squirmed in her seat. *Stuart's here? All this time she figured today's event would be family only. The thought hit her. He's Millie's dad and Ethan's uncle, so he* was *family.*

A part of her wanted to see him, but after he ignored her last night at Lou and Millie's, a bigger part of her feared more rejection. Stuart had been the first man she'd ever bonded with emotionally, and she knew the sizzle between them wasn't her imagination. She rubbed the fingers he'd held that night at Perky's. When Stuart released her hand, the expression on his face made it obvious he'd felt the electricity too.

The earnest way they'd opened up to each other had shaken her world. It probably measured a 7.6 on the Richter scale. She braced for a personal aftershock as Stuart entered the room with children hanging off his arms and clinging to his legs.

A chorus of kids' voices sang throughout the room. "Do you have gum, Poppy?" Chubby little hands patted the pocket of his lightweight jacket.

"I sure do."

Sue quickly became captivated with the children's enthusiasm as they jostled each other and formed a crooked row.

Arms flailed. "Me first. Me first."

"You were first last time, Charlie." JJ crossed his arms. "You're 'posed to be in the back."

"I can't help it if I'm faster 'an you."

Stuart knelt on the floor and each child received a stick of Juicy Fruit along with a fist bump.

A four-year-old little girl stood behind him with her hand clutching his denim jacket. She waited patiently while he spoke to the others.

Once the kids emptied Stuart's pockets of the Juicy Fruit, he turned to the pigtailed girl and gently pulled her thumb from her mouth. His voice softened as he held up a lone stick of gum. "Do you want some too, Lark?"

She nodded, put her arms around Stuart's neck, and kissed his cheek.

He closed his dark brown eyes, and his broad smile made him appear years younger.

Sue melted on the spot. Watching Stuart meet the

emotional needs of a child strengthened her attraction to him and was almost her undoing. She licked her lips, arms aching to hug him too . . . with or without the Juicy Fruit.

Visions of taking Lark's place ran through her mind. She swallowed hard and mentally smacked herself around. *Jealous of a four-year-old, Sue?* Her face flushed with guilt. So not right! These crazy thoughts had to stop.

She couldn't help but smile as the children grouped on the floor around Stuart's chair and sang "Frosty the Snowman" with him. With a glowing face, the surrogate grandpa acted out the song and set the boys and girls laughing.

The front door squeaked again. Marty Rush came inside with his nephew, Brian, and ranch hands, Flapjack and Juan Garcia following close behind.

Marty smiled. "Merry Christmas, everyone."

"Merry Christmas." Ethan closed the front door behind them. "Glad you could join us this year. I think you know everyone here."

The adults cheerfully waved and called out as the men found seats in the brightly decorated living room.

Marty took a chair by Stuart. "We old goats better stick together." He removed his wire-rimmed glasses and wiped the lenses.

"Old goat? Speak for yourself." Stuart nudged his shoulder and laughed. "Compared to you, I'm still a kid . . . baa-aa-aa."

Brian's eyes zeroed in on Sue, and a smile creased his face. His steady gaze made her shiver, but were they warm or cold shivers? Being closer to her age, it made more sense for her to be attracted to him instead of Stuart. Why wasn't that the case? Surely, she had more integrity than to hold his profession against him. Today, she'd make more of an effort not to judge the future judge; after all, he was nothing like Grady.

"Hello, Sue." Brian exuded charm as he sat a little too close and casually draped his arm behind her on the couch.

His self-assurance nettled her, but she endeavored to smile. "How are you, Brian?" She bit her lip and tried to scoot over to put an inch between them. *He's not Grady. He's not Grady . . .*

This was going to be a long day.

Brian pointed to the kitchen. "Would you like me to get you a soft drink while we're waiting to open gifts?"

"Sounds good. Thank you." His left lid drooped in a fleeting wink, making Sue cringe.

Leaning over, Carol whispered in her ear. "Handsome and accommodating. You can't beat that combination."

Sue forced a smile. Brian could be likable, as long as he simply remained a friend.

"You owe it to yourself to let loose and have fun."

"Carol, please don't try to push me into a relationship. I've told you I'm not interested beyond a simple, platonic date. Period."

With a nod, Carol raised her hand and sent her an OK sign. "I'm sorry. Honest, Sooze, I didn't mean to be pushy. Friends only. Got it."

After a few minutes, Brian returned with her cold drink. "I hope regular Coke is okay. Rikki said you like it."

She took the red plastic cup. "Perfect. Thank you." She sat awkwardly and sipped the cola. Now would be the time to come up with a bit of small talk. Her wild animal question didn't seem to work at the speed dating fiasco. Time for new chitchat material. She frantically searched her mind for something clever to fill the verbal hiatus. "Are you taking any time off during the holidays,

Brian?"

"I'm off today and tomorrow." He wiggled his eyebrows and gave her a mischievous grin. "Since I'm alone and you're alone, did you want to be alone together?"

Sue's stomach dropped, and she faked a smile. Why didn't she stick with the stupid wild animal question? "Do you have anything particular in mind?"

"We could go up in a hot air balloon. That's always fun." He scratched his chin. "I know, how about the Eagle Valley train ride?"

Carol leaned close and took her hand. "You deserve to have a good time."

Sue gave her cheerleader an elbow to the ribs. "Thank you, Brian. A train ride does sound interesting." Not to mention safe.

"Great! It's a date. I'll pick you up at nine in the morning." Brian pulled out his cell. "Which reminds me, you'll need to give me your phone number."

"Eight-zero-two, zero-one-one, nine-eight-four-four. I'll be ready at nine o'clock." Sue made the mistake of glancing in Stuart's direction. Their eyes met and held for several seconds. Did she see a look of disappointment? He turned his head to watch the children play. Brian might be nice, but she'd much rather go on this train trip with Stuart.

The unsettling exchange between the couple led Stuart to battle conflicting emotions. It was his fault for suggesting she date the man. He swallowed. As much as he didn't like to admit it, this is how it should be. The natural order of things. They were closer in age, after all, and had several things in common.

Ines Garcia, the ranch cook, came from the kitchen and called the group for dinner. The other kitchen workers were lining a table with platters of fried chicken, side dishes, and fresh vegetables. Bags of potato chips and other snacks filled out the menu. Following a mealtime prayer, plates for the children, Andy, Ethan, and the ranch hands, were quickly prepared. They took their Christmas dinners outside to enjoy on the spacious wrap-around porch.

The adults gathered at the farmhouse table. Stuart settled on the bench, placed a napkin on his lap, and looked across the table. Sue's large blue eyes peered back at him. Her beauty sent a flash of internal panic as he tried to drag his gaze away.

When Brian sat next to her, Stuart's stomach tightened. *You gotta let her go, Drake. It's the best thing for her.*

He turned his head, took a large bite of chicken breast, and focused on chewing. It wasn't long before a lump gathered in his throat. A bead of sweat broke out on his forehead and a small flicker of alarm rose. The bite might have been a little too ambitious. He couldn't chew. His lungs needed air. Where could he spit the superfluous fowl?

The buzz of voices around him faded. Everything began to spin. The room kept getting darker. He couldn't lose consciousness. Not now, not in front of Sue.

Someone grabbed him from behind. A crushing blow hit his ribs.

At the moment of impact, a wad of semi-masticated chicken launched from Stuart's mouth. He gasped, finally able to breathe again.

"You okay, buddy?" The voice came out of nowhere.

Stuart couldn't bring himself to face Sue. He ran a

hand over his sore gut. "Sorry." His voice croaked, and he pointed to the door. "Fresh air."

With Lou's help, he stood, ambled outside, and took a deep breath. "I'm okay. Why don't you go inside and finish your dinner while it's still hot."

"Are you sure? I'm happy to stay with you."

"Naw, I'm fine." Stuart waved him off. "Give me a minute to compose myself. Thanks for your help, Lou."

"Frank brought a glass of water for you." Lou handed it to him and went inside.

Stuart took a drink, then breathed in deeply. *Lord, help me to surrender my feelings for Sue into Your hands. You know I want what's best for her.*

A loud screech caught Stuart's attention. A brown kid goat came running full gait around the house, with JJ waving his arms close behind. Stuart knew how the poor animal felt.

A few minutes later, JJ's yell changed to one of terror as the boy made another pass around the house in the opposite direction. This time the protective nanny goat chased him at Mach speed, her head down and nostrils flared.

Flapjack came from the barn and waved his lasso at Stuart. He raced after JJ and the angry goat while Juan Garcia came from the opposite direction.

Which one would be hogtied, the boy or the nanny? Stuart rubbed the nape of his neck and grinned. Yet another lesson the scamp had to learn the hard way.

As Stuart reached for the door handle, Little Lark came outside to stand beside him. "C'mon, Poppy." She licked her lips, then reached for his hand and tugged. "Miss Rikki got pies ready."

"Let's go get a piece." Stuart held the door open for her. With eyes straight ahead, clinging to what little self-esteem he still had, he followed the munchkin into the house. He couldn't look at Sue . . . and with every ounce of control within him, he wouldn't.

"Here he is. Poppy wants pie."

Millie smiled as she took the girl's hand and led her to the dessert table. "Why don't you show me which one Poppy likes?"

"I get to choose?" Lark's dark eyes grew wide.

Holding his paper plate, Stuart followed them, hoping Lark would choose a pie that he could easily swallow.

She circled the table twice and eventually decided on several desserts. Stuart smiled. At least he wasn't going to go hungry.

Stuart clenched his teeth and reluctantly slipped into his chair across from Sue and a grinning Brian. One mention of the choking incident or the flying chicken wad and Stuart couldn't guarantee his reaction would be cordial.

Other than a little smirk, Brian kept wisely kept his trap shut.

Following the meal, everyone hurried to the living room and found their seat. The doorknob rattled and bells jingled.

"Ho-ho-ho!" Santa Claus stepped into the room with a large bag over his shoulder. "Merry—" He cleared his throat and tried again. "Merry Christmas!"

Stuart smiled. The words came out deeper, but he'd recognize his nephew's voice anywhere. Andy was a natural with kids like his brother, Ethan. Carol raised them right.

"Have you been good boys and girls?" Santa sat in an overstuffed chair by the fireplace and opened his pack.

"Yes!" The excited children squealed as they ran to his side. Two of the older boys examined his white, fluffy beard, while a girl around ten years old poked at his well-padded tummy.

Placing two fingers in his mouth, Ethan whistled. "Okay, kids, let's settle down. I want you to sit on the floor in front of Santa and wait for your name to be called."

Stuart whispered to the little girl beside him. "Don't you want to sit with the other kids so Santa can find you?"

Slowly, Lark joined Sandy on the floor. She glanced back at Stuart with a look of pure adoration on her cherub face.

He allowed his weary eyes to study Sue. Her expression lit as she observed the children receiving their gifts. How he longed to stroke her beautiful blonde hair. The mere thought of it turned his bones to pudding.

Who was he kidding? What made him think he deserved someone as special as Sue North? If they got together, she'd be stuck caring for him in his last days. What kind of life would that be? She deserved better. He'd rather deny himself than reveal his true feelings.

Stuart noticed Sue's head turn his way, and he quickly looked elsewhere before their eyes could meet. His chest grew heavy with sadness while refocusing his attention on Lark.

A half hour later, Santa left with a wave of his gloved hand and a hearty "ho-ho-ho." The children yelled thank you and good-bye in unison before returning to their new toys.

Lou strummed a few chords of "We Wish You a Merry Christmas" on the guitar, and Gabby quickly joined in with her banjo. Faces lit as they sang the familiar holiday ditty.

When the song ended, Brian stood. "Thanks for your hospitality, folks. Are you ready to go, Marty? I have big plans for tomorrow, and I need my beauty sleep." He nudged his uncle's shoulder and then looked at Sue. "Do you need a ride home?"

"No, thank you. I came with Frank and Carol."

"Okay then." He leaned over the couch to give Sue a quick peck on the cheek. "I'll see you in the morning, babe."

Babe? Stuart bristled at the lawyer's forwardness. How gutsy to call her that in front of family and friends. Sue blushed and the flustered expression on her face said it all. The sudden need to take care of her filled his heart.

Why did he push her into dating Brian in the first place?

CHAPTER SIXTEEN

Sue followed Rikki into the empty kitchen while the others continued to sing Christmas carols in the great room. They set out the washed casserole dishes for their owners to take home.

"You did a wonderful job of being hostess today." Sue gave her daughter a hug. "I'm such a proud mom. I loved watching you and Ethan interact with the children. It seemed to come naturally."

Millie poked her head around the corner of the kitchen. "Hope I'm not interrupting anything, but we're leaving in a few minutes, and I need a drink of water before we go."

"You're not intruding at all." Rikki pointed to the refrigerator. "We have bottled water, take one with you."

Sue stepped out of her shoes and wiggled her toes. "Gabby said you and Lou are going to Seattle with her tomorrow. Sounds like fun."

"Lou can't wait to tell his brothers that we're expecting. Even Gabby managed to keep the secret."

Leaning against the counter, Sue slipped her shoes on. "Did you notice how Lark latched on to your dad, Millie?"

"I did. Isn't she the cutest little girl with those pigtails and button nose?" Millie opened the fridge door, reached for the water, and unscrewed the cap. "Dad talks about her all the time. I couldn't wait to meet her."

"It looked like you enjoyed making your own connection with her too."

"Once Lark realized Poppy loved me, she accepted me into her little world. We had fun playing with her doll for a few minutes." Millie's face glowed. "She said Poppy named her doll Princess Rainbow."

Rikki joined their conversation. "Stuart's the first person she's opened up to. Her alcoholic mother abandoned the poor little thing when she was almost three. The first time we met her, she hid under the table and refused to speak to anyone."

"Aww." Millie's eyes teared. "Bless her heart. I'll make it a matter of prayer that Lark gets her very own mommy."

"I feel bad for the mother too. It's a shame she's missing out on her little girl's life." Sue's heart ached. She couldn't help the mothers but determined to find a way to make things better for their precious children. "I wish I was young enough to adopt her."

Rikki lowered her voice. "Let me tell you a cute story. The day she came, Stuart saw her crying under the table. He looked at me, pulled out a stick of gum, then knelt down to talk to her. They've been best buddies ever since."

"Dad did the same thing with me when I was little and scared. I'd make a blanket tent in my bedroom to hide and made it my safe place. Sometimes he joined me and made up stories." A wistful look came to Millie's eyes. "Once upon a time there lived a beautiful princess named Millie."

"That's the sweetest thing I've heard in a long time." Sue's voice tightened with emotion. "I can see why the two of you are close."

"Sounds like they've quit singing." Millie proceeded to the table and picked up her ceramic bowl. "This has been such a wonderful day; I don't want to see it end. Thanks for including Gabby, Lou, and me. You're not only giving the children happy memories, but the rest of us too."

Rikki ran over and hugged her. "I'm glad you could be here. Thanks for bringing the delicious sweet potato casserole."

"My mother's favorite yam recipe. She made it every holiday." Millie rubbed the small of her back. "Our family had the yam and sweet potato debate every Thanksgiving and Christmas."

"And it wasn't Christmas without it, right Mills?" Carol came into the kitchen, gave her cousin a hug, and then turned to Sue. "Frank said it's time for us to leave too. We still have to pack for our trip to Desert Springs tomorrow."

"Thanks again for your hospitality, Rikki." Millie waved. "Come on, Carol. Let's say our good-byes to the kids."

Sue took Rikki's hand. "I came with Frank and Carol. Guess I'd better get my things together. They're leaving early in the morning to go to his daughter's for their family Christmas."

"Would you do me a favor before you go, Mom?" Rikki lowered her voice. "Make sure you say something to Stuart. I'm kind of worried about him. He's been quiet all day."

"I've noticed it too. It's hard to see him acting depressed." Her skin prickled as she wondered if their last conversation turned out to be the root cause of his sadness.

Putting her arm around her mother's shoulder, Rikki pulled her close. "Today went by too quickly. I wish you could stay a little longer. We haven't had a chance to really talk since you've been in Arizona. I've missed our mother-daughter times."

"I'd love to, honey, but I wouldn't have a ride home."

Rikki peeked into the living room. "Uncle Stuart's

still here. I'm sure he'd like company on his way to Apache Pointe."

Not completely sold on the idea of being alone in the car with him, Sue agreed with a slight nod. It would be the perfect time to bridge the gap between them, however nervousness kept her from asking him for a ride.

Stuart entered the kitchen and cleared his throat. "Lark, Sandy, and JJ want to feed the chickens with me. Is that okay?"

"Of course they can go with you. By the way, I'd like for Mom to stay a little longer. We have a lot of catching up to do." Rikki tilted her head and sent him an innocent look. "You wouldn't mind driving her home in a couple of hours, would you?"

Sue and Stuart braved a quick exchange of glances.

His gaze strayed somewhere behind her. "I don't mind taking you to town. It can be a tiresome drive back to Apache Pointe."

"Are you sure?" Icy cold fingers of uneasiness gripped her stomach. She shivered. "I-I'd hate to put you out."

"It's not an inconvenience at all. I wasn't planning to go this early anyway." His hand shook as he pushed back his shirtsleeve and checked his watch. "The kids usually want me to read them a story if I'm here at bedtime."

Rikki clapped her hands. "Thanks, Poppy! I knew we could count on you." She lightly squeezed his cheeks and kissed his forehead.

"I do appreciate it, Stuart." Sue smiled, reached to touch his arm, and stopped. *Careful Sue, don't scare him off – he's already skittish.* "I'll tell Carol I have another way home."

Following their overdue chat, Sue embraced her daughter at the front door. "I'm glad I got to stay a little longer. This has to be my favorite Christmas present."

"Mine too, Mom." Rikki gave her an extra squeeze. "I hope you'll be happy with your new life in Apache Pointe. We're thrilled you're close by."

She moistened her lips. "I know I'll feel at home in time."

"Apparently Brian is showing you around the area to help you get acclimated sooner." Rikki winked. "Is there something going on you need to share with your only daughter? I did notice a little smooch on the cheek earlier."

Sue held her hand up and spoke with all the confidence she could muster. "Brian's getting a little ahead of himself."

"How so? Don't you like him?"

"Of course, but not that way. As I've mentioned many times, I have no intentions of getting romantically involved with another man."

Rikki's eyes narrowed. "But you're dating him, Mom."

"Dating is one thing, Rikki, getting serious is quite another." She bit her lower lip. Confiding in her daughter about the attraction to Stuart had become a real temptation. But she couldn't say anything until their situation improved.

Rikki lowered her voice. "Have you told him you're a wealthy widow?"

"Who?" Sue's face heated as her mind scrambled to catch up.

"Brian, of course. Where have you been?" Rikki giggled. "Does he know you're a woman of means?"

"Good question. I've been wondering the same thing." Uneasiness wandered into her mind. "He's been a confirmed bachelor for fifty-five years, why is he in a hurry to cultivate our relationship?"

"It's always a good idea to keep your personal information to yourself. But, I don't need to tell you that, do I?" Rikki stuck her index finger in the air. "It's the one thing Dad drummed into my head since I was a kid."

"Your dad was extremely protective of you." Sue attempted to smile. She would have taken Rikki and left the oppressive Grady in a heartbeat, had she not been under his controlling thumb. Hopefully, Rikki would never find out his master plan.

The hinges on the door squeaked. Ethan, Stuart, and the kids came into the house after caring for the chickens.

Sandy ran into the kitchen and held out her hand, exposing a small, white object. "Miss Rikki! I lost my toof in Poppy's gum." Her eyes darted to Sue. "Nobody gots to pull it out!"

Lark yanked on Stuart's finger. "Read us a story now, Poppy? Pretty pwease?"

The other kids chimed in and led him to the couch.

"I'll read one story after you get cleaned up and ready for bed." Stuart ruffled JJ's hair. "Don't forget to brush your teeth, young man."

"Aww, Poppy. I don't like the toothpaste. It tastes like Lark's feet."

Stuart laughed at the boy's joke.

A short time later, the younger children sat on the living room floor with their blankets and pillows.

Sue and Rikki watched from the kitchen door as Stuart's gentle voice spun a tale of Christmastime in the forest.

CHAPTER SEVENTEEN

SUE HELD ON TO HER PURSE as Stuart's car bumped along the rutted dirt road. Silent uneasiness still hung between them. Stones and gravel pelted the undercarriage, and desert wildlife scurried from the bright headlights until they reached the highway. The flat road extended before them like a smooth ribbon.

The stillness allowed her mind to revisit the day's family-oriented activities and measure it against her solitary life in Powder Ridge, Vermont.

The excitement of a houseful of kids generated much needed joy. She could sense a bit of healing from their innocence. It was as if the Lord compensated for her inability to have the large family she had desperately wanted.

Sue put her hand to her mouth to capture a yawn. "Excuse me. Guess I'm more tired than I realized." She glanced at Stuart. "It's been a long day, but I loved it."

His gaze never left the road. "Always a lot going on at the ranch. If it's not JJ, it's Sandy coming up with all sorts of shenanigans. Those little rascals."

Tension between them loosened as they laughed about the children's antics. The mellowing edginess helped Sue relax.

At the side of the road, a pair of yellow-green glowing eyes caught her attention. A jackrabbit sprang in front of the car. One more hop and it vanished safely into the brush. Sue smiled. It was just like the Lord to bring her out of the wilderness of a stress-filled life and place her in a physical wilderness to find contentment and peace.

Sue endured another round of tranquil silence before the lights of Apache Pointe appeared in the distance. She glanced at her watch. Only a few more minutes and they'd be pulling up in front of her home.

They needed to talk about the spark that happened between them, but how should she approach it? Her thoughts returned to the Christmas dinner. "It scared me when you choked on the chicken."

"I was a little concerned myself." Stuart cleared his throat. "Brian and Marty watching the whole thing made it worse. They probably think I'm a first-class ninny."

"No one thinks you're a ninny. Who hasn't choked one time or another? I'm glad you're okay." She patted his shoulder, got a roll of Sassy Lassie mints from her purse, and offered him one. Another round of quiet returned to the car, and for the next ten minutes, she watched out the side window. If ever there was palpable silence, this was it.

Traffic in downtown Apache Pointe had become sparse, most storefronts were dark, and the sidewalks strangely empty. A minty fragrance filled the front seat as they continued to suck on their candy.

"I guess we both got talked out today, but I had a good time." Sue settled comfortably into her leather seat and finally inspiration hit. "Watching your tenderness with Lark warmed my heart. When she climbed into Millie's lap and showed Lou her special doll, I nearly cried."

"I love the sweetie. She reminds me of my little girl at that age." They came to a stop sign, and Stuart flipped on the left turn signal.

"You were a good dad, Stuart. I heard the story behind the doll's princess name and why it was near and dear to Millie's heart."

"I made a lot of mistakes." He made the left-hand turn. "Unfortunately, the same ones over and over again."

"Everyone has things in their past they wish could've been different. What a sad commentary on the human condition, but it's true." Sue glanced at his profile as the streetlights illuminated his face. "Our mistakes can't be changed, but they can be forgiven."

"Fortunately, Millie's a forgiving soul." Stuart pulled into her driveway, put the car in park, and leaned against the door.

"Thanks for the ride home. Having extra time with Rikki meant a lot to me." She grabbed the house keys from her purse. "I know it's been a long day, and you're probably tired, but would you mind if we talked here in the driveway for a few minutes?"

Stuart glanced her way and turned off the ignition. "Sure, is something wrong?"

"I hope not." She searched his face, fighting the sting in her heart. "May I ask you something?"

He unfastened his seatbelt and rolled the window down a crack. A moment's hesitation, then he spoke. "I s'pose so. What's on your mind?"

"Why have you been ignoring me the last couple of weeks?"

He wiped the tip of his nose with a knuckle. "I have a lot of things to think through."

She narrowed her eyes and tilted her head. "I've been concerned about our friendship. Even Carol remarked about how you've stopped calling me Suzie."

"Oh, sorry." Stuart lightly coughed, sniffled, and straightened his shoulders. "I-I don't know what to say."

She lowered her voice to a whisper. "Have I done something wrong?"

"Of course not. You're fine." He must've sensed the

distress in her tone. He released a deep sigh.

"Were you disappointed in me over my hate for Grady?" She looked into his eyes. "Please be truthful with me, because I've asked the Lord to help me overcome the problem. I'm doing a lot better."

"It's not about Grady. I want to be honest with you, but for now I'm dealing with personal issues." He sighed deeply and pushed his fingers through his hair. "It's best for me to work through those problems before I share with anyone."

Sue drew her shoulders up tight. "I'm afraid if we don't keep the lines of communication open, we could lose our friendship. I don't want that to happen. You're too important to me."

His features softened. "You're impor—"

Tap-tap-tap!

Stuart jumped.

Yelping, Sue pressed a hand to her pounding chest.

Phoebe glared into the windshield, her mouth puckered. The mega flashlight she carried beamed brightly into the front seat of the car, hitting Stuart between the eyes. Then she trained its stream of light on Sue.

"Everything on the up and up, North?" Her abrasive drill sergeant voice echoed around the cul-de-sac.

It took a minute or two, but Sue's racing pulse finally returned to its normal rate. She quickly lowered her window to quiet the sarge's barking. "We're right here, you don't have to yell. Everything's fine." She clenched her teeth. Right now, Phoebe Ferguson was as welcome as an infected cold sore.

Holding his forehead, Stuart began to laugh, his shoulders shaking. "I think we ought to call it a night." He looked up and added, "Suzie."

Stuart inched his car out of the driveway and headed east toward his home, which the family now called the pink mausoleum. He shook his head. The place had become a shrine to his unfortunate marital incarceration.

The wounds from his marriage to Penny were still raw. He'd been a free man for seven months, but only recently began to chip away at the bars of his mental prison.

The blinking neon Feed Bag sign came into view and lured Stuart to the drive-thru. He ordered a large sweet tea, paid for it, and parked in the farthest spot available. Closing his eyes, the image of Sue appeared.

Stuart felt like kicking himself for being on the verge of confessing romantic feelings to her. What would've happened if Phoebe hadn't knocked on the window? He would've blurted out his love for Sue. Stuart groaned. He not only feared Sue's rejection, but also of hearing her refusal echoing in his mind forever. That would be another miserable situation with no means of escape.

The reflection in the rearview mirror scowled. "This is crazy, Drake. Here you are, a man past your prime, acting like an awkward adolescent digging his toe in the sand of love." He hissed a sigh. This lunacy had to end.

With eyes closed, he bent his head in prayer.

"Lord, You're the One I always turn to for help. The Bible says Your healing grace mends broken hearts. This growing love for Sue seems wrong because of the age difference, but I have no control over these feelings. My confusion is indescribable. Should I run from a possible relationship or embrace it? You understand my weakness, please provide wisdom. In the precious name of Jesus, amen."

CHAPTER EIGHTEEN

UNABLE TO SLEEP, STUART ENTERED THE flower shop at half-past dawn. He fixed a pot of strong coffee, raised the blind in the workroom, and stared into the morning sky as the first sliver of the sun peeked over the skyline. The night Sue's soft fingers entwined in his at Perky's kept revisiting his mind. Memories of her gentle smile and warm eyes made his pulse race.

His attraction to her puzzled him. Here he stood, an older man who'd fallen in love for the first time in his life with a beautiful woman who happened to be fourteen years his junior. How could it possibly work? His pathetic, old body would disintegrate long before hers did. He released a heavy sigh and shook his head. Some dreams were too dangerous to toy with.

Surely, he could overcome this adolescent infatuation. After all, retirement age hung low over his head. His face warmed. Sue still had plenty of good years ahead of her. She needed to be with a man closer to her age. Someone like . . . he mentally spat the name, Brian Campton. His stomach curled at the thought of anyone's lips, except his own, touching Sue's. The man was taking her on a train ride. Would they be in a private car together?

Stuart had nearly finished his third cup of coffee by the time the sun had fully revealed itself.

A pessimistic voice crept into his thoughts. *What would Sue want with an old fool like you? You had your big chance at love and blew it.* His heart nearly stopped.

The strain and fatigue from the lack of sleep made the words cut deep.

"Stu? Are you okay?"

Coffee slopped from Stuart's cup, and he jumped at the sound of his brother's voice. "Max. How long have you been here?" He wiped his mouth and chin, turned from the window, and forced his shoulders to relax.

"Only a couple of minutes, but I've called your name three times. I know something's been on your mind for the last few days. You hardly said a word at Millie's Christmas party." He hung his coat in the locker. "Did you have an argument with someone?"

"Don't be silly. I'm fine." He looked at his brother and gave a half-hearted shrug. "Really, I'm fine."

"If you say so." Max held up a white bakery bag and shook it. "I brought donuts for our breakfast. Glad you remembered to get the coffee brewing. Smells great." He began to pour a cup. "Hey, there's only half a pot here."

"I've been here a while." Stuart rinsed his mug and reached for the coffee can. "I'll make more."

A short time later, the door swung open. Millie and Carol laughed as they entered and hung jackets and purses in their lockers.

"Coffee and donuts." Carol poured coffee into her cup, took a sip, and looked at her uncle. "Made it a little strong didn't you, Uncle Stu?"

"Sorry. I needed a pick-me-up this morning." Stuart smiled at Millie. "Can I pour you a cup, Princess?"

Millie rubbed her expanding tummy and chose a bear claw from the bag. "I haven't felt like drinking that stuff for a couple of months now, Dad. I brought juice from home."

The girls gave morning hugs and kisses to Stuart and Max, and then gathered their pastries and headed for the showroom.

Max swallowed his bite of cruller then washed it down with a gulp of coffee. "While we're alone, are you ready to talk about it?"

"I'm not sure it's the right time to share it with anyone." He paced to the worktable and back. "It's hard enough to wrap my own head around this tangle of feelings."

"Feelings? Oh, Stuart, no." Max groaned. "Please don't tell me you're having some kind of woman trouble."

Frowning at his brother's glib response, Stuart spun around to face him. "What makes you say that?"

"You've been moping around here like a sick pup for a while. It doesn't take a genius to see you're miserable." Max stared at him eye-to-eye. "Is there anything I can do?"

"Not sure anyone can help me with this one."

"If you're holding something in, it'll keep eating at you. Usually helps to get it off your chest."

Stuart closed the workroom door and took a moment to get his thoughts together. "This has to stay between you and me, okay?"

"Look at me, I'm your big brother. Haven't I always had your back?"

"Okay, you guessed right. It is a woman." He rubbed his eyes with his fingers and sighed. "I've tried to ignore my attraction, smother it, and even run from it, but it's no use. My willpower is kaput. She's what I missed in my marriage."

"Aww, Stu. I'm happy for you." Kindness filled Max's voice as he pulled Stuart into a quick bear hug.

"But you don't understand. There's too much of an age difference. How can I justify that?"

Max flashed a grin and patted Stu's shoulder. "You know what they say, age is simply a number." He raised his index finger in the air. "Seize the moment, Brother.

Trust me, neither of you are getting any younger.”

“We talked about our difficult marriages, and she made it clear she’s not interested in getting involved with another man.”

Confusion settled on Max’s face. He crossed his arms. “I thought she had a good marriage. She always speaks highly of Bart, Sr.”

“Who?” Stuart frowned. “What are you talking about? Her husband’s name was Grady, and he was a brute.”

“Wait. You mean we’re not discussing Gabby Blythe?”

“Heavens to Betsy, no! Whatever gave you that idea?”

“I saw you and Gabby having lunch the other day at Perky’s, and you were deep in conversation. I definitely saw hand patting.”

Stuart laughed and rubbed his jaw. “Of course you saw hand patting. We were talking about her son, my daughter, and the grandbaby we have in common. We were deciding what to get him or her for the baby shower.”

“I’m sorry, but when you mentioned an age difference, I jumped to the logical conclusion.”

“You jumped in the wrong direction.” Stuart shook his head. “Gabby’s great, but she’s more like an older sister to me.”

“Then who is she, pray tell? One of the gals from your speed dating experience?”

“No, it isn’t her. She’s nice, but our date missed the mark.”

“It can’t be Myrtle Faye or Veda from church. I give you more credit than falling for one of those two.” Max snapped his fingers. “Well, the only other one I can think of is Sue . . .”

Stuart peeked up and sheepishly nodded his head. “Go ahead and say it, I’m a cradle robber. Are you shocked or ashamed of me?"

"Shocked, yes. Gotta tell ya, Stu, I never saw that one coming." He rubbed his balding head, trying to absorb his brother's news. "First of all, I could never be ashamed of you. My only question is, are you sure?"

"You and I both know my huge mistake with Penny, and why I've been leery of making any decisions about women." He scratched his ear. "Every time Sue touches me, my heart pounds like a jackhammer. I try to stay focused on other things, but it's no use."

With his hand on his forehead, Max softly whistled. "You got it bad, Bro. You've not said anything to Sue about this growing attraction for her?"

"I haven't felt free to share it with her yet. What if she's appalled and never speaks to me again?" Stuart blurted an abrupt laugh ending in a harsh cough. "In spite of my geriatric infatuation, I've encouraged her to go out with Brian Campton. My thought was, I'd have to stay away from her, but then, I'm miserable because she's with him and not me."

"Talk about a drastic decision. I assume you've taken this to the Lord, right?"

"I've invested a lot of prayer in this catch-22, but most of all I want to be in God's will." Stuart rubbed his neck. "Even if it means a life without Sue."

"The next step is to have faith and wait for Him to work." Max's expression turned thoughtful. "In the meantime, I'll agree with you in prayer. Now, let's get busy with the day's orders."

His brother had the right idea. Faith would get him through. Stuart's lips were firm. Although the thought of a life without Sue made his heart heavy.

After a long night of tossing and turning, Sue woke early on December twenty-seventh to prepare for her train ride date with Brian. Why had she agreed to go on this trip? Exhaustion from all the Christmas preparations had drained her, and the chat with Stuart the night before added to her mental fatigue.

After setting the timer, she shuffled to the table with a cup of coffee, a piece of toast, and her open Bible. She prayed over the day's events, her attitude, and for Stuart. "If a new relationship for me is in Your will, please prepare my heart. Help me release my negative feelings for Grady, and forgive me for passing them on to Brian."

The timer beeped. Sue cleared the table and hurried to dress.

She'd tried on a couple of outfits before finding a camisole and tailored slacks which allowed her to move with ease. She pushed her arm through the sleeve of her blue blazer.

It wasn't long before Brian arrived. His angular face beamed when she opened the door. "You look beautiful today."

"Thank you. We have a nice morning for our trip." She dropped her house key into her purse, closed the locked door, and took his offered arm.

Brian kissed her cheek as he helped her into the front seat.

Well, that was ho-hum. Why didn't his display of affection do anything for her?

They headed north along I-17 for the two-hour drive to the Eagle Valley Train Station. Brian's cheery glances coupled with the bright sun shining through the window warmed Sue's face. Did he have something up his sleeve? She wondered if Rikki might be right about him knowing of her wealth. So far this morning he hadn't mentioned wanting to help with her finances, but the day wasn't over yet.

Her conscience troubled her about the judgmental thought. Brian had gone out of his way to be attentive and give her a fun, relaxing day. Time to rein in her imagination. She sat back determined to enjoy the remainder of the drive.

Brian checked the rearview mirror before passing a semi. "I've been giving some thought about fun things the two of us could do together. New Year's Eve is less than a week away, and our office is having a big bash. Would you like to go with me?"

"Thanks for the invitation, but I have other plans."

"Can you get out of it?"

Was she ready to kiss him on the lips at midnight? A shiver ran down her spine. "I've been to a lot of my husband's New Year's Eve parties in the past, and I'm not up to it this year. So, it's best to stick with my original plans."

A crowd had gathered inside the depot by the time they arrived. Sue's eyes took in the scene of activity around the small shops. The tempting aroma of smoky bacon coming from The Kopper Kettle Kafe, located at the end of the depot, made her stomach growl.

Brian pointed to the restaurant. "We're going to be eating on the train, but shall we get a cup of coffee while we're waiting to board?"

"Why not?" Sue smiled. She wouldn't turn down a couple strips of bacon, either. Her mouth still watered as they entered the cafe.

She and Brian ordered their coffee at the counter. They stood next to a man sitting alone in a booth as Brian's eyes searched for an empty table.

The man blinked once behind his black, horn-rimmed glasses, and then a smile of recognition brightened his face. "Brian Campton, down here." He broke the yolk of his egg with a corner of toast, took a bite, then wiped his mouth.

"Hey, Benny. Good to see you, buddy." He reached down and shook the offered hand. "Sue, this is Benny Jefferson, a-a client of mine. Benny, this is my dear friend, Sue North."

Brian's friend reminded her of a heavyset Johnny Cash with his dark, wavy hair. She half-expected him to break into a rousing rendition of "Ring of Fire."

"This place is hopping, would you like to join me?" Benny added a spoon of sugar to his coffee, stirred, then took a swig. "I insist."

"Sure thing. Thanks." He motioned for Sue to slide into the booth first, then scooted in next to her. "I heard you moved to Yuma."

Sue wedged her purse between them. Why did Brian always have to sit cheek-to-cheek? Marking his territory seemed to be his M.O. lately. She clenched her teeth trying to tune out their dull conversation. How much time would it take for her to feel at ease with him as she did with Stuart?

While the men talked about the changes in their lives, Sue watched a chubby little girl with a Cabbage Patch Kid face and red corkscrew curls sitting with an elderly man.

"I want more hot chocolate, Grandpa." Her yellow bar stool spun around, and she kicked her feet.

"Looks like you've had more than enough sugar, Trixie." His face reflected weariness as he stood and lifted the screaming youngster from the stool. Taking her hand, he hauled her out of the restaurant like a limp bag of orange peels.

Benny pushed his plate away, lowered his double chin to his chest, and rendered a muted odiferous belch.

Brian emptied his coffee cup and left a tip on the

table. "It's been nice catching up with you, Benny." He took Sue's arm, and the two headed for the combination gift shop and museum. "Sorry about his lack of table manners, but he's a client, and I have to deal with it."

"The storyboards hanging on the wall are fascinating." Brian walked her to the first one. "It tells the history of this area."

"I want the big eagle, Grandpa." The red-headed girl pointed to a rack of stuffed animals above her head. "Get me that eagle."

The stooped and balding old man shook his head. "Not now, Trixie."

"I want an eagle." Trixie wrinkled her freckled button nose and stomped her foot.

With a sigh, he glared at her. "What do you say?"

"Now!"

"Let's get it after the train ride."

Her voice rose with a screeching command. "I said now, Grandpa!"

The grandpa laughed. "If I get it for you, will you shut up?"

Trixie nodded with a sly grin, then grabbed it from his hand. She ran around the gift shop, making raucous raptor noises. "Caw-caw, caw-caw!"

Brian offered his arm to Sue. "That kid's driving me nuts. Let's get out of here. I sure hope they're in a separate car on the train."

In the Eagle Valley Railroad Depot, a mannequin, dressed as an old-fashioned train conductor, stood by a large chest with a satchel and suitcase on top. A mother and a runny-nosed toddler sat on a trunk while a man took their picture.

"Oh, no! Not another kid." Brian laughed and led Sue across the depot to an unoccupied bench next to the window. His hand searched his shirt pocket. "Why don't you wait here while I step outside for a minute? I'll be back soon." He disappeared into the crowd.

Sue dusted off the pew-like seat before sitting and gripped her purse tightly. She gazed at a man standing beside the large antique clock hanging on a wrought-iron post. Could it be Stuart? He had the same build, and the jade jacket appeared eerily familiar. Had he come to rescue her? Her pulse accelerated. She squinted and leaned forward in hopes of getting a closer look, nearly falling off the bench in the process.

She took a deep breath as he turned. Their eyes locked. All air squeaked from her lungs as the Chinese man nodded and walked away. Her face burned with embarrassment. At least she hadn't run to him calling his name.

The train whistle blew in the distance announcing its arrival. The hum of conversations grew silent when the call came to board the train.

Brian hurried to her side. "Are you ready to board?" They walked to the platform where he took her arm and helped her up the steps of the passenger car.

Once they settled into their seats, the train whistled again as it pulled from the station. A few minutes later, the valet offered the first-class passengers a choice of Champagne or sparkling cider as the luxury train trundled along the track.

Outside the panoramic windows, desert scenes passed by, once again reminding her of the changes in her life. Sue focused her attention on the huge vultures circling overhead in search of a rotting cadaver. She glanced at Brian's stern profile, which suddenly resembled the predatory birds.

She reprimanded herself for continuing her judgmental attitude. Brian proved to be a perfect gentleman, giving her the space she needed for once.

CHAPTER NINETEEN

Two large boxes marked photos and keepsakes sat on the floor in the spare bedroom waiting for Sue to unpack. The beginning of a new year was a good time to tackle the project. She struck a match and lit a vanilla candle on the nightstand. Knowing tears would be a part of the process, she brought in a new box of Snuffs tissues.

Sue sat on the bed, sliced the silver duct tape on the first box, and opened the flaps. On top laid a small shirt box. She lifted the lid, drew out the small bundle covered in white tissue paper, and held the unwrapped item to her chest. Rikki's embroidered christening dress had been saved to pass down to the next child. Unfortunately, Grady's selfish anger ended the tradition before it started.

Picking up the tissue paper, Sue gave it a little shake until the well-preserved ultrasound pictures of Baby Boy North fell from its folds. Hot tears stung her eyes as she openly grieved over their second child, who had been stillborn shortly after Rikki's second birthday.

An uneasy feeling settled over Sue as she stared out the spare bedroom window. The Palo Verde tree had dropped all of its leaves. Her soul felt as bare, as the long-ago scene replayed in her mind.

It had been a difficult pregnancy twenty-two years ago, and Grady's temper added to the stress. Events of the morning flooded her memory. The ordeal began when she left the stove to help Rikki with her spilled drink. It only took a few minutes, but long enough to overcook his eggs.

After she sat his plate on the table, Grady threw his breakfast into the trash. Plate and all. He slammed the lid and turned to face her. "We've been married six years, and you still can't fix my eggs right. I hate hard yolks." He raised his hand to strike her.

She inched away, one hand over her head and the other covering her swollen stomach. "I'm sorry. Rikki needed my attention for a minute."

"You always have an excuse." His fist hit the counter. "Take your role as wife and mother seriously."

"I had a choice, Grady. The baby or the eggs, and I put Rikki's needs ahead of yours." She adjusted the strap on the high chair, then stepped to the trashcan and pulled out the plate. "You could've helped with her leaky sippy cup."

"And ruin my new suit?" His voice grew louder as he opened the back door. "Quit sniping at me, woman."

The choice she made next changed her life. She followed him to the porch. "What time will you be home?"

"I'll be here when you see me." With flaring eyes, Grady grabbed her arm. "If you'd fix yourself up and have a decent meal ready, maybe I'd want to come home." His harsh tone and cruel words bruised her soul.

"I can't have a meal ready if I don't know when you'll be home."

He shoved her. At seven months pregnant, her reaction time was slow. She lost her balance and reached for something to stop her fall, but only caught air. She stumbled down the concrete steps, landing on her side.

Searing pain shot through her abdomen making it hard to breathe. Time stood still before Grady reached out to help. He took her inside and left for work.

With a bruised and swollen wrist, she struggled to grip the wall phone's receiver to call Carol. She told her friend about falling and needing help with Rikki. The sharp pains intensified and grabbed at her stomach before she could hang up. The phone dangled out of reach as labor started.

Carol arrived and called 9-1-1 to take her to the hospital.

The fall had fractured her wrist, and an hour later, they wheeled her in for an emergency C-section. A hysterectomy followed which meant there would be no more children. Alone in the hospital room, she held her last baby until finally surrendering his tiny body to the nurse.

With her trust and respect for Grady severed, she could never love the man again. Perhaps she'd never love any man. *Help me not to hate him, Lord.*

Sue stared at the ultrasound picture again. Her son would've been twenty-two-years-old now. Fighting tears, she packed her most precious items back into the shirt box, returned it to the larger container, then scooted it to the closet. She walked out of the room, closing the door behind her.

After putting on a fresh pot of coffee, Sue pulled out two large mugs from Stuart's kitchen cabinet. She felt like an intruder to be in his home while he was at work. On the other hand, he wouldn't be hanging around and making her nervous.

Gabby was due any time to help her paint. Fortunately, the living room's nauseating pink walls were the last on the list to get a makeover.

She unfolded the drop cloth and spread it on the refurbished hardwood floor. Stuart had made a wise decision in ordering an area rug instead of going with wall-to-wall carpeting. They had planned it to be a beautiful room in a western motif. She couldn't wait until Stuart saw the oil painting of the wild horses Rikki found in her attic at the ranch.

The ringing of the doorbell brought Sue out of her interior decorator mode. She opened the front door. "Good morning, Gabby. I've sure missed you. How did your trip go?"

"We had a wonderful family time at Bart's house. They were speechless at Millie and Lou's baby announcement."

"What a blessing. I don't think any of us expected the wonderful news. I'm glad Millie proved the doctor wrong about them not conceiving." Sue headed for the kitchen and called over her shoulder. "Come on and have some coffee before we get to work. I brought cinnamon rolls."

"Say no more. You know I can't turn down your pastries."

Sue's phone rang while she plated the rolls. "Excuse me. It's my lawyer." She put the phone to her ear. "Hi, Jill. What's up?"

"We may have an issue with Grady's will, and I wanted to speak with you about it. Is this a good time?"

Sue clenched her teeth. Another issue with the will? "If you don't mind, I'm going to put the phone on speaker so my friend, Gabby Blythe, and I can both listen. She's been one of my confidants since I moved out West."

"That's all right. Hello, Mrs. Blythe."

"Hello." Gabby poured the cups of coffee and returned to the table where Sue sat.

"Listen, Sue, I received a message today. Seems Carson North is contesting Grady's will. Do you know this person?"

"Unfortunately, I do. He's my late husband's brother.

We met a couple of times over twenty-five years ago, but I wouldn't know him now if I fell over him."

"The man wants equal shares with you and Rikki. There are no other immediate relatives, right?"

Sue glanced out the window and frowned. "Not that I'm aware of. Grady told me his brother was in prison for armed robbery. Has he been released?"

"I don't see any indication of it in my records. All I know is he's not had any other illegal activity. Not even a traffic ticket. His last location appears to be in Florida where he's been incarcerated."

"Good news, right, Jill? It sounds like he's still behind bars. What do you suggest I do about him challenging the will? If I remember correctly, Grady only left him a few thousand dollars." Sue pursed her mouth.

"I don't think Mr. North has a strong case even if he does get out soon, but I'll keep looking into it for you."

"Thanks for the update." Sue hit the end button on her phone.

Gabby crossed her arms. "Those North boys were real winners. They must've been raised by Bonnie and Clyde."

"I never met any of my other in-laws, but from what I've heard they were good people. Grady mentioned his dad being disabled and the family on welfare. Grady always promised himself he'd never lack for money again."

"I see. Once he had a taste of the good life, it hooked him." Gabby finished her cinnamon roll, licked her fingers, and wiped them on a napkin.

"And he totally made the most of it too." Sue put her phone in her jeans pocket and raised her coffee mug. "Grady would've done anything to get ahead. He never had enough. Obviously his brother is the same way."

"Put your mind at ease for now. Your lawyer said he

doesn't have a solid case. If you need additional help, you can always call a local attorney."

Sue shrugged and tossed her napkin into the trash. "The only one I know around here is Brian."

"I'm sure he's reputable because the Native American Missions hired him. They wouldn't have done that if there was any doubt." Gabby shook her head. "If you're not comfortable with him, find someone else. I'll help you look."

"Since I hesitate to mix business with friendship, your help would be appreciated." Sue placed a can of paint on the drop cloth and carefully pried off the lid.

"You got it, girl." Gabby stirred the paint before pouring it into the pans. "I'll do the trim while you start on the walls." She grabbed a brush. "Speaking of Brian, I want to hear all about your train ride."

"At least we had a nice day to get away. I got to know Brian a little better." She reached for the roller and dipped it into the paint. "I discovered he's impatient with young children."

After moving the stepladder to the window, Gabby carefully painted around the trim. "Other than his allergy to little kids, have your feelings for him improved?"

"They've remained status quo. Like I've said all along, I like Brian. He's a nice man, but there are things that bother me about him. For now, friendship is all I need." She rolled antique white paint onto the wall. "Do you think one coat will cover this pink?"

"We won't know until it dries. The can says it covers everything in one coat or our money back."

"It better do the job. Stuart's new rug is coming tomorrow." Sue reloaded her roller. "The only thing left to do is match draperies and curtains. Then we're finally done."

"This calls for a celebration. Valentine's Day is

coming in two weeks. Why don't you and I plan an elegant dinner for a small group? Heaven knows we've had a lot of experience." She ticked the names off on her fingers. "Millie, Lou, Carol, Frank, Brian, you, Stuart, and me. It's only eight people. Won't that be fun?"

Sue barely nodded her head. It would be more fun if she could sit with Stuart. "I don't think our condos are big enough for eight."

"No, but this place is the perfect size. We'll combine the dinner with a housewarming." Gabby motioned around the room. "Let's ask Stuart if he would mind hosting in his beautiful home we graciously de-pinked for him."

"Are you stooping to emotional blackmail, Gabby?" Sue grinned and rolled a huge W on the wall and began to fill it in. "Is this going to be formal?"

"Absolutely. I said elegant."

"And who's going to drop the, um, elegant bomb on the men?"

Gabby released a hearty laugh. "Lou and Frank have wives to do the dirty work, which leaves Brian and Stuart. Surely we're woman enough to handle a couple of bachelors."

"Guess I'll be calling Brian." Turning from Gabby to hide her disappointment, Sue made a few overlapping strokes with the paint. "While you're informing Stuart of the dress code, you can ask him to help us with a floral centerpiece and pillar candles."

"I never get a chance to use my Limoges wedding china and Waterford crystal goblets anymore. I'm glad I brought them out of storage."

"Good idea, Gabby." She laid her roller down and stretched. "I have a beautiful linen tablecloth we can use."

Gabby Blythe was a definite Godsend. What a fun

and down-to-earth friend. Only she would think to combine a housewarming with a Valentine's Day dinner. Sue's excitement and curiosity rose. She couldn't wait to see how handsome Stuart looked dressed to the nines. If only he was her date.

CHAPTER TWENTY

TWO WEEKS AGO, SUE HAD REACHED Brian's voicemail trying to invite him to the Valentine's dinner. She hadn't received a response. Should she be worried? Her stomach churned as the old feeling of neglect resurfaced. It was one more warning bell against him. Had she discouraged his advances one too many times and he'd found another woman? She decided to give him the benefit of the doubt. Maybe he was busy in court.

She dialed Gabby's number. "The guest list for our party is coming together. I have a definite yes from Frank and Carol, but I couldn't reach Brian."

"Have you called his office?"

"Of course, along with his cell phone. His secretary didn't seem alarmed and said this happens once in a while. She promised to give him my message." Sue tapped her foot. "The party's tonight, and he hasn't bothered to respond. Let's assume he's not coming."

Gabby released a moan. "I agree. But, if the old boy calls or shows up, we'll simply have to deal with it."

"I suppose you're right. It's rude not to contact me for two weeks. If he didn't want to see me again, he only had to let me know."

"It's nearly four o'clock. We have less than three hours before our guests arrive. Are you ready to take things to Stuart's for the party?"

Sue glanced at the items on her table. "I couldn't find my linen napkins, but everything else is packed and ready to put in the car. I'll pick you up in a couple of minutes.”

Once they got to Stuart’s house, it didn’t take them long to carry their boxes inside.

Gabby checked the buffet drawers. “While I waited for you to pick me up, I called Stu. He said Penny had several sets of cloth napkins around here somewhere. Different patterns and sizes.”

“Let’s hunt for eight of the same style.” Sue’s phone beeped with a text. She quickly scanned it. Brian. Rats. “You’ll never guess who’s finally sending me an RSVP text. We’ll have four couples after all.”

“Nothing like waiting until the last minute.” Gabby closed the drawer. “Good grief, all her napkins are pink. Plaid, paisley, stripes, and floral. You name it, Penny probably had it. While your phone is out, why don’t you see if Stu can get some red napkins?”

She nodded and dialed his number. “Hi, Stuart. Would you pick up red cloth napkins on your way home from work?”

“I suppose so. Couldn’t you find Penny’s?”

“We found them, and they’re lovely, Stuart, but they’re pink.” She looked at Gabby and grinned. “All ten sets.”

“And that won’t work, huh?”

“I don’t have time to explain. We need large, red napkins. At least eight of them.”

“Got it. Eight red napkins coming up. I brought the candles home last night. Are they what you wanted?”

“They’re perfect.”

“See you in a few minutes with the flowers and napkins.” A click on the line ended the call.

Sue turned to face Gabby. “Did I give him a clear description for the napkins?”

“I don’t think we have anything to worry about. Stu can follow orders.”

As they completed setting the table with Gabby's gold-trimmed white china plates, caterers from the Hollow Coyote delivered the food in shiny chafing dishes.

Soft instrumental music played as Sue and Gabby placed candles on the table and in various spots around the dining room.

Sue blew out her match and took in the soft glow. "The last candle is lit. What do you think, Gabby?"

"Very romantic." She turned her head. "I think I hear Stuart in the garage. Why don't you get the napkins while I finish pouring water in the goblets?"

Sue met Stuart at the door, took the centerpiece from his hands, and placed it on the counter. "Were you able to get the napkins?"

"Boy did I get lucky. These were in the discontinued items bin." He grinned and proudly presented a Kolonial Kubby bag. "In here you'll find one package of a dozen red dinner-sized napkins, as ordered, especially for you, Suzie."

"Thank you." Sue pulled out the cellophane package, then peeked up at Stuart. She kissed his cheek and hurried to the dining room before she burst out laughing. He got the paper kind? Shaking her head, she placed a stiff and scratchy napkin at each setting. Hadn't she specified cloth? Zero hour had finally arrived. These would have to do.

Gabby retrieved the floral centerpiece from the counter. "This is beautiful, Stu. Love your choice of flowers. You might want to hurry and get dressed. Our guests will be here any time." She placed the fragrant arrangement in the middle of the table.

After he ran up the stairs, the front door opened. Millie and Lou took in the home improvements as they walked through the door. Frank and Carol were close behind.

Carol gave Sue a hug. "I love the color you and Gabby chose for this room. It's warm and inviting, isn't it, Frank?"

His eyes scanned the area. "What an amazing transformation. You had a great idea to combine Stu's housewarming with a Valentine's dinner."

Motioning the couples into the living room, Gabby held up a silver tray overflowing with various appetizers. "Once Brian gets here, we'll take our seats. Meanwhile, would you like hors d'oeuvres?"

Millie helped herself to a bacon-wrapped treat. "I love what you've done with the house. It looks like a completely new place. How does Dad like it?"

"I think he loves it. He's crazy about his new couch." Sue pointed to the camel-colored sofa in the far corner.

Frank headed for the sofa. "This looks comfortable. I gotta try it out." He sank into the soft cushion. "Lou, come check this out. We're talking man cave quality right here."

He took his place on the other end and ran his hand across the seat. "I'll bet it's real leather, isn't it?"

Stuart came down the stairs and hugged Millie. "What do you think of my new and improved home, Princess?"

"It's beautiful, Dad. You all did a wonderful job. I'm sorry I couldn't be a part of it." She walked to the fireplace. "I like this painting of the running horses. It looks like it could be on the ranch."

Gabby nodded for Sue. "My hands are full with these hors d'oeuvres. Will you be a sweetheart and help Stuart with his tie?"

"Of course I will." Sue gently pulled on his arm. "You look dashing, Stuart, but your tie is slightly crooked. Gabby wanted me to fix it for you." As her fingers repositioned the fabric, their eyes locked. Her hands jerked away. She whispered, "Sorry."

Stuart's cheeks turned a light shade of pink, and he quickly glanced to the floor. As if on cue, the doorbell rang. Relief settled on his features, and he hurried to answer it. "Come on in, Brian."

With a slight look of scorn, Brian handed his jacket to Stuart. He then walked to Sue and gently kissed her hand. His gaze slowly traveled from her shoes to the top of her head. "You look magnificent in that dress."

For some reason, the compliment fell flat. She smiled. "Thanks, Brian." Her mystery date had been gone for two weeks with no reason or explanation. Now he wanted her to pick up where they left off? Fat chance.

Gabby clasped her hands. "Everyone's here, shall we go to the dining room and have our meal?" She took Stuart's arm and led the way. She pointed to the candlelit buffet where the prepared meal waited for them.

"How dreamy." Millie handed a plate to Lou and motioned around the room. "I love all the candles."

Lou released a soft moan as he scooped a helping of mashed potatoes. "Eating in the dark has Mom's name written all over it. You wouldn't believe how many times she made her four sons and husband suffer through candlelight dinners."

"It doesn't look like you've missed too many meals, Lou." Stuart took his filled plate to the dimly lit table.

"The Blythe men learned to eat in braille." Lou paused and put a dinner roll on his plate. "Here's a tip, guys. Meat at six o'clock, veggies at three."

Sue could only see the shadows of their faces, but loud chortles came from the general direction of Stuart and Frank.

"Listen here, Son." Gabby took her seat and her dark form playfully poked his arm. "When a lady lives in a testosterone-filled house like I did, she has to inject a shot of estrogen whenever and however possible."

"Don't pay any attention to them, Gabby." Carol's voice came from somewhere in the semi-darkness. "I think I can speak for the ladies when I say, the candlelight brings on such a romantic atmosphere."

"Drink it in now, girls." Gabby giggled. "If memory serves, you won't get this treatment at home."

Three feminine "amens" rose from around the table.

"But-but-but how can I gaze into Carol's beautiful eyes without the lights on?"

Another masculine voice spoke up. "I hope that was Pastor Frank speaking."

Within minutes, everyone was seated at the table. After the laughter calmed, Frank led in prayer.

Sue picked up her fork and glanced at her date's hazy outline. He hadn't bothered to join in the group's fun. Why did he come if he didn't want to be there? "Brian, you're awfully quiet. Are you okay?"

His silverware clinked on the plate. "I'm sorry. I don't mean to be a wet blanket, but my mind is on a major trial coming up tomorrow."

Stuart cleared his throat. "Your Uncle Marty said you were working on the Wilson case. How's it going?"

"It's going okay." The rough paper napkin rustled as Brian wiped his mouth. "I've been working hard on it for the last couple of weeks."

Sue's eyes squinted. Why didn't he have the courtesy to tell her whether he was coming or not? A call would've only taken a minute or two of his precious time, or his secretary's.

"Sounds like you've invested a lot of time." Ice hit the

side of the glass as Stuart took a sip of his drink. He grabbed the napkin from his lap. "I hear the whole thing is going to be televised on Courthouse 90 TV."

"That's right. I'm a little tense about it." Brian buttered his dinner roll and placed half on his plate. "It's a lot of pressure, but my team's in place, and I'm ready to take it on."

Silence followed. Sue sighed into her napkin. Brian took part in the conversation, and then he had to brag. Her conscience niggled. Why did she have to judge him all the time? Maybe he wasn't bragging, but showing self-confidence.

Frank set his fork down and wiped his mouth. "I know we gave you ladies a hard time about the candles earlier, but all kidding aside, this is delicious."

Gabby rested her forearms on the table. "Thank you. The Hollow Coyote catered. It's always nice to have a good meal with close friends. To be honest with you, I thought with a half-dozen candles on the buffet, having two candles on the table would be plenty of light."

"It's no big deal. You and Sue did a good job at planning all this." Stuart pushed his plate away. "It doesn't hurt us to be formal and romantic once in a while.

"Thank you, Uncle Stu. See, Frank?" Carol nudged her husband's elbow. "You should take notes."

Brian leaned closer to Sue and whispered. "The candlelight enhances your beauty." He rubbed her cheek with his knuckle.

She closed her eyes, embarrassed at his public display of affection. Maybe the candles weren't such a good idea. Sue glanced across the table where Stuart squirmed in his seat.

His grunt was barely audible.

"I had a call from Ethan today." Carol scooted to the

edge of her chair. "He said the kids were playing outside and JJ went missing. It took Ethan almost an hour to find him."

Stuart smacked the table. "The little rascal does that too often. I'm afraid that one of these days he's going to get hurt hiding in those obscure places and how will we know?"

"You're right, Uncle Stu. There are so many poisonous snakes and things out there. Ethan's warned him about it, several times."

"Sometimes kids have to learn things the hard way." Gabby folded her napkin. "I'm sorry to say, but it may take a crisis before JJ gets the message. The key is to find something to interest him."

Brian wiped his mouth. "Good luck with that. He's just a kid with nothing but a good imagination and wide-open spaces. I grew up on the reservation and did the same things at his age. What kept me pumped was the adrenaline rush I got watching them try to find me." Beep-beep-beep. He put his hands on the table and stood. "I'm sorry, but my alarm's reminding me it's time to go."

"I'll get your jacket." Stuart scooted his chair from the table.

Brian raised a hand to stop him. "Don't bother getting up, I know my way out. Thanks for everything, I had a good time." He leaned down and kissed the top of Sue's head. "Bye, my love."

She patted his hand kneading her shoulder. "Good-bye, Brian. Best of luck on the trial."

A chorus of good-byes came from around the table.

"Excuse me, folks." Millie awkwardly got to her feet. "Save some dessert for me. Make it a big piece of whatever it is. I'm eating for two."

Gabby took a drink, wiped the moisture from her

lips, and relaxed in her chair. "A televised trial. How O. J. Simpson! I might have to tune in to see Brian at work."

A squeal came from the hall. "Carol! I need you."

Carol jumped to her feet. "It's too early for the baby." She scurried from the room. It didn't take long before Carol's voice called from the bathroom. "Uhh . . . Sue . . . would you come here, please?"

She stood and headed that way. "Is it the baby?"

Lou groaned and cracked his knuckles.

"No, just come here."

As Sue got closer to the open powder room door, she heard the women laughing. "What's going on?" It only took a few seconds for Sue's shriek to hit the air.

The thunder of feet stomped down the hall.

"What's wrong?"

Sue, Carol, and Millie turned to look at them. Each one wore bright red splotches and streaks on their mouths and cheeks.

"It won't wash off with regular hand soap." Millie held up her equally red hands. "I tried several times."

Stuart flipped on the hall light. All seven stood with mouths agape at the red-faced horror.

When the laughter finally eased, Sue smacked Stuart's shoulder. "It's all your fault, Mr. Bargain Hunter. The dye from the napkins got on our hands and faces every time we used them."

With a new onslaught of chuckles, Stuart snorted twice, then fell against the wall. "I just remembered, our buddy, Brian, has a televised court date tomorrow. Talk about must see TV!"

Sue's stomach coiled as she paced the floor. She had to call and explain the red dye to Brian, hoping he wouldn't be angry with everyone.

Stepping into the dining room, she lifted her phone.

"I'm going to my car to call Brian. My conscience is bothering me, and I need to apologize. Like you said, he's going to be on TV tomorrow."

"Do you want me to call since I'm the one who bought the cheap napkins?" Stuart's brown eyes twinkled as his mouth quirked into a semi-smile. "I'll be as sincere as I can."

"That's what I'm afraid of. Let me handle it on my own, thank you. You've done quite enough for today." She couldn't help but love his crooked grin. "This will only take a few minutes, then I'll be back to lend a hand in the clean-up."

Sue climbed into the front seat of her car, took a deep breath, and auto-dialed Brian's number. How would she break the news gently?

A click on the line. "Brian Campton, here."

"This is Sue. Did you get home yet?"

"No. I live in Phoenix, remember? I still have twenty minutes to go. Why do you ask, did I forget something?"

"Oh, Brian." She gulped. *Lord, give me the right words.* "You have no idea how much I hate to tell you this. By the way, is there any place for you to pull off the road?"

"You're scaring me, Sue. Why should I pull off the road?" His voice held an irritated edge.

"Trust me."

"There's a gas station ahead. I'll stop there, but remember I have to get home soon."

She took another deep breath while he parked the car. "Please don't get angry, no one is to blame. After you left, we turned the lights on, and discovered that all of us have red dye on our hands and faces from the napkins."

He must've been speaking in his native Apache tongue, because Sue couldn't understand a single word, although the delivery came through loud and clear.

"The trial is being televised tomorrow. Oh, crud! I have red streaks all over my face and hands. It won't rub off. How do you get rid of this mess?"

"Soap and water doesn't seem to work. You might try peroxide, lemon juice, or something with rubbing alcohol. Use it on your hands first to see if it works, then try it on your face."

"I don't have that kind of stuff in my house."

"You're on the way home. Stop at a pharmacy and buy a bottle. Maybe they can suggest something else to try." She hesitated before breaking her final idea to him. "If all else fails, you may have to use makeup." A click on the other end of the line told Sue he didn't care for her suggestion.

Stuart met her at the door when she headed inside. "Sorry, Suzie. I hope the red napkins haven't caused a rift in your relationship."

After the intense look she and Stuart shared earlier, the statement came as a surprise. Did he truly want her to be with Brian?

The day after the napkin fiasco, Stuart finished with a customer then hurried to the flower shop breakroom. He rubbed his red-stained hands together and quickly turned the TV to Courthouse 90. Brian Campton and the infamous Wilson trial was about to start. He offered Max a box of Jujubes. "You know, I shouldn't be enjoying this as much as I am."

"Can't say as I blame ya." Max shook colorful candy pieces into his palm. "It's natural since you have a thing for Sue."

"Shh. There he is. Is that a red streak on his nose?"

The camera zoomed in on Brian for a close-up. Stuart slapped his knee. His chuckle ended with a snort. "It is!"

Max glanced at him. "Did you do it on purpose?"

"Of course not." He half-chuckled. "I was in a hurry and grabbed the first package of red napkins I could find."

"You laugh now, but aren't you afraid Sue will feel sorry for Brian? She might continue to go out with him to make up for his embarrassment."

Stuart's toothy grin flatlined as he fixed his eyes on the pointed toe of his cowboy boot. Leave it to Max to take all the fun out of a simple mishap.

CHAPTER TWENTY-ONE

STUART HUNG UP THE WALL PHONE in the workroom of their flower shop. He turned to his brother. "Hold on to your teeth, Max. That was our realtor, Harry. He said someone put in an offer for Scent-sations."

"Ye-haw!" Max pumped the air with his fist. "Harry listed the shop at the end of December. It's only the beginning of March and we have a bite, talk about an answer to prayer. What's our next step?"

"There's one little speedbump on the road to retirement. The buyer wants us to come down fifty thousand dollars."

"We can't do that, Stu. It's a flower shop and a landscaping business. Considering the property and inventory, we made a point to be more than generous with the asking price. Our turn to come back with a counter offer."

"Let's be careful to not scare the buyer off, but we can't give our company away, either. I'm glad the realtor knows what he's doing. He'll help us with the negotiations."

Max's expression turned thoughtful as he placed his clippers on the counter and sat on a nearby stool. "Let's see if we can get with Harry before noon and work something out. I don't want to drag this out any longer than necessary."

The children's pleading brown eyes melted Sue's heart. She'd only been at the ranch twenty minutes before they pressured her into milking a goat.

Rikki handed her the washed and sanitized buckets. "I wish I could milk Gretchen with you, Mom, but it's time for the second graders' math class, and the others have homework." She wiped her hands on a towel. "One of the ranch hands will be there if you need help. Oh, and you'll want to wear those rubber boots by the door. Trust me on this."

Sitting on a bench in the mudroom, Sue donned the yellow rubber boots. She grabbed the shiny bucket and then clomped behind the younger children to the barn.

The old building had seen better days. Decades of baking desert sun had taken its toll. Inside, the smell nearly sapped her breath. She blinked, allowing her eyes to adjust to the dimness of light, and soon made out the shapes of wooden enclosures and the loft overhead.

Flapjack was mucking a stall when JJ ran to him and yanked on the leg of his jeans. "Miss Sue's gonna milk Gretchen."

He tousled the boy's hair. "This should be fun." He caught Sue's eye. "Have you done this before, ma'am?"

"Not in this life. Could you help me get started?" She watched as JJ scooted the milk table from the corner and called the mama goat. Gretchen's eyes moved, but she didn't.

After coercing and wrestling a rope around the feisty goat's neck, Flapjack handed the lead to JJ. The boy dragged and jerked the bucking animal from the dirty stall to the milk stand. The process looked borderline abusive.

Gretchen's stubbornness began to crush Sue's hopes of pleasing the children. She watched them bribe the beast with a trail of food up the goat stand ramp. They dumped the remainder of grain into her trough.

Once Flapjack locked the nanny in her head catch, he stepped aside and grinned. "She's all yours, ma'am." He leaned against the barn wall, stuffed his hands into his pockets, and waited.

"Okay, Gretchen." Sue stared into the pale, slit eyes and took a deep breath. "I get to milk you today, you sweet, old goat."

The boys and girls clapped. "Come on, Miss Sue."

"Here we go." Could she really do this? One peek at those hairy udders, and she nearly lost her nerve. She wondered if Rikki could see her from the kitchen window. She would double over with laughter at the sight of her mother attempting to drain poor Gretchen.

JJ stepped between Sue and the goat and pointed. "You gotta grab those hangy-down things and pull on 'em. But not real hard."

"Hold on." Flapjack handed her a bottle of udder wash. "Gotta git 'em all nice and clean before you start."

Sue eyed the spray bottle. "Am I supposed to use this on my hands?"

With a hearty laugh, Flapjack shook his head and handed her a clean cloth. "Nope, I'm talkin' about those hangy-down things."

Because of the nanny's kicking, it took Sue nearly ten minutes to swab poor Gretchen who had almost finished her grain.

"Eat slow, girl. I still have to milk you." She grabbed the shiny silver bucket and gave the goat's udders a squeeze. "Nothing? Okay, let's try this again." She clenched her teeth and gripped a little harder. Squeeeeeeze.

Gretchen bolted and bleated her displeasure.

"Sorry girl. I'll get this." The next attempt squirted milk to Sue's jaw. Her eyes popped open as the warm liquid dribbled from her chin.

The children squealed and laughed in delight. The ranch hand seemed to be enjoying the comedy routine too.

Sue squeezed again. Finally success! She was not about to loosen her grip now. Ready, aim, fire. "Watch me, kiddos. Two hands!"

"Look at you go! Milkmaid extraordinaire."

Her breathing halted at the sound of the familiar voice in the shadows across the barn. She turned to find Stuart leaning against the tack room door, his arms loosely crossed. He flashed his debonair grin while the ranch's Australian Shepherd sat beside him.

"It's Poppy!" Lark sang out. The little girl broke from the group, ran to him, and clutched his shirttail. "Hold me, pwease Poppy!"

Ol' Shep barked as Stuart lifted her into his arms and carried her to Sue's side. "Miss Sue is doing a good job, isn't she?" He kissed Lark's forehead and lowered her to the barn floor. Peeking into the pail, he gave a light chuckle. "Would you look at that, kids? She almost has the bottom filled."

"Gretchen seems to like her soft touch." Flapjack pushed the straw hat to the back of his head exposing his sandy-colored curls. "Since she's experienced now, we'll git her to milk one of the cows."

Laughing, Sue kept a steady tempo going. "If I'm going to milk Ol' Bossy, then you'd better put me on the payroll, Flapjack."

Stuart leaned forward and winked. "Think you'll be done in a couple of hours?"

"You're hilarious, Farmer Drake." Her gaze skittered away. If her eyes held a hint of interest, she didn't want him to witness it. "Don't you have something more constructive to do than watch me make a clown of myself in front of all these kids?"

"I guess you don't need my help, huh?" Stuart shrugged, then headed for the tack room with Shep at his heels.

Sue's hands continued to milk the nanny while her eyes followed him to the door. She wished his presence didn't boost her heart rate to a dangerous level. Taking a deep breath, she noticed Flapjack's dark blue eyes still watching her. He raised his brows and sent her a knowing grin.

The pitter-patter of little goat nuggets hit the table. Sue clenched her teeth, removed the pail, and looked at the nanny eyeball-to-eyeball. It took great restraint to keep from choking the animal. She roughly swiped the table and udders clean . . . again.

Then, returning the pail, she soon got into rhythm. Without forewarning, the nanny jerked and stepped into the bucket.

"No, Gretchen! Get your dirty hoof out of the milk." Sue hung her head and her shoulders drooped, then she hoisted the goat's hind leg.

"It's no big deal, we're not losing too much milk." Flapjack shook his head. "Sandy, go git us another pail."

The six-year-old immediately obeyed.

Glancing into the container, Sue's heart sank. Her face warmed as she turned to the ranch hand. "Are those floaters what I think they are?"

"Yup." A deep chuckle rose from his chest. "We can't use this milk, but at least you're learning a skill set."

"I'll be sure to add it to my resume." Sue took the clean bucket from Sandy, placed it under Gretchen, and soon developed a milking cadence. Aim and squirt. Aim and squirt. Sue smiled at the sound of white liquid splashing against the side of the bucket.

Gretchen wiggled and squirmed, but this time, Sue

dodged the wicked assault of an airborne hoof. Why wasn't Gretchen enjoying this?

Sue stared at the half cup of milk in the bucket. What would the cooks do with a whole four ounces?

Stuart returned to the tack room which smelled of saddle soap, oil, and horse sweat. After grabbing a harness from a hook on the whitewashed wall, he threaded a heavy needle with black cord. If he stayed busy enough, maybe he could keep his mind off Sue.

He grinned. Even with goat juice dripping from her chin, she had to be the prettiest woman he'd ever met. Hands down. He found it more and more difficult to keep his distance. Every time they were together, he wanted to haul her into his arms.

A voice in the nearby paddock caught Stuart's attention. He stuck his head out the door and found seventeen-year-old Colt Richardson talking to a stallion while brushing its tangled mane.

"What am I going to do Shadow? The younger ones get adopted, but nobody wants us older kids." Colt rested his hand on the horse's shoulder. "I only have a couple of months to live here, and I'm scared."

Shadow nickered softly and shook his head in response, as if understanding the boy's broken heart.

Stuart stepped outside and leaned on the fence. "Hey there, Colt. I admire the gentle touch you have with Shadow. He always seems to respond well to you."

"Hi, Poppy. I didn't know you were here." The boy turned his head and rubbed Shadow's nose. "Animals accept me no matter what I look like or how old I am. I've loved them all my life."

"Have you ever thought of making a career out of working with animals?" Stuart scratched his chin. "I can see you becoming a veterinarian, a horse trainer, or even a wildlife rehabilitator. There are a lot of jobs out there for someone with your God-given talent."

"Sounds good, but I don't have the money to go to college."

"You might be able to become an apprentice or an assistant and save up for tuition—and of course, there are also scholarships. Why don't you get online and see what's available, and I can get in touch with a few friends."

"Thanks for your help. The only problem is where am I going to live when I have to leave the ranch in a couple of months?"

Stuart's heart clenched as he gave Colt a side hug. "We'll pray about that too. You'll be surprised at what God can do with you."

CHAPTER TWENTY-TWO

THE SECOND WEEK OF APRIL AND Millie was overdue. Stuart hadn't been able to sit still all morning. His grandbaby would be born any day now. Maybe buying supplies for the ranch would keep his mind occupied.

Entering the home improvement store, he pulled out a shopping cart and headed for the paint department. Another two gallons of brick red should be enough to finish the barn. He grabbed three roller pans as his phone rang. "This is Stuart."

A deep, shaky voice responded. "It's time!"

"It's what? Is this Lou?"

"The baby's coming. Millie's in labor." Tires squealed and horns honked. "We're going to the hospital."

"Be careful, Lou. That's my daughter and grandbaby in the car with you."

"I'm not driving." Lou groaned. "My momma's at the wheel."

Stuart laughed. "I'm on my way." He ended the call and ran to the parking lot. If only he could share this life-changing moment with Sue. Pushing the thought aside, he jerked at the car's door handle, but it didn't budge. He pointed the key fob directly at the blue door and pushed the unlock button. Nothing. Stupid fob. Maybe he needed to replace the batteries.

Wait a cotton-pickin' minute. He hadn't owned a blue car in five years. At least it was the same model. Holding the keyless remote over his head, Stuart pressed the horn button. It honked two rows over, and he hurried in that direction.

Happy for the light traffic, he made his way to Apache Pointe Memorial. Once inside the hospital, the lady at the information desk directed him to the green elevator which would take him to the maternity floor.

He walked down a long corridor and saw a door marked 'Deliveries.' The woman surely didn't mean that one, it wasn't green. Time to ask for help. A custodian led him in the opposite direction and to the proper elevator door.

When Stuart entered the waiting room, Gabby and Carol were leafing through well-worn magazines. He leaned over and kissed his niece's forehead, then took the seat next to Gabby. "Any news, yet, Grandma?"

"It's only been a half hour, Stu. First time babies aren't in a hurry." Gabby tossed the magazine on the blond end table. "We may be here a while."

Stuart pointed to a coffeemaker on a nearby counter. "Would either of you like a cup?"

"Yes, please." Gabby rubbed her hands together. "I'd like to warm my hands. It's chilly in here."

"I'll pass." Carol shook her head. "I remember their coffee tastes like tar."

Stuart filled two disposable cups with the dark liquid and handed one to Gabby. "It smells a little old, but at least it's hot. Would you like cream or sugar?"

"Black is fine, thanks. I don't mind strong coffee." She laughed and took a sip. "Trust me, I've had worse in other countries."

Carol returned her phone to her purse. "Sue sent a text saying she's on the way to the hospital."

At the mention of Sue's name, Stuart's last swallow of the hot drink went awry, and dribbled down his chin. He quickly turned his back to the women and wiped his face. *C'mon, Drake. Be more discreet in hiding your feelings.*

After they watched a few minutes of a muted *Leave It to Beaver* rerun, Sue joined them in the waiting room. "Did I miss anything?"

"Not a thing. Millie went into labor this morning." Gabby looked at her watch. "Lou and I brought her here about an hour ago, but he hasn't updated us yet."

"Which reminds me, I need to call Max and let him know why I'm not at the shop." Stuart got to his feet, shuffled to the hall, and breathed a sigh of relief. He had come for the birth of his grandchild, and Sue's dazzling presence kept blocking his concentration.

After leaving a message for his brother, Stuart paced the hallway. Sue looked exceptionally pretty in the lavender outfit today. Maybe he could've kept his eyes in their sockets had she worn the non-descript brown one.

The only safe way for him to keep his mind off her would be to start a deep conversation. An idea struck. This was the perfect opportunity to tell everyone about his recent talk with Colt.

He opened the door and reminded himself to focus only on Gabby. Fortunately, the task wouldn't be too difficult since Sue and Carol were now sitting together on the couch.

"I had a good talk with Colt Richardson a couple of weeks ago. He's become anxious about having to leave the ranch soon." He continued to disclose his opinion about the boy's situation.

Gabby listened with great interest. "I've been concerned about the older kids too. All four of them are gifted. If they don't continue their education, I'm afraid they'll drift along with the wind after they leave the ranch." She took another gulp of coffee. "You mentioned Colt's interest in animals. I've noticed Kathy is good with math."

"Oh, yeah, she's always helping the younger kids with their homework." Stuart nodded and smiled. Gabby understood the importance of the children's future. "That gal's a whiz with figures."

Gabby put her paper cup down. "Sharla always wants to play my guitar and banjo. She has great musical ability and can play almost any instrument."

"Then there's Becky." Carol looked at her uncle. "Rikki says she has tons of patience and works well with children. I can see her as a great teacher someday."

Leaning forward in her seat, Sue's fingers drummed her purse. "Maybe we can all work together to prepare them and even supply some of their needs."

"You're right, Sue. Those kids need a fighting chance to make it in the world. The four of us have the means to help." Stuart stood and tossed his half-filled cup into the trash. "Our first course of action should be to ask Marty Rush about the possibility of mentoring or sponsoring the kids who age out."

Gabby clapped her hands. "I think it's a wonderful idea. Marty knows the reservation's tribunal regulations as well as Arizona's state laws."

Excitement filled the small waiting area. Stuart's gaze automatically travelled to each lady's face. As soon as his eyes lit on Sue, his prearranged guard fell flat. Her countenance reflected admiration and respect, something Stuart had never experienced before. A heady rush of emotion swept through him. Had the time come to tell her of his love, instead of trying to push her away?

The waiting room door flung open, and Lou stepped inside. His scrubs were soaking wet. Whipping off his damp surgical cap, he fanned himself with it. "We have a baby!"

Gabby ran and gave him a bear hug. "Congratulations, Son."

"So, is it a boy or girl?" Carol grabbed Lou's arm.

A blank look came into his eyes. "A girl. A sweet little girl with dark hair like her momma."

Stuart had to lower himself into his seat. A granddaughter. At long last, he had entered the illustrious portal of grandparenthood.

"Come on, Gramps. She's waiting for us." Gabby grabbed one arm and pulled him to his feet. "Let's go see our grandbaby."

Sue and Carol followed them to the nursery window. The new daddy scanned the incubators and finally pointed to the newborn on the left, blessed with an abundance of hair. The tiny infant's red face scrunched as she cried.

Oohs and awws came from the picture-snapping quartet as Lou proudly stood with his nose pressed to the over-sized window.

Gabby turned to her beaming son. "Your daughter is precious. It's about time we had another girl. So, give me the particulars, how long is she and how much did she weigh?"

"I was so worried about Millie, I forgot to ask." His face flushed. "I'll go find the nurse. Be right back."

Lifting her cell phone, Gabby took more pictures as Stuart leaned against the glass.

Lou returned and sheepishly pointed to the window. "Oops! Wrong baby. Ours is still getting her first beauty bath."

The new daddy's mistake in identity brought on instant laughter from the family which echoed down the busy hospital corridor.

"Oh, great." Stuart stared at his phone. "Do you realize how many pictures we've taken of somebody else's baby?"

Gabby cackled. "That's nothing, I've already sent most of the ones I took to Lou's brothers and other family members.”

"The nurse said it might be a while before Millie and the baby are ready for visitors." Lou cracked his knuckles. "Why don't you go to the cafeteria for a snack? I'll text Momma when it's time."

"Sounds like a plan." Gabby held up her phone. "Meanwhile, I'll text your brothers and tell them to disregard the previous photos."

Stuart called Max and Sylvia to share the good news as he followed the ladies to the cafeteria. He waited in the hall while Carol, Gabby, and Sue stopped in the hospital gift shop to check out baby clothes.

By the time Gabby received Lou's text, the women had their arms full of gift bags, a vase of flowers, and a colorful bouquet of balloons.

The baby's whimper greeted them as Stuart opened the door to Millie's room. His heart raced as he saw his daughter cuddle her newborn.

The three ladies gave Lou the gifts, sanitized their hands, and crowded around the bed. Suddenly, it was a woman's world, and Stuart felt left out. He and Lou swapped glances.

A tug on his shirt cuff pulled him to the side of the bed. Sue whispered, "Congratulations." She linked her arm through his as they took in the miracle of new life.

"She's beautiful, Princess. I'm proud of you." Stuart's voice cracked. "What have you named her?"

"Meet your granddaughter, Gracelynn Joy." Millie kissed the baby's head. "We'll call her Grace because God taught me a lot about His grace this past year with Mother." She looked at her dad and grinned. "We gave her Mother's middle name, Joy. Is that okay with you?"

He returned her smile. "Of course it is. It's a very fitting name for our tiny bundle." The baby grabbed his finger, and his voice softened. "Hi, Gracie. I'm your Poppy."

CHAPTER TWENTY-THREE

THE CHILDREN AT MAVERICK RANCH HAD never celebrated Memorial Day. Sue came up with the idea of having a party for them in the community building at her condo. She and Gabby went together to reserve the facility. They wanted to take every opportunity to instill patriotism in their young hearts.

The children were pumped to have an indoor picnic with everyone they loved. Sue had asked Rikki to have the children make red, white, and blue paper chains to drape around the walls of the dining area. Color coordinating balloons and streamers hung from the ceiling.

The kitchen hummed with activity while the ladies prepared hamburgers on several electric griddles. Hotdogs were heating in the oven.

Sue brought out potato salad and a tray of vegetables and placed them on the table with bags of chips, condiments, and sandwich buns. She had to remember the cubed watermelon chilling in the refrigerator. Gabby carried a large serving bowl of baked beans which the men had insisted be a part of the menu.

The burgers were coming off the griddle when Lou and Millie arrived with Baby Grace. The children swarmed around them to get their first peek at the infant in the carrier. As usual, Lark stood off by herself.

Stuart knelt down beside her. "I bet you'd like to see the baby too."

Her face brightened. "Yes, Poppy."

Holding her in his arms, Stuart lifted the girl to see Grace. "Isn't she tiny?"

She reached out and with one finger, touched the baby's chubby cheek.

The man's tenderness with children flamed Sue's admiration for him. She'd never forget the loving scene.

Ethan clapped his hands loudly and called them together. "We're going to pray first, then the children can line up to fill their plates." He asked the Lord's blessing and by the time he said, "Amen," the children scattered with JJ rushing to the head of the food line. He stuck a hotdog between his teeth and precariously balanced two more on his plate while adding a handful of potato chips.

The room's noise level escalated with silly giggles and happy chatter.

"Lou, would you help Lark get her food?" Stuart handed her to his son-in-law and tweaked her chin. "See ya in a bit, kiddo. Gabby wants to talk to me."

When Sue managed to fill her plate, JJ headed back for seconds and jumped ahead of her in line. She shook her head and watched him fill a hamburger bun with globs of baked beans, Cheddar Doodles, and a dill pickle. "Are you going to eat all of that?"

"Sure I am. Not the seed things on the bun, though." He gave her a plucky grin and hurried to his seat beside Juan Garcia and his wife, Ines.

Sue sat across the table from them and watched as JJ busied himself with picking sesame seeds off his hamburger bun and laying them on Juan Garcia's paper plate.

It hadn't taken Sue long to understand why everyone watched out for the little guy. The six-year-old was loveable, but his overactive imagination, coupled with a dose of bad luck, always got him into trouble.

Taking the seat next to Ines, Millie set Grace's carrier

on the floor. Her hands shook as she held the crying baby to her shoulder. The new mom dug into the diaper bag and brought out a bottle.

Ines touched Millie's arm. "May I feed the little one while you eat?"

The tension left Millie's face as she gently passed her infant to the woman's outstretched arms. "Thanks, you're an angel." She reached for the plate of food that Lou left for her and scooped a bite of potato salad.

A short time later, Sue finished her lunch. She made her way to the kitchen and brought out dessert for everyone.

Thirty sets of brown eyes watched Sue and Rikki bring trays of chocolate cupcakes decorated with tiny American flags to the serving table.

Ethan climbed onto a chair and clapped his hands. "Listen up, kids." The room grew quieter. "I want you to come up and form a line like we do at home. Take one of Miss Sue's cupcakes and Poppy will give you a bowl of ice cream. Go back to your seat and eat it quickly before it melts."

When JJ returned to the table, Sue took pictures of him devouring ice cream. Then he carried his cupcake and stood between Juan and Ines. Baby Grace faced JJ as the older woman patted her back. A large burp erupted, surprising the boy.

Sue lifted her phone again and captured him licking the top of his cupcake. He ran his finger through the frosting and looked at the baby. She could almost see the wheels turning in his head.

His icing-covered finger neared Grace's mouth and Juan grabbed the boy's wrist. "Vamoose, amigo. She is too young." When the ranch hand laughed and wiggled his dark, bushy mustache, JJ ran off.

Gabby strummed her banjo and began to sing "This

Land is My Land." The adult voices around the tables were loud and clear as they joined in. At the end of the chorus, she stood. "Lou, would you and Juan like to come up here and bring your guitars? Sharla, you've been practicing on my banjo all week so I want you to come too. Stuart, I heard you brought your harmonica. The four of you can lead our friends in a few fun songs."

They stepped forward. Gabby handed her banjo to Sharla, then sat next to Sue at the table.

"I have forty minutes to get to the meeting at the reservation. Marty and I are going to discuss our idea of mentoring and sponsoring the older kids. I'll take him one of your cupcakes to sweeten the deal."

Sue patted her hand. "I'll be praying all goes well, and he sees the benefit of the whole concept."

Playing the harmonica left Stuart lightheaded. Or did the wooziness come because Sue had been relentlessly watching him? He stood, glanced her way, and struggled with an intense need to be close to her.

Stuart pocketed his harmonica and sat at the table across from Millie. He smiled as his daughter held her sleeping newborn.

Tiptoeing to Millie's side, Lark spoke barely above a whisper. "We gots this many new kitties at home." She held up three fingers on each hand.

"I bet they're cute. Do they have names?"

She nodded and held her fingers up once more. "Cycwops, Hercawees, Zeus, Thor, and 'Dusa. My kitty is Fwuffy." She put her hands behind her and swayed as she watched the baby nap. "I wuv you, and I wuv your baby too." She ran to Stuart and hid her face in the front of his shirt.

Millie leaned over the table. "Lark?"

The little girl peeked at her.

"I love you too." Millie wiped a tear rolling down her cheek. "Will you come and let me give you a big hug?"

Stuart thought his heart might fly from his chest as he watched Lark and his daughter bond. He knew Millie understood the child's needs.

"Hey, everybody." Ethan loudly clapped his hands again. "Our time is about over, and we need to get this place in ship-shape. Let's all pitch in." He assigned each age group a task.

After they finished cleaning the community room, Gabby returned from her meeting at the reservation. She and Sue gathered the adults around Millie's table.

"First of all, Marty loved the cupcake, Sue." Gabby grinned. "I want you all to know, he was especially impressed with how we organized our proposal for the older kid situation. He's eager to be involved and promises to take it to the tribunal next week. He'll let us know their decision as soon as possible."

Stuart glanced at Colt helping Juan pull trash bags from the cans. The young man hadn't smiled much all day. This would be a good time to pick up his spirits. He walked to the boy. "Colt, could I talk to you?"

"Yes, sir." A questioning look came over his face.

The two wandered to a quiet corner. "Remember when we talked about your future? I spoke with my veterinarian friend in Arrowhead about your ability with animals. He wants to see you about a part-time job after you graduate in a couple of weeks. "

Colt's eyes grew wide. "Is this for real? Do you think I'm good enough to do it?"

He nodded. "Of course you are, but this is a decision you have to make on your own, son. No one can do it for you. If it doesn't work out, you can find something else."

"I have some news too, Poppy. This scholarship came in the mail yesterday." He smiled and pulled a folded envelope from his back pocket. "It's all because of you. Thanks."

Stuart gave him a man hug. "God gave you a special gift of working with animals. Continue to please Him with a strong work ethic. Reach high and study hard. It'll pay off. Stay in touch so we can see your accomplishments. I'm proud of you, Colt." Stuart noticed Colt's demeanor had become more self-assured with the promise of a future.

CHAPTER TWENTY-FOUR

"I HAVEN'T BEEN ON A HORSE since my seventeenth birthday." Sue gave Brian a sideways glance. "Hope I remember how to ride."

Brian adjusted the red bandana around his neck. "Trust me, it's like riding a bike. You never forget." He drove his black Porsche through the gates of the ranch. "This is a perfect day for a horseback ride."

"If you say so. It's seven o'clock in the morning and the temperature has already climbed to the upper eighties."

"This is about as cool as Arizona's going to get in June. Just wait until July and August." He parked in the large circle drive of the ranch house and turned off the engine. "I called Ethan yesterday to remind him we'd be here at seven."

"You're punctual." She donned her wide-brimmed hat and stepped out of Brian's car. The heat nearly bowled her over. She roughly adjusted her hat. *This* was a perfect day for a horseback ride?

"Why don't you take care of the horses while I say hi to Rikki and the kids?" She headed for the ranch house and called over her shoulder. "Wait here for me."

JJ came running from the barn with a basket load of fresh eggs. He climbed the porch stairs with her. "Look how many eggs I got, Miss Sue. Did you come to milk Gretchen again?"

"Not today." Sue ruffled the boy's coal black hair. "Mr. Brian and I are going to go riding."

"Can I go with you, pleeeze? I'm a good horse rider. Ask Miss Rikki."

The front door opened and Rikki stepped out. "There you are, JJ. I thought maybe you were hiding in the chicken coop again."

"That mean ol' rooster don't like me. He chases me all the time."

"Then stay away from his house." Rikki kissed her mom's cheek. "I hear you and Brian have plans this morning."

"We do. I'm a little leery of riding in the desert in this heat."

Rikki proceeded to the refrigerator and handed her two large bottles of water. "Stay well hydrated and you should be fine. Brian knows where to get out of the sun."

"Thanks. He's waiting for me. I'd better go." She walked through the kitchen and headed for the rear door.

"Ethan and I are driving the kids out for a nature hunt in a little while. We'll be back in a couple of hours. Have a good time, Mom."

Brian had led the saddled horses from the barn and waited for her by the gate. He handed Shadow's reins to Sue. "Hold these in your left hand and put your left foot in the stirrup. Grab the saddle horn with your left hand while your right hand grasps the cantle."

She frowned. "The what?"

"The back part of the saddle that sticks up." He patted the raised area.

Following his directions, Sue put her foot in the stirrup.

"Give a good jump and lift yourself straight up with all of your weight in the stirrup. Your body will be against Shadow." He paused while she did as he said. "Okay now, release the cantle and with the same hand, take hold of the horn. Good. Swing your right leg over and put your foot into the stirrup. Do you feel balanced?"

"Kind of." Sue prickled at Brian's laugh. She wiggled a little until she felt centered in the saddle.

"Okay, you're good to go. Walk Shadow here beside me, and we'll go around the paddock until you feel secure."

Sue let Shadow set the pace as she gently tried the reins from one side to the other. She pulled back slightly to stop the horse, amazed the animal quickly obeyed. Rikki and Brian were right. She did remember.

"Are you doing all right, Sue?"

She nodded. "Let's go. I'll follow you for a while."

"No, I want you right beside me." Brian waved her toward him. "I want you to copy how I control the reins."

The farther they rode, the more relaxed she became as Shadow's gentle rocking motion soothed her tension. "I'm enjoying this more than I thought."

"I knew you would. Now you can take in the beauty of the surroundings. Help me look for an outcropping that overlooks a watering hole. We'll rest while Shadow and Marmalade get a drink. Since it's sweltering, we'll head back to the ranch. No need to overdo it your first time out." He quickened his mount's pace.

Sue nudged Shadow with her heel and caught up with Brian. He smiled, evidently satisfied at her increasing equestrian aptitude.

Before long, the crest of rocks came into view. At the watering hole, Brian dismounted, walked around Shadow, and reached for Sue's waist. Suspended by his powerful hands, she caught his penetrating gaze while he slowly lowered her to the ground.

His strength and nearness left her feeling awkward and a little frightened. The look in his eyes bordered on dominance, and after living through the same thing with

Grady, she wasn't about to give Brian the upper hand. Sue reached inside herself for all the fortitude she could muster and glared at him. He seemed to back off.

Feeling a bit stiff, Sue raised her shoulders to stretch. How long would she have to ride before her legs began to take on the shape of parentheses?

As he led their horses to the water, Sue's eyes scanned the desert landscape. "It's odd to see green trees growing out here in such a dry place. What kind is this?"

"It's called a desert willow. They can grow twenty feet or better." Brian kicked the grassy area around the tree.

"What are you doing?"

"We have to keep our eyes open for scorpions and snakes. They're good at hiding anywhere and everywhere. This area looks pretty safe."

Sue jumped. "Wait! Have you looked in the tree? I don't want any dangling tree snakes falling on me."

"No, but I will." Brian looked up into the blue-green leaves of the willow before spreading a blanket out in the shade. He held her hand and guided her to the blanket.

She reluctantly sat, eyes darting in search of venomous critters. And to think, she'd only been worried about sand fleas.

"Relax. We're safe." His irritating laugh cut through the hot air. "I'll fetch our water from the saddlebags." He quickly returned with the bottles and slowly reclined next to her on the blanket. A chill sprinted down her spine as she caught his dark eyes raking over her body from beneath the rim of his Stetson.

"You're a beautiful woman."

She took a drink and hoped her aloof response would fend off his unwanted advances. "This water hits the spot."

"Listen, Sue, we've been seeing each other off and on for about eight months. My position in the firm is secure, and I have a bright future ahead of me. It's time to settle down, and there's nobody I'd rather be with than you." He took a deep breath. "Have you given any thought about making a real commitment?"

How should she handle this? Stalling for time, Sue took another drink of fresh water and swallowed hard. *Lord, please help me be tactful.*

"So, what do you think?" Brian reached out and softly rubbed her arm. "Would you do me the honor of becoming my wife?"

"We have a nice, friendly relationship, Brian. You've helped me to become acclimated to living in Arizona. For that I thank you, but the idea of getting serious scares me." Sue's eyes diverted to the horses ripping grass from the sod. Marmalade stopped mid-munch, eyeballed her, and nickered as if agreeing with her statement.

Brian frowned and jerked his hand away. "I see." His clipped tone showed how offended he felt. "Is it because of my Native American heritage?"

"You know better." Her anger doubled as she sent him 'the look.' "My answer wasn't meant to hurt you, and I'm sorry if it did. You have to realize my last commitment was a twenty-six-year disaster. Making a lifetime decision is a lot harder to do now."

"Think about it, we could have a lot of fun and be a power couple."

The remark settled heavy in her chest. "I've already experienced that phenomenon. It wasn't a happy time in my life, and I don't care to repeat it." She stood. "I think it's time we returned to the ranch."

A distinct hardening of Brian's eyes appeared as he finished his water and hurled the bottle at the tree.

Witnessing his outburst filled her with fear, which morphed into disgust, and then outright anger. She marched to the tree and snatched the plastic container from the ground. "This is exactly why we can't have a deeper relationship."

He looked away. "I thought we had something special, Sue. You seemed to understand me and my desire to succeed."

She walked to Shadow without replying to his comment. Determined not to ask him for help, she stuck her foot in the stirrup and jumped three times before mounting.

Brian kicked the sand with the toe of his boot. "Oh, I get it. You're going to give me the silent treatment." He climbed into the saddle and led the way.

Silence hung heavy as they headed to the ranch. After twenty minutes, Brian slowed and let Sue catch up with him. "Listen, no hard feelings. Even if you don't want to get married, I still worry about your financial status. You've dropped a lot of serious money on the ranch in the past few months. There's always a chance you'll over-extend your budget. We don't have to have a personal relationship for me to help you with your finances."

Sue clenched her teeth. "I already have a financial advisor."

"Sure, back in Vermont. You need someone to look out for you and keep your portfolio in check here in Arizona."

"We've talked about this before, Brian. I'm happy where I'm at."

"I've got a handle on some great investments. You don't want to be a loser."

Sue grew tired of the conversation. He'd never get it. Rikki's question came to mind. Did Brian know she was a woman of means? At least she'd discovered his genuine feelings about her. Hot wind dried her tears of frustration and whipped at her hair. Fury churned like a boiling geyser waiting to erupt.

As the barn came into view, Shadow surged forward, harder and faster, causing her grip on the saddle horn to slip. "Whoa! Please whoa." Her legs instinctively hugged the sides of the horse to stay in the saddle, but she didn't think to pull on the reins. He galloped even faster. Sheer terror overtook her.

Brian came up beside her. Before she knew what was happening, he grabbed hold of her and pulled her onto Marmalade's back. The horse jerked aside and whinnied as Shadow ran off.

Grateful for his sturdiness, and too relieved to dwell on their differences, Sue clung to Brian's waist until they entered the barnyard. He helped her dismount. Desperately in need of support, she fell into his arms, shaken and exhausted.

He pressed his mouth against hers. "We'd make a good team. Do you want to reconsider my proposal?"

"Thank you, but no." Sue struggled to catch her breath. "You asked me to marry you twice, and love wasn't mentioned either time." She turned and took a few steps toward the barn, hoping someone would be there.

Brian stomped after her. "You want love? I'll show you love." He grabbed her arm and pulled her to his chest. A rough kiss followed.

"Stop it! Let go of me." The first three buttons of her blouse tore off as she wrenched from his hold.

Stuart seemed to come out of nowhere. "Get your paws off her." He threw his shoulder into Brian's, catching him off balance. The lawyer's feet flew out from under him, and he landed hard on his hip.

Brian jumped to his feet with both fists ready. "Come and get it, old man."

Sue screamed as the two of them squared off.

Knowing Brian's skill in boxing, her blood turned cold. She held her breath. *Please Lord, take care of Stuart.*

Successfully dodging Brian's first punch, Stuart caught the next one straight on the jaw. He staggered for a moment but stayed on his feet.

She dug her phone from her pocket and dialed 9-1-1, hoping to reach the small police station on the outskirts of the reservation.

Holding his chin, Stuart stepped forward. Suddenly, his fist caught Brian's nose.

Blood spurted as Brian's head jerked backward. Regrouping, he threw three rapid punches to Stuart's gut. Left-right-left.

Stuart doubled over and gasped for air.

With another swift blow to the chin, Brian knocked him into the massive barn door. He breathed heavily and watched as Stuart's limp body slid to the straw-covered floor.

"Stuart!" Sue ran to his crumpled form.

Flapjack ran in from the paddock and grabbed a wheelbarrow. He thrust it into the back of Brian's legs. The man tumbled into the one-wheeled cart. His arms and legs thrashed as the ranch hand hauled Brian outside and dumped him face first into the manure pile.

It didn't take long for Brian to scramble from the stinking mound. He swore, shook his arms, and ran to the horse trough. Tearing off his shirt, he threw it to the ground, then plunged his head and hands into the water. He splashed the muck from his face and walked briskly to his Porsche. Gravel flew when the car peeled out of the drive.

The sound of sirens in the distance encouraged her as she cradled Stuart's bleeding head on her lap. The left side of his jaw had swollen and began to bruise. She stroked his temple, avoiding the goose egg forming.

"Hang on Stuart. I love you."

Flapjack put his hand on Sue's shoulder. "He'll come around, ma'am. Loosen his collar, and I'll get him water."

"Thanks." She kissed Stuart's forehead and spoke softly in his ear. "How do I make you see that we belong together?"

Running into the barn, Ethan yelled, "I hear sirens!" He knelt beside his mother-in-law. "What happened to Uncle Stu?"

Rikki came close behind. "Mom, are you okay? Oh, no, Poppy."

Stuart moaned, but didn't open his eyes.

The ambulance pulled into the drive accompanied by two squad cars. The EMTs rushed into action, checking Stuart's vitals.

A policeman approached Flapjack, who stood aside with the water, while another officer began to question Ethan.

"I don't know what happened, sir. I wasn't there." Ethan rubbed the nape of his neck. "My wife and I had thirty children on a nature study in the back pasture. We heard the sirens on our way home and got here only minutes before you arrived." He laid his hand on Sue's arm. "This is Sue North. She'll be able to tell you."

"Ma'am." The officer pointed to her with his pencil. "Were you an eye witness to the altercation? Do you know how it began?"

She held the front of her blouse closed. "Brian Campton sexually assaulted me, and Stuart interrupted him."

"You mean Brian Campton, the attorney?"

Sue nodded. "Yes. I've been dating him off and on for a few months. We went on a horseback ride this morning. I rejected his marriage proposal twice, and he became downright furious." Tears trickled down her face.

Rikki put an arm around her shoulder, giving her the fortitude to continue. "He ripped my blouse when he tried to force me to kiss him."

A groan came from Stuart as they strapped him to the gurney. "Suzie?" His moaning increased. Ethan hurried to his uncle's side before they loaded him into the waiting ambulance.

Stuart had called her name. The inability to run to him filled her with the sting of frustration. She stared at the floor and cried, willing herself to continue with the policeman's questions.

"I'm sorry, Mom. Don't worry, Stuart will be okay." Rikki pulled her into a tight hug and looked at the cop. "Mr. Campton tricked everyone connected with the ranch into trusting him."

"Yes, ma'am." He tapped on his notebook. "Now, Mrs. North, can you tell me what happened after Campton tore your shirt?"

Sue's heart twisted as she watched the ambulance leave, lights flashing, siren blaring. She faced the cop as Ethan stood by Rikki. "Things happened in a flash. Both of them were throwing punches, but Brian's been boxing for years, so Stuart didn't stand a chance."

"I see. Is that when Campton knocked him out?"

Sue nodded. "Brian's final blow came to Stuart's jaw. He fell against the barn door and collapsed." She pointed to the ranch hand. "This man, Flapjack Wolf, saved Stuart's life." She proceeded to fill him in on the details.

The officer chuckled as he took down the note. "Nice job."

Ethan stepped up. "When my wife and I came outside, we saw him taking a quick rinse in the horse trough, and then he left in his Porsche."

The man's pen stopped writing, and he seemed to be gathering his thoughts.

"Officer, are we done here?" Rikki frowned as she took Sue's arm. "My mother needs to change her clothes before we take her to the hospital to be with Stuart."

Without waiting for the policeman's reply, Sue sprinted to the house. She had an ominous feeling about Stuart's wellbeing.

As the ambulance sped through town, Stuart's mind shifted back to the fight with Brian. He moaned when they turned a sharp corner.

"Lie still until we get your ribs checked out." The paramedic's eyes showed concern.

Stuart tried to take a deep breath. A burning pain shot through his stomach and chest. His jaw hurt as he talked through clenched teeth. "Where's Sue?" He took a shallow breath. "Is she okay?"

"Try not to talk, sir." The young woman put her hand on his shoulder, then placed an oxygen mask over his mouth and nose. "No one else was injured."

Good. Sue wasn't hurt. He moaned again. Apparently neither was Campton. So much for being her Sir Galahad. Anger grew in his battered chest, but if the opportunity arose, he'd do it again in a heartbeat to protect her.

The ambulance turned into the emergency drive. The paramedics pulled the gurney from the vehicle and rushed him inside.

Stuart was glad when the exams and X-rays were over. His right hand was bandaged, jaw was swollen and jutted forward, and the knot on the back of his head ached. The orderly wheeled him back to the emergency room cubicle where Sue and Ethan were waiting.

Even though he was embarrassed for her to see him all boogered up, he still wanted to hold her.

"You poor thing." Sue hurried to his side, clutched his good hand, and kissed it. "Thank you for taking care of me."

He squeezed her hand. "Welcome."

"I wish you hadn't been hurt in the process. I'm so sorry, Stuart." Tears welled in her eyes as she pushed the matted hair from his forehead.

"Not your fault." If only he could pull her into his arms and share how much he loved her.

A tall nurse opened the curtains. "We'll have to ask you to leave, now. Mr. Drake needs his rest."

CHAPTER TWENTY-FIVE

Sue's heels clicked down the long hospital corridor as she searched for room 234. Her stomach balanced on the brink of nausea thinking about yesterday's fistfight and the awful beating Stuart took. She'd prayed all night that he hadn't sustained any internal injuries.

Standing outside his partially open door, she took a deep breath as guilt continued to plague her. If she hadn't pushed aside her feelings for Stuart, the heated situation with Brian would never have taken place.

Facing him again would be difficult. He said he didn't hold her responsible, but after several hours of thinking about it, had he changed his mind?

Max's cheerful voice coming from the room gave her hope and a dash of courage. She cautiously peeked inside.

The curtain hanging from the ceiling surrounded the bed and provided scant privacy. Four legs were showing beneath it. Obviously, one set belonged to Max, and she deduced the other must be Millie's. Were they going to hold her accountable for Stuart's injuries?

What would be the appropriate way to thank her hero? She wanted to run to him. However, with his family looking on that might prove to be more than a little awkward.

Sue took another deep breath, pasted a smile on her lips, and walked around the curtain. "Good morning." Did she sound cheerful enough? She winced at Stuart's good-natured face, battered and swollen. The sight of him made her mouth go dry. In her peripheral vision, she noticed Max and Millie staring at her.

She continued to focus on Stuart's puffy face. However, upon seeing her, a little gleam danced in his good eye.

Her chin quivered and hot tears streamed down her face. Not caring that Max and Millie were there, she ran to Stuart's side. "I'm so sorry."

Even with a swollen jaw, and split lip, Stuart strained to parrot her words.

"You have nothing to be sorry about." She gently placed her hand on his. "Thank you for protecting me. You'll always be my hero, Stuart Drake."

His one eyebrow shot up as he tenderly looked at her. "You're okay?" He squeezed her hand.

"I'm fine." Tilting her head, she leaned forward, longing to press her lips on his forehead. "What did the doctor say? Will you be going home soon?"

Millie smoothed a wrinkle from his blanket and tucked the corner under the mattress. "He said Dad can probably go home tomorrow."

"Can't wait." Stuart rubbed the salt and pepper stubble on his chin.

"Stu sprained his left shoulder, but the doctor said he'd feel better in a couple of days." Max straightened his back. "It'll take a good six weeks to completely heal. He also has two bruised ribs on the same side as his sprain, and a good-sized knot on his noggin."

"Don't forget about his poor broken thumb." Millie carefully lifted her dad's bandaged right hand.

"Yeah, I socked his snout." Stuart's chuckle was brief.

"I remember. It wasn't a pretty sight." Sue closed her eyes and pictured Stuart's one and only good blow. "You really let him have it. Did Max and Millie tell you the rest of the story?"

Max shook his head. "We decided to wait for someone else to tell him since we didn't see it ourselves."

"You got at least one good lick in." She pointed to his bandaged hand. "God was watching out for you because Brian's been boxing since his college days."

"Glad I didn't know that 'fore I tangled with Sugar Ray."

Sue beamed and forged ahead with her story of Flapjack's deeds of derring-do.

A short laugh came from Stuart's puffy lips which ended in a dry cough. He groaned and held his chest. "Quit, quit. It hurts."

Millie faced the other way, and her shoulders shook.

Throwing his head back, Max released a burst of laughter. "Justice prevailed. That Campton sure fooled everyone."

Sue agreed with a nod. "I hope we never see him again."

The room grew quiet. Stuart broke the silence. "What day is it?"

Checking his watch, Max answered. "It's Sunday, June tenth."

"Max, give me a red rose from the bouquet, please." Stuart's good eye twinkled, and he managed a quick half-smile as he took the flower from his brother. He offered it to Sue. "Happy birthday."

She could think of many other ways to spend her fifty-first birthday, and all of them featured an uninjured Stuart.

The next day, Stuart shaded his eyes from the sun's

glare and leaned on the armrest of the emergency room wheelchair as Max pushed him to the parking lot. "Go easy on the bumps. I still have a doozy of a headache."

"Hold on a little longer, Stu, we're almost there."

Millie ran ahead and opened the front door of her uncle's car.

"Why don't you go with us, Sue?" Max cleared his throat. "We can always come back for your vehicle later."

Stuart took Sue's hand. "Thanks for staying with me during the fight, Sue. I had no idea Brian was so strong." His temples throbbed, and coupled with his bruised ribs, he wanted to scream in pain.

"Both of you were acting like Brahma bulls. I half-expected to see you two lower your heads, snort, and paw the ground." She kissed the top of his bandaged head. "I appreciate you standing up to him. You're a pretty special man, Stuart Drake."

"He's a good man but a terrible patient." Max put his arm around Stuart's shoulder to help him up from the wheelchair.

Stuart winced as he stood next to the front passenger door. Bending to get into the car, he nearly passed out from the searing pain in his ribs.

"That pretty little nurse gave you mighty potent pills." Max pushed the wheelchair aside. "They should've kicked in by now."

Sue and Millie climbed into the backseat and fastened their seatbelts.

Millie leaned forward and patted her dad's good shoulder "I called Lou and he has the guest room ready for you. Thankfully, it's far enough away from the nursery, Gracelynn's crying won't disturb your rest."

"No way she'd disturb me." His head bobbed and eyes crossed as the painkiller took hold.

Stopping at a red light, Max looked over at his

brother. "After I drop you off, I'll run to your house to pick up your clothes, toothbrush, and razor. Anything else you want?"

"Can't think of anything else." Stuart lowered the visor and glanced in the mirror. Sue in triplicate. Sweet. He couldn't tell if his lips were smiling as he focused on the middle image. "I-I'm sorry. I shouldn't-a had my sweetheart date the guy." He mentally kicked himself. Did he really say that out loud?

"Those pain pills are definitely working." Max chuckled. "You're a bit more candid than usual, Stu."

Sue smiled at his reflection in the visor mirror. "None of us realized Brian would go spastic. Don't be upset about it." She sighed. "I didn't have to go out with him."

"We're almost home, Dad." Millie's voice quivered.

Stuart dreaded getting out of the car and walking into the house.

As the car pulled into the driveway, Max looked his way. "I promise to be as careful as I am with Sylvia. We'll go at your pace."

True to his word, Max got Stuart settled into the guest room, then left with Millie and Sue in charge.

"Can I get you anything, Daddy?" Millie pulled up the sheet. "A drink of water or something?"

"I'm okay."

"Before we leave, I need to say something." Millie put her hands on her hips. "You know, I've been watching you two for months. Why don't you admit you have feelings for each other once and for all? I'll be in the next room." She walked out the door.

"She's right, you know." Stuart sent a quick glance to Sue and kept his voice low. "I have feelings for you that I shouldn't have."

"Good feelings or bad?" She sat in a small, upholstered chair beside the bed.

"Oh, definitely good." His eyes grew blurry. He closed them and gingerly touched the stubble on his swollen jaw. "Are you disgusted this grungy old man finds you attractive?"

Her tone remained warm and steady. "There you go, putting yourself down again. We both know you're not grungy, and I certainly don't think of you as an old man."

He looked up, trying to give her his full attention. "The first time at Perky's, I saw a beautiful, caring lady with a shattered heart. I wanted to hold you."

"I wish you would have." Sue watched for his reaction.

Stuart's eyes grew heavy. He drew in a breath, and slowly released it. "My feelings for you aren't right, Suzie." His determination to stay awake failed.

CHAPTER TWENTY-SIX

LATER THE NEXT WEEK SUE SAT at her daughter's kitchen table. "I haven't been that scared in a long time, Rikki. Brian got angry over my rejection of his proposal." She sipped her coffee. "But he totally flipped out because I refused to put him in charge of my finances. The man's temper frightens me. If Flapjack hadn't been there, he could've seriously hurt Stuart and me."

"His Uncle Marty is heartbroken. He told Ethan the Native American Missions wanted to be open about the accusations and not try to hide it. They removed Brian from their board of trustees."

"It would be natural for them to protect one of their own." Sue swirled the remainder of her coffee in the cup. "I'm glad they've taken action."

"Marty said the Mission will be looking into his records for any other improprieties. He's pretty sure the partners in Brian's law firm will be keeping a close eye on him too. He'll probably lose his job."

One of the children ran into the house and slammed the door. "Miss Rikki, JJ did it again. We can't find him." The youngster looked at Sue and grinned. "He's the bestest hider we got. Is it time for snacks yet?"

"Soon." Rikki sprang from her chair. "This is the second time this week." She took Danny's hand. "Where did you last see JJ?"

"We were looking for the kittens in the barn." He shrugged. "Then he wasn't there."

"That boy is sorely testing my sanity. We'd better

look for him, Mom." Rikki's voice shook. She pointed to the refrigerator. "Grab a bottle of water in case we need it. I'll get my shoes on."

Sue hurried to get the water. "I'll tell Ines to get snacks ready now."

Rikki stepped out the back door, rang the large triangle, and yelled for the kids. "Time for morning snack." She turned to Sue. "We'll wait a few minutes to see if JJ heard the signal."

They watched out the window for any sign of him. Ten minutes later, when the boy didn't return, Sue followed Rikki outside. "I suppose we start looking in the barn since it was the last place the kids saw him." She wasn't eager to go where Brian had tried to assault her.

"It'll be faster if we split up. I'll check the barn and you can look around outside." She handed Sue a whistle. "Blow this if you find him. I have one too."

Sue headed to the side of the barn where Ethan and Juan Garcia were working on the tractor. "Have either of you seen JJ recently?"

"Don't tell me he's hiding again." Ethan wiped his face with his bandana and put the wrench in the toolbox.

The ranch hand took a step closer to him. "I think maybe this boy hides away 'cause his mama does not want him."

"Good point, Juan. Thank you." Ethan stretched his arms. "Where have you and Rikki looked, Sue?"

"She's in the barn. Danny told us they saw JJ there, apparently on a kitten hunt."

"That means he could be anywhere. Juan, do you want to check the bunkhouse? If he's not there, go to the big house and check under the porch. I'll see if he's in the bed of the pickup. Sue, the goat pen is over there, and you know where the chicken coop is."

Sue decided to start with the goat pen since JJ said

the rooster didn't like him. After checking the perimeter, she stepped inside the wire enclosure and peeked into the small shed. "JJ, are you in here?"

No answer.

Old rubber tires were stacked in the pen for the goats to climb on. Sue examined them. No JJ, but it gave her an idea. Outside the barn, an old tractor tire had been propped against the back wall, waiting for Stuart to turn it into a small flowerbed.

Sue scurried in that direction. As she approached the large tire, a kitten climbed from it. Her heart rate picked up exponentially. JJ had fallen asleep inside the tire well, snuggled with two kittens on his belly. She reached for the whistle in her pocket, squinted, and decided to wake him up in a kinder, gentler fashion. Sue nudged his shoulder.

The boy woke with a start. "Miss Sue!"

"Everyone is looking for you, JJ." She blew the whistle two times.

"Uh-oh. Am I in trouble?"

Ethan came running and pulled the boy into a tight hug. "We've told you how dangerous it is to hide in secret places. There could be a snake, tarantula, or a scorpion hiding there too." He gave him another hug. "We love you and don't want you to get hurt."

"I'm sorry. The kittens were playing in there. I didn't mean to fall asleep."

Ethan held on to the boy's shoulders. "Why don't we go to the house and let everyone know you're okay? But you'll have to be punished for disobeying."

With tear-filled eyes, JJ lowered his head as they walked to the house. "Whatcha gonna do to me?"

"First of all, you don't get dessert after supper." Ethan took his hand. "You'll go to bed early and miss popcorn and movie night. You have to learn to stay with the other kids. Do you understand?"

JJ nodded. "I'm a good hider, ain't I?"

Ethan gave Sue a cross-eyed look, then picked up the boy and carried him. "One more thing, son, if you ever get lonely or need a hug, come to Miss Rikki or me."

"Welcome to Floral Scent-sations." Stuart pushed aside the order form he'd recently filled as a jet stream of cologne entered his nostrils. He wiped his nose. "Hi, Mrs. Eichenbaum. May I help you find anything on this fine July morning?"

The grandmotherly woman reached for her trifocals hanging on a chain around her neck. "Oy vey! Would you look at those bruises on your pretty face?" She placed her multi-ringed hand over her heart.

"It looks a whole lot better than when it happened."

"At least you're still amongst the living." She gave her usual tweak to a curl by her temple. "My canasta club friend, Vayla Abrams, said it's all over Apache Pointe that Attorney Campton gave you such a beating over the love of a woman and then left you for dead."

"Wow, that's quite a tale." He chortled carefully to keep from hurting his ribs. "Trust me, it's not how it came down at all."

"Vayla worked at the hospital when the ambulance brought you in. She heard the whole story from her nephew who is the father of one of the first responders." Long, glittery earrings wobbled and sparkled when she shook her head. "I don't think they'd make up something like that."

"Campton threw a sucker punch and knocked me out cold." Stuart touched his sore jaw. "But wait, the story gets even better. While I was out cold, Flapjack Wolf, one of the ranch hands, shoved him into a wheelbarrow and dumped him end-over-appetite into a fresh dung pile. You got it straight from the horse's mouth, and you can pass it around as the truth."

"Serves him right. Too bad they had to schlep his sorry tochus out of the pile." Mrs. E. wiped her bright red lips with a tissue.

"I wish someone would've videoed that part."

"Vayla said her rabbi's cousin works at the coffee shop next door to Campton's law firm. Those waitresses hear the confidential information from all the secretaries. They say he brags about winning a middleweight boxing championship all the time. I certainly hope you're going to press charges."

As much as Stuart wanted to have the man arrested, he'd rather spare Sue the embarrassment of the courtroom and media. "We'd rather settle out of court, but no one's been able to reach him for a deposition. From what I understand, he's taken a leave of absence."

Her amply rouged cheeks dimpled. "You mark my word, Stuart. The schmendrik is on the run."

"Schmendrik?" Stuart held his healing ribs as he laughed. "Schmendrik doesn't sound nice. What's it mean?"

"To put it nicely, a jerk. Ptui, ptui, ptui." She pretended to spit her contempt. "If he did anything to me, Mordechai would squeeze out his last penny, then have him tarred, feathered, and catapulted to Siberia."

"As it is, Campton's reputation has taken a major hit."

The bejeweled woman opened her large embroidered purse and dropped in the lipstick-loaded tissue. "Now I have the scoop directly from your mouth. I'm here to buy a tchotchke for my mother-in-law's ninety-fifth birthday."

She glanced around. "Where are your discounted items? I have to hurry and get to the meat market and buy lamb chops for Mordechai's supper."

Stuart pointed to a table in the corner. "We put new trinkets out this morning."

Mrs. Eichenbaum poked around the bargain tchotchke bin and within minutes decided on a scented candle. "This will work. Her house always smells like burnt latkes." Her attention shifted to a display of chains for eyeglasses. She picked out a gold one with small, red stones and laid the items on the counter. "Mordechai will want me to have this. It matches my earrings."

"Well, if it isn't Mrs. Eichenbaum. Good morning." Max stood beside his brother. "I like the chain you've picked out. It highlights your rosy cheeks."

"You want I should fall for such schmaltz?" Twisting her curl, she cackled and pulled out her paisley billfold. "I'll buy two."

The corners of Max's mouth quirked. "Stu, I need to talk to you as soon as you're done here."

"I'll be with you in a minute." He turned to the customer. "That'll be ten dollars and fifty-nine cents, please."

She handed him the correct change and waltzed to the door. "Mosel tov."

Closing the register drawer, Stuart sighed and waved off the lingering scent of Mrs. E's heavy perfume. "What's on your mind, Brother?"

"I got a call from Harry Reitenoffer. He said the Bransons were happy with our counter offer. Their loan to buy Floral Scent-sations finally went through."

Stuart lowered himself onto a stool and planted his elbow firmly on the counter. Sixty years' worth of mental images flooded his mind. "Do you remember the time when the local Silver Saints group had a St. Patrick's

Day banquet and Dad over ordered shamrocks?"

His features brightened as he nodded. "The director told him they had six tables and needed six planters. He misunderstood and thought they needed six for each table."

"It was an expensive mistake, but everything turned out okay." Stuart drummed his fingers on the order pad. "Good ol' Dad sent the extras to shut-ins and nursing home residents who had no family."

"God has certainly blessed our family with this flower shop, and He'll continue to bless us after retirement. Even though this chapter in our lives is coming to a close, those old memories will live on in us." Max rubbed his hands together. "It's time for us to get out there and make new ones."

CHAPTER TWENTY-SEVEN

Stuart rang Gabby's doorbell as the August sun poured out its relentless heat.

Gabby answered the door. "Good morning, Stu. I'll be ready in a minute. I have coffee and brownies in the kitchen. Help yourself while I finish packing."

"Don't mind if I do."

Gabby returned, wheeling her suitcase behind her. "I think I'm set to go. We still have an hour before we need to leave for the airport." She pulled out a chair and gaped at her watch. "Would you look at the time? It's brownie-thirty. Pass the coffee."

"Your wish is my command, fair lady." He filled her cup.

"Want to know what my real wish is?"

Stu squinted. "Maybe."

"My real wish is for you and Sue to get your acts together." Gabby sipped her coffee. "We all know how you feel about each other."

"Is it that obvious?" He squirmed and bit into a brownie. "There are technical difficulties."

"Because she's a bit younger than you?"

"I admit age is a big part of it." Stuart looked up and caught her studying him. He quickly averted his eyes. "Another reason is, Penny's only been gone a year and my mind is only now adjusting to my new normal."

"I understand what you're saying. It takes a while for your system to adapt to the changes of being alone." She patted his hand. "I'm sorry, Stu, but they sound like excuses."

"It's more than excuses." He paused. "How can either of us enter a new relationship when we're both healing from dysfunctional marriages?"

"Good question. I agree you need time. Both of you are stuck in the fear of ending up with another disaster." She moistened her lips. "You and Sue weren't the failures. Your spouses were."

Stuart hung his head. "I never thought of it that way."

"What I see are two brave and selfless people who did everything possible to hold their families together. That, my friend, is honorable."

"All I know is God helped us push through the pain day by day." He lifted the coffee pot and offered a refill. "There are a couple of gulps left."

Gabby held her hand over the cup. "Normally, I'd love more, but we need to get going. Lou and Millie are waiting for us." She took the coffee cups to the kitchen and put them in the dishwasher.

Stuart carried her luggage to the car and put it in the trunk. Honorable? How many times had Penny referred to him as the biggest disappointment of her life? He slammed the trunk lid. It had been painful enough to hear it from her, but if those words ever came from Sue, it would crush him.

Stepping from the house, Gabby pulled the front door closed, and checked the lock.

He helped her into the front seat. Silence filled the first few minutes of their drive to Lou and Millie's house. There was a lot of truth in what Gabby said. Still, his one bad decision to marry Penny resulted in many years of pain, not just for him, but also for the entire family. A choice which turned out to be a tough burden to carry.

"I only have a few more things to say." Gabby set her

purse on the floor. "Let's consider your first marriage. Penny was a stranger who wrote beautiful letters to a lonely soldier in Vietnam. This naïve young man desperately wanted to believe everything she claimed in her love notes. She gave him the hope he needed to make it through the war."

"How stupid could I be?"

"No, the word is naïve. Big difference." Gabby touched his arm. "You eloped only a few days after returning home, right?"

"The same week and despite my family's warnings."

"Nevertheless, my point is you didn't take time to know the real Penny. You married a fictional character from a dime store novel." She moistened her lips. "The Stuart I know learned from his mistakes and now has a realistic view of the world."

"Yeah, I try not to be as irresponsible and spontaneous now." He stopped at a light and flipped on the right turn signal. He wanted the memory of that spur-of-the-moment decision gone forever, but it refused to go away.

"The difference now is you've taken time to know Sue's heart. She's a genuinely kind soul, unlike your first wife. She's been Carol's friend for over twenty-five years, and that alone should tell you you're not buying a pig in a poke."

Stuart laughed as he stopped in Lou and Millie's driveway. He looked her in the eye. "Thanks for the pep talk." Still chuckling, he walked to the door and rang the bell. Gabby had opened his eyes to the possibility of an enduring romance with Sue.

He stepped out of the way when Lou brought Gracie's bags to the door.

"Millie says we need this pink diaper bag in the backseat." He hung the strap on Stuart's shoulder and wandered into the house for more.

While the young couple finished last minute details, Stuart got into the car to wait with Gabby. "I forgot how much stuff you have to take to transport a baby."

"It's been a long time since I've been a young mother, but I still remember the hassle." Gabby buckled her seatbelt again.

"She's well worth it." Stuart didn't care if he sounded like a smitten grandpa. "Looks like they're finally ready."

When everyone settled in, they headed for Sky Harbor Airport.

Stuart felt a sense of relief from Gabby's talk. She made a good point. He and Sue would never intentionally hurt each other. He'd have to have a serious conversation with her tonight on the way home from the ranch.

"I want you to think long and hard about what I told you earlier." Gabby sent him a motherly smile.

Stuart shrugged. "She's going shopping with Rikki this morning, but I'll be taking her home from the ranch this evening. We can discuss everything then."

"Are you talking about Sue?" Millie tapped him on the shoulder.

Gabby looked into the backseat. "I was telling him that he and Sue belong together."

"That's what I told him. Go for it, Dad."

He nearly sprained his neck turning to see his daughter. Another confirmation. "You wouldn't mind if I dated her?"

"I want you both to be happy. You're perfect for each other."

Hope rose in Stuart's chest. Tonight he would express his love to Sue. His heart soared at the thought of holding her tight.

CHAPTER TWENTY-EIGHT

LATER THE SAME DAY, SUE STOOD on the wrap-around porch. The intense August heat had sapped her energy. The kids were playing a game after completing their chores, but something seemed wrong. It was too quiet. She quickly counted heads and called out. "Where's JJ?"

Sandy ran to her and pulled her arm. "We didn't see him go. Would you help us look so he doesn't get in trouble?"

"I will, but Ethan needs to know first." Great. This had to happen on her watch. She hurried into the house, letting the door slam behind her. The sound of pots and pans drew her into the kitchen. "Ines, I need Ethan right away. Do you know where he is?"

"Si. He is in the barn giving Poppy a short list of supplies to get in town."

Sue turned on her heels. Outside, she found her son-in-law walking toward her as the pickup truck drove away. "Ethan!" She rushed to his side. "JJ's hiding again."

"What am I going to do with that boy?" Exasperated, he threw his hands in the air and called to the other kids. "How long has JJ been missing?"

Sue lowered her head. "I'm sorry, it's my fault. They were playing tag and I thought it would be safe to go inside for a few minutes."

"Okay, obviously he can't be too far." He looked at the kids, and his voice became more strict than usual. "You know the routine. Spread out."

Two hours later, Ethan called the sheriff's department. "This is Ethan Mason at the Maverick Ranch. We have a six-year-old boy who's been missing for nearly three hours. Also, my uncle, Stuart Drake, went for ranch supplies and never returned. We've tried calling him but didn't get an answer."

For the next few minutes, he patiently answered their questions the best he knew how. He hung up and turned to Sue and Rikki. "The deputy will be here soon."

As per usual, Stuart gave the bed of the pickup a quick check for any stowaways before leaving the ranch. Finding no one, he drove off to get provisions.

Five miles into the journey, a motorcycle raced across the hot terrain, pulled about twenty yards in front of the truck, and stopped.

Stuart had to use both feet on the brakes. The truck veered to the right onto the shoulder of the desert road before coming to a halt.

After the cyclist dismounted, he came to the truck and rapped on the driver's window with the barrel of his gun. "Out. Leave the keys."

The sun's glaring reflection on the large, tinted visor of the helmet, made it impossible for Stuart to see the man's face. He quickly jumped from the truck, hands in the air.

"Phone." The biker's voice was gruff. He held out his hand.

Stuart patted his pockets. "It's in the truck." He squinted. "Look, I don't have any money if that's what you want."

"Turn." He motioned with his gun. "Hands behind

back."

As Stuart turned, his mind searched for a way out. Did he know this guy? Suddenly his wrists burned as the biker tied his hands together. Now he couldn't defend himself. Movement in the truck bed caught his attention. A little head popped up. *Please, Lord, not JJ.* Stuart tensed. Leave it to that boy to make a bad situation worse.

Soon, the youngster jumped from the truck bed as the biker blindfolded Stuart.

The man's deep voice called. "What are *you* doing here, kid?"

"I wanted to be with Poppy. Who are you? Is that a real gun? Can I touch it?"

The man swore. "Get over here or he dies."

"You said bad words. I'm gonna tell Ethan, and you're gonna get in trouble."

Stuart's mind whirled. "Don't make things worse, boy. Do what the man says." His stomach clenched as he heard the shuffle of feet and the truck's gate creaking open. They were going to a second location and that's never good.

"Get in the truck, squirt." Another shuffle. "Hands behind yer back."

"You're hurting me, mister."

"Aw, shut up. Scoot all the way in."

"Poppy, help me! I can't see."

A hand grabbed the neck of Stuart's shirt and forced him forward, causing Stuart to stumble into the side of the truck. The man shoved him against the lowered gate.

"Get up there."

The boy cried. "Poppy, don't leave me."

Stuart sat on the tailgate and lifted one leg. "Why are you doing this?"

No answer.

Stuart grunted when the man used both hands to give his wounded shoulder a hard push. He fell onto his side. Then the man forced him further into the truck bed and slammed the gate.

Something heavy fell next to him. He jerked when it hit against his leg. "Is that you, JJ?"

"Yeah. I can't see and my hands hurt, Poppy."

A motorcycle engine started and rode away.

Beneath the blindfold, Stuart's brows drew together. *Why would he capture us and ride off? This might be a good thing or a bad thing.*

JJ's voice squawked. "Is the bad man gone?"

Suddenly the truck door squeaked open and slammed shut. The engine revved, and the truck started to move.

Here we go. Stuart tried to envision their location by the turns the driver made. They headed south and turned right off the highway onto a dirt road. He was sure they were going west.

The truck turned right again. Were they going to the ranch? Then it took another bumpy right. Stuart's sense of direction floundered. Were they even on a road? He heard the toolbox and tire iron sliding in the back of the vehicle. Another sharp turn and the toolbox hit Stuart's foot.

How were they going to get out of this? He had to get his hands free to protect the boy. *He's only six years old, Lord. Help us.*

"Ouch!"

"Are you okay, JJ?"

"I banged my head. I'm scared, Poppy."

"Listen to me, son." He spoke louder. "We have to stay calm and not make this guy mad. Understand?"

"What's he gonna do?" JJ sniffled. "Is he gonna shoot us?"

"I don't think he'll use the gun, but he could still hurt us. Remember, it's important to do what he tells you." Stuart struggled to free his hands, but only succeeded in skinning his knuckles.

"I hope snakes and spiders bite him hard."

As they bumped and rumbled across the desert, Stuart felt JJ's small body shaking beside his. "Hang in there, kiddo. Now's the time to pray and we'll be okay."

The truck inclined at an angle and came to a stop. The door opened and Stuart waited for the man to put the tailgate down. If only he'd been able to grab the tire iron.

"Get out."

Stuart used his legs to scoot to the edge of the truck.

The man yanked off Stuart's blindfold, grabbed his arm, and pulled him to his feet. "Stay put while I get the kid."

Stuart blinked as his eyes adjusted to the bright sunlight. The guy still had the helmet on and a gun in his hand.

JJ cried while being pulled from the tuck. "I wanna go home."

"Shut up, kid, and I'll take your blindfold off." After the bandana fell from the boy's eyes, he gave Stuart a nudge with the barrel of the gun. "Now we got us a hill to climb. You two start movin', slow and steady."

With their hands still bound, the hike was rough with loose rocks falling along the way. Stuart's foot caught between two rocks, and he stumbled to his knees. He felt a strong hand under his arm, jerking him upright, and to a standing position.

"Where we goin', mister? We sure are goin' up high. Are we gonna be vulture bait?" JJ's footing slipped.

"Wait there, kid. I'll get ya by the arm."

"Thanks. You watchin' for snakes? Ethan says

there's lots of snakes out here. I like snakes. Do you like 'em?" He stumbled again. "You're not helpin' me very good."

"Will you shut yer trap?" He smacked JJ's head.

"Go easy on him. He's just a little boy."

"Keep movin', old man, and you can shut yer trap too."

"You're mean." JJ cried out. "Leggo my arm, you're squeezin' too hard."

"Don't worry, I'll leave you alone in a bit. There might be enough vittles in the box to hold you for a couple of days. Go easy on it."

Stuart's knees felt like they were about to give out. He guessed they hiked another twenty minutes. By this time, his shirt dripped with perspiration, and his mouth felt like a wad of cotton. "JJ and I need a drink."

"A few more yards. You can drink then." The man pushed an abnormally quiet JJ into the mouth of a cave.

Dear Lord, You know where we are. Keep us safe in the presence of danger. Help someone find us soon. We trust You.

The man returned. "Don't be a hero, I've got a gun. I'm gonna record yer voice, so read this note, and tell them the kid's with ya." He drew the trigger back, then held the cell phone close to Stuart's mouth.

"This is Stuart. JJ is with me." His voice shook as he held the paper. "My truck is fifteen minutes from the ranch house on Maverick Road. There's a note inside. No police. I'm serious."

After the man recorded the message, he clicked off the phone and held it high. "Money in the bank."

"Now, get in the cave with the kid." He led Stuart forward and shoved him to the ground. "This'll give you shelter."

The cave offered instant relief from the sweltering

heat, but the fall didn't help Stuart's sore knees at all.

"Water's inside. Now, gimme yer shoes."

"How are we supposed to get to the water when we're tied up?" Stuart pried his boots loose with his heels.

The man yanked them from his feet. "That's yer problem." He left the cave and called over his shoulder. "You have plenty of time to figure it out."

Stuart cringed at the condescending laugh fading in the distance.

"Are you okay, JJ?" No answer. "JJ?"

The boy's weak voice answered. "I'm okay, Poppy."

"You've been brave today. I'm proud of you." Stuart paused. "I need you to listen to me right now. Do you think you can help us get loose?"

"I'll try."

"Good. I want you to come over to me so I can untie your hands."

The boy moved to Stuart's side. "Whatcha want me to do now, Poppy?"

"We have to sit back-to-back. Then scoot as close as you can to my hands. My fingers need to reach your ropes." Stuart waited while JJ inched behind him. "Good job!"

After a few attempts, Stuart realized it wasn't going to work. He looked around the small cave. "We need something sharp to cut the cord."

"Poppy, I stole something from your truck."

"Why are you telling me this now? What did you take?"

"I'm sorry, Poppy. I was lookin' for gum and found your pocketknife in the glove box. There's somethin' else. I took your matches, too." He took a deep breath. "Are you mad at me?"

Freedom! Stuart realized they could signal with a fire—if they ever got their hands free from the binding cord. But first things first. "Listen to me closely, JJ. I'm not mad at you, but I am disappointed. It hurts when you take things from people. Stealing is always wrong, but this time we can take the wrong thing you did and use it to help us escape. Where'd you put the knife?"

"It's in my back pocket."

"See if you can put your fingers in your pocket and pull the knife out."

The child followed directions as Stuart cheered him on. "I got it, Poppy!"

Stuart's heart soared. "Yay! I want you to hold it still, then I can get my fingers wrapped around it."

"Okay. I'm a good helper."

"Yes, you are. Try not to move. I have to get it with my thumb too." JJ remained perfectly still while Stuart grasped the gadget. Now to open it. "You'll need to scoot away from me so you don't get hurt." He repositioned the knife carefully in both hands and got his thumbnail on the blade's stud. "Dear Lord, thank You for helping us and keeping us safe. You know we need this knife to open. Don't let me drop it."

Stuart felt the blade give but it hit the rope and closed again. He carefully repositioned the casing and tried again. With determined focus, he managed to swing the blade through its arc until it came fully open. "Thank You, Lord."

Hands sweating and teeth clenched, Stuart slowly began to cut through the layers of thick cord on his own wrists, trying not to injure himself.

"How long is it going to take, Poppy? I'm hungry. And thirsty." JJ kicked at a stone. "Wonder what the kids at the ranch are doing now?"

The boy's constant chatter hindered all of Stuart's efforts to concentrate. *Please Lord, I need to focus. Calm my hands, my mind, and JJ's mouth.*

The rope slackened and finally dropped to the ground. A flood of relief loosened the tension in his shoulders. After flexing his fingers and rubbing his wrists, he grabbed a bottle of water and shared it with JJ before going to work on the child's bindings.

By the time the boy was free, the sun had begun to set. Like it or not, they were going to spend the night in the cave. Judging by the position of the sun, there may be a good half hour before darkness hit.

Would they be warm enough? They needed a fire. At least they had matches and a few big branches to build one. But, he couldn't trust a six-year-old to leave the matches alone.

"Listen to me, JJ. Will you take the food out of the box for me?"

"Why, Poppy?" The boy's eyes were wide with curiosity as he pulled out a large bag of beef jerky.

Stuart removed a bag of apples and placed it by the water bottles at the wall of the cave. He figured the box measured about 18x12x9 inches, big enough for what he needed. "I'm going to get firewood." It might be a good idea to check around inside to make sure JJ would be safe. Taking one of the branches, he swept the dirt floor, searching the cracks and crevices for any unwelcome inhabitants.

"Where do you find firewood? Can I help?"

"Not this time. I need you to stay here with the food while I go get things." He squatted and held out his hand. "Why don't you give me the matches first?"

JJ reached into his left pocket, pulled out a book of matches, and handed it to Stuart.

"Thanks for helping me. You'll have to wait in the cave while I'm gone, understand?"

"Don't leave me, Poppy." The boy wrapped his arms around Stuart's neck and clung to him. "I'm scared."

"Everything's going to be okay." Stuart pulled an apple from the bag and buffed it on the front of his shirt. "Sit still, eat this, and we'll pretend we're camping. Won't that be fun?"

He took the fruit from Stuart. "Yeah. We'll play like we're camping. Cool. I'll stay here and watch for bears." Grabbing a long stick with his free hand, he brandished it like a sword. "This'll scare him."

"I feel safer already. Behave yourself and don't go anywhere without me. It'll only take a few minutes to gather what we need." Not wanting to leave JJ alone for long, he referred to his watch to keep track of the time.

Sharp stones gouged his stocking feet as he hobbled outside. His boots sure would be handy about now. He glanced around and waved at the child who appeared extra small and vulnerable.

Stuart kept his eyes open for any harmful critters while gathering dry bark and twigs from the straggly Mesquite and Palo Verde trees. Thistles poked his feet, but he didn't care. They needed a fire in the cave. He quickly filled the remainder of the box with anything to make fire starters.

With socks torn and feet bleeding, Stuart ventured back to the cave. He whistled "Jesus Loves Me" to let JJ know he was returning.

"Is that you, Poppy?" A timid voice called in the twilight.

Stuart came closer and saw the boy sitting against a rock with his knees pulled tightly to his chest. "I thought I told you to stay inside the cave."

"Bunches of birds came outta there. They scared me."

"Are there birds in the cave? We'll have to chase them out with your sword, won't we?" Stuart knew they were probably bats, but JJ didn't need to know. He felt the boy's body shake next to him. "You're okay now. Let's go inside, make a fire, and get something to eat. How does that sound?"

JJ rubbed his tummy. "Good. I'm hungry. What we gonna eat?"

"Whatever the man left for us. When we get our fire going we'll be able to see better." Stuart carried the tinderbox to the middle of the cave, made a ring of rocks, and built a little pyramid out of sticks with bark beneath it. When he struck the match, JJ cheered him on. It didn't take long for the small fire to take the chill off their new home.

Following a meal of dry Cheerios, beef jerky, and a bottle of water, JJ fell asleep while coyotes howled at the rising moon and owls softly hooted in the distance.

He closed his eyes and the image of Sue came into his mind. Thanks to Gabby and Millie, he'd gained enough confidence to admit his love to Sue, and now this happened. Would he ever see her again?

CHAPTER TWENTY-NINE

Sue, glad the ride home from church had been a quick one, wiped the perspiration from the nape of her neck. The first Sunday in August, and the temperature had climbed to a whopping 106 degrees. She'd felt a bit guilty thinking of Stuart and JJ through this morning's worship service instead of listening to Pastor Frank's sermon. But how could she not worry about them? They'd been missing twenty-four hours.

Entering her condominium, she kicked her navy blue pumps off at the door and took them to her room. She changed into jeans and a short-sleeved shirt then headed for the kitchen. Lunchtime, but who could eat when Stuart and the boy had been missing this long without a word? Not wanting to waste the sheriff's time, Sue shook off the temptation to call him. She checked her voicemail for any updates.

She jumped as the cell phone in her hand rang. Her heart soared at the sight of Stuart's number. His face flashed before her eyes. "Hello?"

"This is Stuart. JJ is with me." The monotone voice paused.

"Stuart, where—"

"My truck is fifteen minutes from the ranch house on Maverick Road. There's a note inside."

During another short break in the dialog, she heard a faint mumbling and JJ's high-pitched voice in the background. At least they were both alive.

Stuart spoke again. "No police. I'm serious." Click.

She grabbed a pencil and looked at the time. 12:45 p.m. What did Stuart say? With shaking hands and thoughts whirling, she scrawled the information: truck fifteen minutes from—her mind went blank. Where did he say it was? Oh, well, she'd fill it in later. She scribbled: Note in truck, no police.

She immediately called Ethan.

"Hi, Sue. What's up?"

She swallowed and licked her lips. "Ethan, listen to me. Oh, I have it, Maverick Road."

"Hold on, you're not making sense. What are you talking about?"

"This is important, write it down. I got a call from your Uncle Stuart. I know it was a recording, but he sounded scared and said he had JJ." She looked at her paper. "They left his truck on Maverick Road, fifteen minutes from the ranch, and he said to look for a note in the truck." When Sue finished giving the information, she took a deep breath.

"Shouldn't you notify the police?"

"No, Stuart emphasized no police. You're closest to where the truck is and can get to it quicker. It may be a ransom note. Please be careful. I'm wondering if Brian Campton is involved."

"What makes you say that?"

"Brian's been missing since he and Stuart had the fist fight in the barn a couple of weeks ago." She tapped her pen on the table.

"It does sound pretty fishy."

Tears slid down Sue's face. "I'm going to call your mom and Frank, and we'll meet you in your office at the ranch, and remember, no police."

Sue, Carol, and Frank disappeared into the cramped storage room which Ethan often referred to as his office. They settled around his cluttered desk. Soon, feeling the sting of frustration, Sue paced the eight-by-eight-foot room, while they waited for her son-in-law's return. She looked at her watch. It had already been half an hour.

She heard a car door slam, hurried to the office window, and watched Ethan run to the house.

He was pale and out of breath as he handed the note to her. "It's addressed to you."

Sue's fingers could barely hold the paper as she unfolded it and read silently.

We have Drake and kid. Put two hundred and fifty thousand dollars in a brief case. Go to junction of Saguaro Highway and Devil's Backbone. Leave case in phone booth at abandoned bar and grill promptly at 1 a.m. on Tuesday. Don't inform police of the drop-off, or Drake and kid will die. Any mistakes, your daughter is next.

Feeling her blood turn ice cold, she lowered herself onto a chair and looked at the others. "I'm supposed to get a quarter of a million dollars by early Tuesday morning?" She handed the note to Frank. "They repeated no police or they'll kill Stuart and JJ and then go after Rikki. How am I supposed to get my hands on that much money in such a short time? It's not like I have it sitting in my safety deposit box."

Frank rested his hand on her shoulder and gave it a reassuring squeeze. "Let me call Myron Hogan and see if he can meet us at the bank."

Sue's eyes darted here and there waiting for someone to agree or disagree with Frank's suggestion.

"Wait a minute, Frank. It's Sunday, and the bank won't be open." Carol frowned.

"Are you forgetting Myron's the bank president? He has connections and the authority to help us."

"Is this going to work? Will he have enough time to gather that much money? What if he asks why she needs it?" Carol's eyes grew wider as she considered the options. "Sue can't say it's for the ransom, and we don't want her to lie."

Ethan leaned in his chair and crossed his arms. "Good question, Mom. Why don't you say something unexpected came up at the ranch? After all, it's true."

"Think about it." Frank loosened his necktie and scratched his jaw. "You contacted the sheriff's department yesterday with a missing persons' report, so they already know JJ and Stuart are gone. Myron's a smart guy with strong ethics. He'll figure out why she needs to withdraw that much money It won't take him long to contact the authorities. They know how to handle it. From that point it's out of our control, and completely in God's."

Pressure showed on Ethan's youthful face. "I'm afraid of taking unnecessary chances with their lives. Remember, he threatened Rikki too."

"But the Lord knows we trust Him to help us all through this." Frank stood abruptly and buried his hands in his pockets. "We have to make a decision, here and now. Let's not waste time, since, like you say, two, possibly three, lives hang in the balance."

Sue nervously shifted in her chair and relived the moment Stuart took her hands in his and gazed into her eyes. They shared a bond she'd never dreamed possible. The thought of losing him now brought panic to her stomach. "We have a plan, why are we waiting? Stuart and JJ are counting on us."

"You're right. I'll call Myron now." He reached for the phone in his pocket.

In her mind's eye, Sue pictured Stuart lying in a heap at the barn door. *Lord, keep Brian from hurting him again.*

"I'm glad you understand the severity of the situation and why we need to keep this confidential. We're leaving the ranch now and will meet you at the bank as soon as possible." Frank headed for the door with phone in hand. "Come on, Sue. Myron will be there before we are." He stopped and kissed Carol's cheek. "We'll be in contact when we learn anything."

The long, silent drive to the Apache Pointe First National Bank seemed endless. What a blessing for Frank to know Myron well enough that he agreed to come to the office on a Sunday evening. He would aid them in getting the ransom money. Stuart and JJ should be free sometime on Tuesday.

Sue's thoughts repeatedly wandered to her growing love for Stuart. She longed to wrap her arms around him. Two hundred and fifty thousand dollars was a small price to pay to get him and JJ back.

Sitting in the bank president's office, Sue willed herself to remain calm.

Myron leaned back in his office chair and steepled his hands on his belly. "Now, Pastor Frank, from what you said in your prayer at church this morning, I need to ask, have Stuart and the boy from the ranch been abducted?"

"I'm afraid so." Frank nodded to Sue. "She received a call after the worship service telling us where the ransom note could be found and warning us not to contact the police."

"He threatened to take my daughter if we did." Sue bit her pinky nail. "Can you help us?"

Frank patted her hand. "We came here first to see if it was possible to get the ransom together by the time it's needed."

The banker sat up straight and made a note on a legal pad. "Before we go any further, I need to tell you the authorities will have to be notified to get your loved ones back safely."

"But they said not to. I don't want to put my daughter in danger."

"I understand." Myron's voice remained calm. "But even with that warning, the police are still your best bet in situations like this."

Frank stood. "We know you're right, but how do we set it up without someone seeing us with the police?"

"I'll call the chief and ask him to meet with us. He can come in the back so he won't draw attention." Myron dialed his desk phone. "While you talk to him, I'll make other calls to procure the monies."

Several minutes later, Apache Pointe's Chief of Police arrived at the bank.

CHAPTER THIRTY

SUE, CAROL, AND FRANK SPENT MOST of Monday helping Rikki at the ranch, trying to keep the kids occupied indoors.

While eating lunch, Frank's cell phone rang. He went to Ethan's office to answer the call. It wasn't long until he asked Sue and Ethan to join him.

Sue closed the door behind her. "Do they have a plan?"

"First of all, Myron is getting the money. Ethan and I will get the ransom and leave it at the drop site, as ordered, and then we'll come back here and wait.

As the drop-off time neared, Sue stood at the door with Carol and Rikki when the men left for the bank. "It sounds like the kids have finally settled down. I wish my stomach would too." Sue sat on the couch with her cup of tea. "It's in the Lord's hands now. All we can do is pray that all of them will be safe."

Carol closed the door and checked her watch. "The eleven o' clock news will be on in five minutes. I wonder if they'll have another update on the kidnapping."

Rikki picked up the remote and plopped beside her mother. "I didn't like the spin KAPP put on their segment yesterday. They made Stuart sound responsible for kidnapping JJ."

"Sounded like it to me too. It certainly wasn't impartial coverage." Sue glanced at the window. "Is the wind picking up?"

"The weatherman predicted major storms tonight." Carol looked at Sue and Rikki. "I hope the weather holds off until after the stakeout."

Rikki turned on the TV and settled into the couch. "That Sheridan fella better get the facts straight this time, or I'm going to send Ethan to complain."

The Channel 2 news logo appeared on the screen.

"Welcome to KAPP's Eleven O'clock News." The light-brown haired news anchor offered a radiant smile. "I'm Kent Sheridan and this is Monday, August fourteenth. KAPP's meteorologist, Will Scott, is standing by with the latest monsoon update for parts of the Western Valley and surrounding areas. What do you have for us, Will?"

"Thank you, Kent." Will Scott pointed to the map behind him. "We're keeping a close eye on thunderstorms and high winds expected to arrive within the next few hours.

"A strong dome of heat remains over the southwestern states, and storms are expected to pummel mid-Arizona and most of New Mexico." The meteorologist droned on, Sue's blood pressure rising with each word. "This active weather pattern will appear off and on for the next couple of days. Rainfall could be in excess of three inches in the deserts and over the mountains. Anyone in these areas should continue to keep watch for flash flooding. I'll have your complete weather forecast later."

Rikki muted the TV. "Monsoon? Flash flooding? Doesn't sound good. I hope Stuart and JJ are in a safe place out of the storm."

"Sometimes these storms don't reach monsoon level." Carol rubbed Rikki's shoulder. "Let's pray for the Lord to protect and guide them in this awful situation. We also need to pray for the safety of Sheriff Rowe and his men."

"Turn the sound up, Rikki, so we can watch the rest of the news." Sue's hand shook as she sipped her tea.

Sheridan looked directly into the camera. "New details have emerged of the alleged kidnapping of six-year-old JJ Lopez. The young boy is a resident of the Maverick Ranch for Children outside of Apache Pointe, Arizona.

"Deputy Josiah Stanford responded to a call about the boy missing from the ranch on Saturday. The juvenile was last seen playing hide and seek with a group of friends and has not been found.

"At the same time, ranch volunteer, Stuart Drake, mysteriously vanished. Sixty-four-year-old Drake is the co-owner of Floral Scent-sations in Apache Pointe. This is a recent police photo of Drake taken after his physical altercation with the prominent attorney, Brian Campton. Campton has also been missing since—"

Rikki stomped her foot and tossed the remote onto the coffee table. "How dare they do another hatchet job on Stuart?"

"I'll tell you what." Carol stood. "I'm going to call the KAPP station and let them know my uncle is innocent of that allegation." She stomped to the window. "People have the right to know the truth."

"Here we go again." Sue joined her friend. "The media is always looking to sensationalize stories and make the good guys look bad. Meanwhile they sing the praises of degenerates like Brian Campton."

Carol gathered the empty teacups. "Unfortunately, it's the way it usually works." She carried the cups to the kitchen and placed them in the sink. "Think it might be a good idea for us to watch out the windows while the men are gone?"

"Absolutely." Sue headed for the front door. "Rikki, while we check down here, why don't you peek in on the kids?"

She rose from the couch. "I'm on it, Mom."

Every twenty minutes for the next hour and a half, the women carried out their routine.

They finished their latest watch and met at the kitchen table.

"Do you hear that?" Carol turned around and peered out the window. "Why does Shep keep barking?"

Rikki shook her head. "Oh, don't worry about it. The wind is picking up. I imagine he's cornered a tumbleweed or two."

The rumble of thunder came with its promise of an approaching storm.

Running to the front door, Sue cracked it open. "I see headlights coming down the lane. Maybe it's Frank and Ethan."

A flash of distant lightning lit the horizon as the car pulled up to the house, its horn blaring.

By now, Carol and Rikki were at her side.

Sue sniffed the air. "Do you smell smoke?" She opened the door further. A gust of wind snatched it from her hand, causing the door to hit against the house.

"Fire, fire!" Frank and Ethan yelled frantically as they hurried to the wrap-around porch and hustled the women inside.

Ethan pulled Rikki to himself. "The back of the barn is burning. I need all of you to stay in the house, but have the kids ready to evacuate in case the fire comes this way."

"We're going to help Flapjack and Juan get the animals out of danger." Frank left and raced to the barn.

Near the paddock, Shep howled with the blaring sirens and ran in circles as the nearby Hawk Township

Sheriff's car and other emergency vehicles raced down the long, desert road toward the ranch.

When the firemen arrived, red and blue lights merged in blinding flashes. The fire chief shouted orders to the men in the yard, and their silhouettes scrambled to aim a hose at the barn window. Other firefighters targeted the tack room area where the heaviest smoke billowed. The fire truck's engine chugged as water sprayed the flames now growing in intensity.

Sue, Rikki, and Carol nervously hurried up the stairs to get the children out of bed and ready to flee should sparks and flames reach the house.

Water hit the building with great force. Sue and Rikki rushed to a bedroom, as a flash of light came from outside. A child screamed.

Rikki ran to the bedside. "It's okay, honey. We're going downstairs."

Another bolt of lightning and a cracking explosion. Sue clenched her teeth. Had the barn blown up? She held the arm of a small child, silently prayed, and raced for the stairs.

Groggy and confused, the sleepy children gathered in the huge living room, with their blankets and pillows. Fear grew evident in many eyes.

The door swung open and Juan, covered with soot and ash, brought Ines to safety with the others. "¡Ay! ¡Caramba! Mucho problems, now a storm. It is not needed." He kissed his wife's cheek and trudged outside.

Songs and games calmed the frightened children while Sharla accompanied them on an old upright piano. When a couple of the younger boys grew tired, Colt built a tent with couch cushions and blankets.

"We need candles, matches, and many other things. You girls check all windows." Ines quickly moved into her customary routine of gathering the cache of emergency supplies from the storage room.

Within another hour, the storm's heavy rain and firemen's brave efforts paid off and extinguished the angry fire. The intense downpour eventually moved out of the area, and a light drizzle replaced it.

Sue stood at the back door as Frank, Ethan, and Juan shed their muddy shoes on the porch. She handed them thick towels before they entered, dirty, exhausted, and smelling of smoke. "Wasn't Flapjack out there with you?"

"Yeah." Ethan vigorously toweled his damp head. "I understand he's the one who called the fire department as soon as he discovered it. We owe him our gratitude. If he hadn't been alert, the whole ranch could've gone up in flames."

Juan nodded. "He heard Marmalade go loco." The ranch hand accepted a cold glass of water from Ines. "After the fire was out, he went to his bunk."

"He needs his rest. We'll be sure to thank him later." Ethan shivered. "I can't wait to get out of these wet clothes. Frank and Juan, you can use the two showers upstairs. Rikki, will you give them something dry to wear?"

"Sandwiches will be ready when you men are." Ines patted her husband's damp shoulder.

Sue hurried to the living room and checked on the children. Colt and Becky were engrossed in a movie while the others slept. She returned to the kitchen and looked out the window. Lightning flashed erratically between two mountain peaks. Instantly, the image of Stuart's face returned to her mind. "Where are they, Lord?"

Carol put an arm around her shoulder. "I'm sure they're okay, Sooze. This is where our faith becomes stronger. We have to believe the Lord is watching over them."

"I'm confident we'll hear something soon." Ethan sat at the table, took a sandwich, and checked his watch. His expression turned pensive. "It's already after two in the morning. I'll call Sheriff Rowe around eight and see if there's any news about the ransom money."

Within a few minutes, Juan entered the room in rolled-up pant legs and a baggy work shirt. Frank followed him in a pair of ankle-length jeans and a navel-baring tee. They grabbed a sandwich and sat across from Ethan.

"The fire chief thinks the barn is a total loss." Ethan wiped ketchup from his mouth. "He said accelerants were found on site, which means we should count on a visit from an arson inspector sometime this morning."

"So this was done on purpose?" Juan's eyes narrowed. "Who would do such a thing?"

Sue caught a look between Frank and Ethan. "What are you two thinking?"

"When the fire chief mentioned possible arson, Ethan and I wondered if the kidnapping and the fire could be connected in some way."

"I paid the ransom. What would they gain by setting the barn on fire?"

Frank leaned forward with his elbows on the table. "Maybe they saw the stakeout."

"And they had to draw attention away from themselves." Ethan steepled his hands. "If that's the case, I pray we didn't put Uncle Stu and JJ in more danger."

"Obviously these guys aren't dumb. They probably planned the fire right from the beginning." Sue gathered the paper plates and headed for the kitchen. She made coffee to busy her thoughts with things other than Stuart and JJ. How much would it cost to replace a barn and improve on the layout and functionality? Fortunately, they had insurance.

Her cell phone buzzed. Nervously pulling it from her pocket, she held her breath and hoped for good news. "This is Sue North."

"We have the money. You can find the old man and the kid around Quartz Peak."

"Quartz Peak? Are they okay?"

The phone clicked without an answer.

The wind grew stronger as Stuart stepped around an outcropping which had blocked his vision. He'd never been this far out to look for firewood, and it proved to be a worthwhile venture. Two dead Mesquite trees lay close together. Within a few minutes, he had filled the box with gnarled branches and twigs while strobes of lightning struck in the distance.

An ominous feeling came over him. The weather pattern seemed right for a monsoon. He hoped he had enough time to gather extra fuel for their fire before the storm hit. If only he could get more of the Mesquite to the cave. He hefted the box under his arm, reached for a branch sticking out from the trunk, and yanked it. Maybe he could drag the whole piece.

He stood and surveyed the terrain from this new vantage point. Beyond the withered tree, he noticed a familiar mountain range. The remaining sunlight glistened off huge white rocks. Excitement grew in his chest. They had to be near Quartz Peak Trail. He and Max had hiked this area many times during their high school years.

Phoenix wasn't far away. At least they'd have a better chance for rescue on the trail, and if not there, certainly by the time they reached a main road.

Stuart picked up his pace as he climbed the rocks with his load. Mist had dampened his shirt by the time he reached the cave. Closing his eyes against lightning, he made his way into the opening. Crackling thunder echoed through the mountains and the ground shook. Shortly after, a deluge of rain hit.

Streams of water flowed past the entrance of the cave. Stuart added more rocks around the fire pit to protect it from the wind and rain. He threw another broken branch on the fire.

The small boy shivered and moved closer to him. "I'm scared of storms, Poppy."

The need to protect JJ rose in Stuart's chest. He pulled the little guy onto his lap and encircled him with his arms. "Remember when I told you God would take care of us?"

"Yeah?"

"He provided this cave to keep us out of the storm, a fire so we can stay warm, and plenty of Cheerios, Cheddar Doodles, and beef jerky to keep our tummies full." Stuart paused as a sharp clap of thunder hit louder than before. "Why don't we sing to keep our minds off the weather?"

"The Cheerios are all gone, and I don't know any songs. You sing."

"You'll know this one." He sang softly. "Yes, Jesus loves me, yes, Jesus loves me . . ."

"Yes, Jesus loves me, the Bible tells me so." JJ grinned at Stuart and finished the song. "Are we still camping?"

Stuart set his jaw with determination. "You betcha."

"Are we ever gonna go home?"

"Sure, but we may have to stay on this adventure until there's a break in the storm." He gave the boy a hug and pointed to the small wall of rocks forming a fire pit. "I'm sure glad you had matches."

"Are birds still in this cave?" JJ climbed off his lap and looked at the ceiling. "Can we eat 'em? I'm tired of jerkies. Do you have any gum?"

Stuart rolled his eyes at the boy's rapid-fire questions. "You know me, I always have gum." He reached in his pocket and pulled out the pack. "Oops, this is the last stick. Why don't you chew half now and save half for later?"

"Okay, and I'll chew it slow."

Finally, the boy grew quiet, giving Stuart a chance to think of a way for them to escape. However, his mind wandered to Sue . . . again. Time to face the facts; he wasn't going to get over her. His gaze drifted to the rain splattering on the outcropping of rocks. *Lord, You've given us a gift of love for each other. I'm surrendering my reluctance and accepting this as Your will.*

Stuart turned his head and saw JJ rummaging through the stash of food.

The boy held up a bag. "I swallowed my gum. Can I have Cheddar Doodles, Poppy?"

"Of course. Bring the bag over and share with me." Grabbing a few doodles, he popped them into his mouth, and washed them down with water. When they returned to civilization, he promised himself never to buy another bag of them.

Lightning and thunder intensified. How were they going to get out of there with bare feet? Glancing at his empty bottle of water, an idea struck him. Stuart rubbed the thick stubble on his chin. It might just work. Pulling out the pocketknife, he deftly cut around the pant leg above the knee. After removing the fabric, he cut it into strips.

JJ crawled to him. "Why are you cutting your

pants?"

"I'm going to try to make some shoes for us so we can get out of here."

"Make shoes with your pants? How are you gonna do that?"

"Watch me." Stuart cut the denim into long, narrow strips. "Would you hand me a couple of those empty water bottles?"

Stuart took the bottles from JJ, then stepped on one until it flattened. With his foot still on the bottle, he wrapped the fabric around the neck and tied it in a knot. One strand went to the right of his foot and the other to the left. He crisscrossed it underneath the bottle and drew it up in back of the heel. After crossing it again, he took it to the front of his leg and tied it above the ankle.

The boy clapped and squealed. "Poppy, you made a shoe! Can I have shoes too?" He lunged for the pocketknife.

Stuart held onto him. "I'll make you a pair when I'm done with mine." He worked on his other pant leg, folded the knife, and put it safely in his pocket.

Within a half hour, he had fashioned three additional plastic sandals. JJ's needed shortened to fit his small feet. The two of them clomped around in the cave, keeping the boy's mind occupied while the storm brewed outside. Stuart noticed a glimmer on the far side of the cave and hurried to investigate. His heart soared when he picked up an aluminum can. Where did it come from? No matter, maybe he could use it to reflect the sun's rays to get help.

Setting it aside, he turned to count the rations. The snacks were getting low, and only two apples remained. If they had enough water, they could set out tomorrow and possibly find a road. Weather permitting.

Without warning, JJ cried out as he lost his balance

wearing his new shoes. He grasped at nothing but air. Helpless to catch himself, he tumbled a few feet outside and into the pouring rain.

"Are you all right?" Stuart hurried to pick the boy up and carried him inside, thankful lightning hadn't hit them. "Let's get you dried off by the fire. These shoes sure weren't made for slippery rocks."

JJ hung his head and sniffled. "Sorry, Poppy. I didn't mean to fall."

"It's okay, son. Don't cry. You didn't do it on purpose." Stuart ruffled the child's wet hair in order to calm him, then added excitement to his voice. "Listen close. I have a plan to get us home."

"Do I get to help?" He wiped his eyes.

"You sure do. The first thing tomorrow morning, we're going to go down the hill in our bare feet and when we get to the bottom, we'll put on our new shoes."

"Why don't we put 'em on up here?"

"You fell on the rocks. The shoes will be safer on level ground." Stuart scratched his scruffy cheek. "I want you to help me carry things we need to take with us." Glad to see the boy's face relax, he felt the tension ease from his own body.

"Night." JJ nestled under the crook of his arm.

"Thank You, Lord, for keeping us safe today. Please give us a good night's sleep, and help our minds to be clear for our trek home."

CHAPTER THIRTY-ONE

THREE HECTIC DAYS AT THE RANCH had provided Sue with little time for sleep and only a quick shower. She couldn't wait to bathe and take a nap, although with constant thoughts of Stuart, falling asleep might prove to be a challenge.

The front doorbell rang as she entered her house from the garage. Phoebe Ferguson stood at the door, hands on hips. "Where have you been, North? You look like a wreck."

Sue's hand went to her hair where her fingers snagged in the messy bun. The last thing she needed was to spend precious naptime explaining things to the meddlesome sarge. "I've been at the ranch. Stuart and one of the boys were kidnapped."

"I know. It's been all over TV. Do you have any more recent news?"

"The ransom money has been taken." Sue released a deep breath and continued to lean out the front door to prevent her neighbor from entering. "The kidnapper called and said Stuart and JJ are somewhere around Quartz Peak."

Phoebe's eyebrows arched. "That's bad. Those foothills are honeycombed with caves hidden by brush and rough terrain."

"The sheriff said the main problem now is to get through the monsoon water to find them. A search and rescue squad and ambulance will be there as soon as they can."

"Do they have any leads on the kidnapper?" The sarge's face took on a serious expression as she crossed her arms.

Sue tilted her head. "Not as of this morning. The storm and fire didn't help the investigation at all. Whoever it is has the money and is probably long gone by now."

"What do you mean, whoever it is? It has to be the Campton guy. He hasn't been to the Bet and Roll Casino for a week, and that's not like him. I go hit the slots at least once a week and he's always there shootin' craps." Phoebe squinted and pointed at Sue's nose. "I never liked his beady eyes."

"Did you say casino?"

"Sure. He's a high roller. You dated him. Didn't you know? Word has it he owes a bundle to a certain dangerous loan shark."

Sue rubbed her brow. Now it started to make sense. No wonder Brian had been eager to get married. He wanted to control her money to pay off his gambling debts, and she would be his lucky charm as he continued his habit.

"Sue?" Gabby nudged her arm, drawing her back to the present. "Earth to Sue."

She jumped. "When did you get home, Gabby? I thought you were in New Mexico."

"We came home early when we heard about Stu and the boy. I came right over." Gabby motioned to the house. "It's hot out here. Can we go inside?"

"Of course." Sue let them in, then grabbed the mail from the box by her door. "I just got here to check my mail and take a much-needed shower. Why don't you make yourselves comfortable, and I'll be out soon."

Gabby called after her. "Have you had lunch yet?"

"I've been too preoccupied with the kids and other

things."

"Tell you what, while you get clean, Phoebe and I will make a sandwich and a pot of coffee for you."

Sue tossed her bills onto the dining room table. "Thanks, gals. I'm famished."

"I'll help with the coffee in a minute, Gabs; I got me an important call to make first." Phoebe marched out the front door.

The hot pulsating shower eased the tension in Sue's shoulders. She prayed while rinsing the shampoo from her hair. "Dear Lord, please continue to watch over Stuart and JJ. Help the search team find them quickly and let the sheriff catch Brian before he leaves the country. In Jesus' name."

With great reluctance, she turned the water off, wrapped the towel around herself, and stepped from the shower. If only a quick nap was possible, or better yet, a long one. As she dressed, thoughts of Stuart and JJ living in a cave filled her mind. Had either of them been hurt, or bitten by spiders and other creepy crawlies?

Gabby spoke on the phone in the hallway as Sue passed by. The aroma of strong coffee lured her to the kitchen where a sandwich and cottage cheese waited for her on the counter.

With Phoebe gone, the living room became a quiet refuge. Sue took her food to the couch, put her feet on the footrest, and clicked the TV's remote.

Gabby sat on the other end of the sofa. "That was Millie. Of course, she's worried about her dad. I've been trying to keep her calm. She wanted to go to the ranch with Lou, but with little Gracie coming down with a cold, Millie didn't want to take any chances."

"I certainly understand. There's nothing going on right now except the children's chaos. Taking care of a fussy infant will wear her out." Sue picked up her coffee cup. "I know she'll want to be available when they find Stuart."

"Warning. Before you take a drink, Phoebe made the coffee, and I know from past experience it might be a little on the thick side."

"Where is she, by the way?"

"After Sarge used her phone, she came in and made coffee. Then she received a return call about ten minutes ago. Didn't say a word, simply up and left in her Hummer."

Taking a sip of the black, almost-liquid, Sue shuddered, and her eye went into a spasm. "Don't ever let that woman near my coffeemaker again." She finished her sandwich. "Would you like to go to the ranch with me in an hour or so? I promised to take a few DVDs and popcorn to keep the kids busy."

"Sure I'll go with you. The DVDs are a great idea." Gabby hesitated. "Did you and Stu make any decisions about your relationship before the kidnapping?"

The question caused Sue's stomach to constrict. "I'm still waiting."

Drowning in a sea of orange puffs, Stuart struggled for air. His eyes opened and he blinked. Was he awake or dreaming? The darkness around him made it difficult to tell. However, the irritating smell of Cheddar Doodles intensified.

The crinkle of a snack bag next to his ear gave it away. He pushed himself up on one elbow and frowned as the outline of JJ hovered over him.

"Morning, Poppy. I made breakfast. Want some?"

Stuart ran his hand through his hair and tried to

shake himself awake. He rubbed a hand over his mouth and hit something hard. "What's this in my nose?" He pulled the object out. "A Cheddar Doodle? Why, JJ?"

"You wouldn't wake up, and I wanna go home." JJ pulled Stuart's hand. "C'mon, Miss Rikki's probably worried."

Stuart got to his feet, dreading the long walk ahead. He stepped outside the cave and peered at the horizon, where the rays of the sun brightened the cumulus clouds. Fortunately, the wind had calmed and the rain ceased.

He stretched his arms and took several deep breaths. They had to decide what to take with them. Water and their shoes were necessary, along with the corrugated box, and ropes which had bound their hands. He couldn't forget to take the aluminum can with possible fingerprints. It was important to leave enough evidence behind to prove they'd been there. The snack bags and fire pit would work.

"Would you help me find all the ropes, JJ?" Stuart put the empty box in front of him and used his knife to make two holes on the side.

"Here you go, Poppy. What are you making now?"

Stuart wiped his hands on his jeans. "I'm making something called a travois."

"What's a tra-boy?"

"It's like a sled made with two poles. I'll show you." Stuart joined the ends of two branches and tied them together. "This part stays on the ground." He tied a shorter stick across the middle to hold them together and put the box above the middle support stick. "Now we'll put the last ten water bottles in the box. You hold the other two ends and pull it behind you."

JJ grabbed one of the sticks. "I'm gonna pull it?"

"Maybe after we get down the hill."

"Are we going home now? Can I wear my shoes? I'll put the Cheddar Doodles in the tra-boy."

"We'll leave as soon as soon as the box is loaded." Stuart put the bottles in and held up their shoes by the denim straps. "These aren't safe to wear until we get down the hill. They'll go in the box too." He took a deep breath. "And leave all the snacks here."

JJ frowned. "Leave 'em here? Why? What if we get hungry?"

"The salty snacks will make us too thirsty, and we don't have much water. There's one apple left, and we'll have to share it at noon."

"Share an apple? You can have my skin part of it."

"That's good. Thank you." Stuart tied a strip of denim around their foreheads and handed JJ a walking stick.

The boy patted the new headband and held his stick high in the air. "We're caveman warriors, Poppy."

Before leaving, Stuart put his hands on the child's shoulder and pointed to the cave. "Look at the home we had for three days. God took care of us here, and He will take care of us on our way home." He looked to the sky. "Thank You for meeting our every need, Lord. Please be with us as we walk in faith through the desert. Continue to keep us safe and lead someone to rescue us. In Jesus' name, amen."

Stuart handed his own stick to JJ. "You can be a big help by taking this down the hill for me. Now, you can use both hands and pretend you're skiing on the slopes." Stuart showed him.

"Like they do on TV?"

"You got it." He lifted the box and glanced at his watch. Six-thirty. How long would it take to get off the hill? "Okay, kiddo, stay right by my side and take your time because I have to carry this box and the travois."

"It's a tra-boy, Poppy."

He chuckled. This was going to be quite a trip. "You're right. Remember to watch for snakes and stuff."

"People on TV eat snakes. We're cavemen warriors, can we eat one?"

"Not today. We can't build a fire in the desert. Let's get moving." Stuart stepped forward on the large stones ahead of him. Their cargo didn't seem as heavy now, but he knew that would change as his energy waned.

CHAPTER THIRTY-TWO

THE DVDS SUE AND GABBY TOOK to the ranch later that afternoon turned out to be a big hit with the children. Sue distributed several batches of popcorn among the kids. The wonderful buttery aroma of a movie theater filled the house.

"I made this bowl of popcorn for us not the kids." Sue placed it on the kitchen table and sat next to Carol.

"We've been through a lot together, haven't we, Sooze?" Carol's hand trembled as she reached for a handful of popcorn. "I never thought a kidnapping scheme would ever hit our family."

Faces around the room were of people she trusted most. Only Stuart was missing.

"Since all of us are here, Gabby and I need to share what Phoebe Ferguson mentioned at my house this afternoon." Sue paused. "She said Brian is a long-time gambler."

"He owes a lot of money to . . . ." Gabby air quoted, "certain people."

Frank leaned forward. "Did you tell the sheriff?"

"We called him right away." Sue confirmed with a nod. "He said they had been aware of his gambling history. He's definitely a suspect."

"That certainly gives him a motive to kidnap." Ethan's eyes showed concern.

Sue wiped her eyes. "Wish I hadn't gotten involved with Brian in the first place. This whole thing has caused such heartache." She went to the porch and sat on the top step.

Rikki followed and pulled her into a hug. "You can't think that way, Mom. Because of you, the ranch has become more of a home to these sweet kids. They all love Miss Sue and so do I."

"But if I'd stayed in Vermont, Brian wouldn't have gone after my money and there'd be no reason for a kidnapping."

"Brian couldn't hide his true colors forever. He probably would've gone after my money eventually."

Before long, a car pulled into the circle drive. Sue stood. "Oh, good. Millie and Lou are here with the baby."

They all gathered in the kitchen to wait for any news on the kidnapping.

Stuart rubbed his tired eyes as he and JJ sat in the minimal shade of a scrub tree. While the boy slept, Stuart kept watch on the lone vulture circling overhead. He wondered what critter was on tonight's menu.

Wanting to keep JJ away from any and all disgusting conversation starters, he glanced around for the carcass. His eyes lit on a black object a few yards away. What was it? Curiosity got the better of him, so he silently made his way to the spot.

A shoe? Had someone been injured during the storm? He looked back to see if the boy was still asleep before venturing toward a nearby rock formation. A solid wall of stomach lurching stink hit him in the face. As he covered his nose and mouth and backed away, he noticed two human legs sticking out from behind the rocks.

A small voice called from a distance. "Poppy, where

are you? Did you leave me?"

"Here I am, JJ." Stuart turned, ran to the boy, and gave him a tight hug. "Let's get our things and find our way out of here."

Stuart guessed it was a half-hour later when they made it to the road which meant civilization was not far away. He'd have to report the body to the sheriff.

They stopped and shook sand from their makeshift sandals and shared another bottle of sun-heated water.

JJ leaned on Stuart's arm. "How much longer, Poppy? I can't stay awake anymore."

"Hang in there, son. We've made it to the road and things will go a lot easier now." A dust cloud in the far distance caught Stuart's attention. Someone was coming! His heart raced as he struggled to his feet to get a better look.

The object grew closer. Stuart squinted, shaded his eyes, and soon began to distinguish the form. Was that a black Hummer? Knowing his luck, it was a mirage.

JJ hid behind Stuart's legs. "Is that the bad man coming after us again? Don't let him tie us up this time."

"Be quiet for a minute." Stuart recognized Phoebe's sweet ride as it came to a stop. He released a deep, weary sigh. "Thank You, Lord. We're safe now, JJ."

Leaving her vehicle, Sarge gave both refugees a bottle of chilled water. "Good seein' ya, Drake. You sure had folks worried." She looked at JJ. "Especially you, squirt."

Stuart grinned, took the clear container, then swept her up into a bear hug. "Phoebe Ferguson, you're the prettiest thing I've seen in a long time." He kissed her forehead.

She clung to Stuart's arm to regain her balance. "Stars and stripes, Drake. Not in front of the kid." She pointed to the Hummer. "Get inside and cool off. When I recognized you, I went ahead and called the nearby EMS to meet us halfway into town."

The trio climbed in the car and sped down the dirt road. Fifteen minutes later, they saw the ambulance and the sheriff's squad car headed their way. Phoebe pulled over.

Sheriff Rowe climbed from his cruiser and slammed the door.

When the bright yellow emergency vehicle stopped next to them, the cave warriors climbed out of the Hummer. Stuart leaned down to comfort the boy and pointed to the man in a white button-down shirt. "This is a medic and he won't hurt you. They want to make sure we're okay since we've been lost for so long. Let him listen to your heart and look in your throat."

"Okay, Poppy. Can I look in his throat too? He's not gonna give me a shot is he?"

The EMT laughed, lifted the boy into the back of the ambulance, and sat him on a stretcher. "Have you ever been in a truck like this before? They're really cool." He put the stethoscope to JJ's chest. "Sounds good. Do you hurt anywhere?"

"Well, these shoes kinda crinkled my feet. And I'm really hungry."

"I can take care of that, kiddo." He pulled out an energy bar and opened it for him.

Stuart moved away from the ambulance and took the opportunity to tell the sheriff about the body he'd found earlier. He gave the officer the general location, then returned to JJ.

After checking Stuart's vitals, the paramedic handed each another bottle of cold water. "You're both looking really good for being out here so long. We're going to let you go, but be sure to drink plenty of fluids when you get home."

Stuart climbed from the ambulance and reached up

to retrieve JJ from the man's arms. "I want to thank you guys for being here for us."

From Phoebe's Hummer window, Stuart watched the sheriff point back to where the body was.

The sheriff spoke into his lapel mic and went to Phoebe's car. He opened the door and poked his head inside. "Sergeant Ferguson is going to take you to the ranch."

Phoebe climbed behind the wheel. "Let's get you home, men."

After helping JJ fasten his seatbelt, Stuart settled into the passenger seat beside Phoebe.

She goosed the engine to release a great roar. "Never gets old." She put the SUV in gear and eased her foot down on the pedal.

Stuart white-knuckled the armrest, and JJ squealed in delight as the vehicle lumbered in and out of the sandy ruts.

Looking out the side window, Stuart contemplated who their abductor could have been. His mind went to the man he'd fought a couple of months ago. Was Campton the kidnapper? He tried to recall the biker's voice, but he'd only heard a muffled tone beneath the helmet. No help there. Were his shoulders the same width as Campton's? Why couldn't he remember?

In another half hour, they turned down the road to the ranch. Stuart rubbed the bristles on his face, wishing he had a cordless shaver. "I'm not smelling too pretty. Maybe I should visit the horse trough before I go inside."

"Grab the package of wipes out of the glove compartment and rag off."

"Thanks, Sarge." He ripped a few lemony-scented sheets from the pack and busied himself with the insurmountable task of removing the four-day stench.

"I have a camo jacket in the backseat. I think the

boy's using it as a blanket."

JJ sat up and looked around. "I'm not sleepin'. Are we home yet?"

By the time they pulled to a stop in the circle drive, Stuart had replaced his smelly shirt with Phoebe's jacket.

"Are we at the right place? It doesn't look the same." The boy pressed his nose to the Hummer's window. "Oh, no! Where's the barn?"

"A big fire broke out the night of the storm." Phoebe opened her door and looked at Stuart. "Arson."

JJ jumped from the SUV and ran into Rikki's open arms. He wiped his eyes with his sleeve. "Don't cry Miss Rikki. We've been campin' in a cave."

Picking the boy up, Ethan held his head close and kissed his forehead. "We've missed you."

"I missed you too. There's my friends." He ran to the group of shouting kids waiting on the wrap-around porch. "Hi, guys! I'm back."

Stuart's knees ached as he climbed the porch stairs. He got about halfway when Sue pulled him into a hug and deeply kissed him. He held on to her upper arm to prevent them from toppling off the steps.

Tears streamed down her cheeks as she cradled his scruffy face in her hands. "I have to say this now before I pop. I love you, Stuart Thomas Drake."

"I love you too, Suzie." His chest nearly burst with sheer happiness. As they moved to the porch, he noticed the others had gone inside. He kissed her forehead. "I hate to cut this short, but I smell a little gamey. Let me take a shower and clean four days' worth of whiskers and grime off before crushing you in my arms." He took her hand and led her into the house.

Millie met him at the door. "I've been so worried, Dad. I'm glad you and JJ are alright."

He pulled her into a hug. "I love you, Princess. God took care of us."

With her eyes wide with fear, Lark peeked from behind a door. She ran to Lou, sitting on the sofa.

"It's okay, Lark." Lou's deep voice calmed her. "That's Poppy. He's all dirty from being outside."

"I'm going to go get clean and then you'll know who I am."

Rikki motioned to Stuart. "It's good to see you safe and sound. There are clothes for you in the bathroom along with a new razor. Help yourself to anything else you need. I'm going upstairs to check on JJ."

"Thanks, honey. One more thing, could you give me a trash bag for these clothes? You may want to burn them." He turned to Phoebe. "Hold on and I'll toss your jacket to you. Thanks for the loan."

Once in the bathroom, Stuart removed the camo jacket and handed it to her out the door. He looked in the mirror, shuddered, and then took a closer gander at the bewhiskered hobo staring at him. How could Suzie kiss such a mangy mug? He turned the shower on, then shoved his dirty clothes in the trash bag while waiting for the water to heat.

Muddy water trickled down the drain before he could reach for the soap. Three shampoos later, he tackled his beard. After toweling off, he dressed and added a little aftershave. The guy in the mirror returned his smile.

Stuart walked into the kitchen in his stocking feet. The ranch kids quickly surrounded him and one by one, offered a hug. He felt a tug on his shirttail and knelt down.

"This is my Poppy." Lark's small arms encircled his neck. She ran her finger on his cheek. "You're soft now."

Ethan stood and clapped his hands. "Okay, kids. It's late, and you need to go to bed. I know you're all happy to see Poppy, but he'll come see you in a few days." He took Rikki's hand. "Let's get this crew tucked in and prayers said. We have a lot to be thankful for tonight."

"I'll bet Stuart's starving." Gabby retrieved deli ham and turkey from the refrigerator. "Let's have something to eat. Hey, Stu. You're by the pantry. Will you grab a bag of chips and Cheddar Doodles?"

"Chips are fine, but please, no Cheddar Doodles. I've been Doodled up to here." He ran his index finger across his nose. "Literally."

Frank took the offered bag of chips. "Sounds like a story to me. Spill it."

"My one and only good night of sleep and I woke up to Doodles sticking out of my nose. JJ told me he had breakfast ready."

Sue laughed. "That's our JJ."

While eating his first real food since Saturday, Stuart shared more tales of the caveman warriors. "The little man became a warrior in his own right."

There was a knock on the door. Ethan came down the stairs and answered it.

Sheriff Rowe followed him into the kitchen. "We ran the fingerprints from the ransom pick-up and an accelerant can from the fire. They match." He laid a paper on the table. "This is his rap sheet. His name is Carson North."

Sue gasped and clutched Stuart's arm. "Carson?"

"Are we related to him, Mom?" Rikki searched her mother's face.

"Carson is your dad's brother. He's been in a Florida prison since before you were born. I didn't think he'd been released yet."

"How come I never heard of him?"

"Your dad had big political hopes, and Carson turned out to be a liability." Sue glanced around the table. "I've only seen him once, and he was still a teenager."

Ethan reached for the rap sheet and studied it. "Call me crazy, but doesn't this picture of Carson North look like a young Flapjack?" He glanced at the sheriff. "He's worked here for the last two years and has never been a problem. We really liked the guy."

"Let me see the picture." Gabby snatched it from his hands. "His hair looks different now, and his cheeks are fuller, but you're right, that's definitely Flapjack."

"I feel like a fool." Sue shook her head. "Flapjack is Carson. He was right under my nose this whole time, and I didn't recognize him."

Sheriff Rowe looked from one person to another. "When was the last time you folks saw him?"

"Our other hand, Juan Garcia, said he helped put the fire out. I'll take you out to his bunk." Ethan hurried to the door. "Follow me."

After the two men left, Sue placed her hand on Stuart's back. "I apologize for my brother-in-law's part in this."

"No one is blaming you. We all know your heart." Stuart took Sue's hand. "I'm bushed. I've been running on adrenaline for three days. Time for me to get home and crash."

"Wait a minute." Rikki left the room and returned dangling a set of keys. "Ethan found these in the truck. How about having him drive you?"

Stuart took them from Rikki. "Thanks, but this will give me time to clear my head. I'll be in touch tomorrow after I get some shuteye. I'm going to take the boots from the mudroom." He took Sue's hand. "Walk me to the car, Suzie?"

She fell in step with him as they left the house and walked into the moonlight. "Are you going to be all right on the way home?"

"Sure. Don't worry about me. You're tired too. We both need our sleep." They slowly approached his car, and his hand tightened around hers. He stopped and swept her into his arms. "I've dreamed about this moment for months. Being lost in the desert made me wonder if I'd ever see you again."

"Me too." She clung to him, pressing close.

A thrill shot through him as his lips feather-touched hers. With a sigh, she rested her head against his pounding chest.

He took a deep breath. "I love you, Suzie. This may sound like a line, but I've never felt this way before."

"Neither have I." She wiggled her eyebrows. "We have a lot of catching up to do."

"Let's get started." Stuart's head bent once more and their kiss turned into a lingering caress. He reluctantly released her. When he opened the car door, he checked in the back seat before getting behind the wheel. "Can't be too careful. We'll talk more tomorrow. Want to have breakfast at Perky's around ten?"

"I'd love it." She leaned into the car window and kissed his lips again. "See you at ten o'clock."

Smiling at her, Stuart waved. As he drove down the lane, he struggled to make himself breathe normally.

Several miles later, a bright light in the rearview mirror brought his wandering mind to the present. Stuart glanced out the side window.

The roar of a motorcycle grew louder as it caught up with him.

CHAPTER THIRTY-THREE

THE NEXT MORNING, SUE WAITED FOR Stuart in their booth at Perky's. It wasn't like him to be late. She checked the time again.

Pickles came to refill her cup. "I heard they found Stu and the boy safe out by Quartz Peak."

"We're thankful. Stuart's supposed to meet me here soon." Her eyes drifted to the window, searching for his car.

Something soft and fragrant touched her cheek. She spun in her seat and came face-to-face with a dozen crimson roses. "They're beautiful, Stuart. Thank you."

"Sorry I'm late, honey. These roses were crying for a new owner." He carefully shook the bouquet and talked in a falsetto voice. "Love me. Feed me. Take me home with you." He laid the flowers on his usual seat and sat next to her.

His eyes sought hers, and once again, the feathery touch of his lips sent a warm and sweet wave through her.

"Let's keep it G-rated, folks." Pickles giggled. "Give me your breakfast order and I'll leave you alone."

They glanced at each other and Stuart spoke. "We'll both take the house special."

"It'll be a few minutes." Pickles' blue-green eyes squinted, first to Stuart and then to Sue. "Carry on."

"I got a little nervous when you were late today. You're never late. I thought something might have happened."

He took her hand and kissed it. "I'm fine, but on my way home last night I had a scare. I'd been thinking about you when a motorcycle nearly ran me off the road like Flapjack did. Talk about déjà vu."

"See, I should have gone with you."

"Are you kidding? If you were there, we'd still be out there smooching behind a cactus." He winked and their lips touched.

She felt all eyes on her. "I hope everyone accepts us as a couple."

"Does it matter?" His finger lightly traced the smile creases around her mouth. "You know Who put us together, right?" He grinned widely. "It certainly tips the scales in our favor." He took her hand and pulled her close. "When we're done eating, would you like to go to the park and walk along the river?"

"Sure," she whispered and then closed her eyes and waited for a kiss.

Stuart gave her another quick smooch and then laughed. "Uh-oh, busted."

Sue glanced up. Pickles stood beside the table with her arms loaded.

"Don't let me interrupt." The smiling waitress placed their breakfast order in front of them. "Two house specials. And I brought you extra syrup."

"Flapjacks?" Sue buried her face in her hands, and her shoulders shook with laughter.

"Thanks, Pickles. You'll get an extra tip for this one." With his fork and knife in hand, he cut into his tall stack with great gusto.

When they were finished eating. Stuart tossed a tip on the table. "Now, Suzie, let's go for that walk."

Mourning doves cooed as Sue and Stuart held hands and strolled along the Saguaro River Walkway. A gentle breeze rippled the water reflecting the sun's rays.

"That's a beautiful area over there. Can we cross the footbridge so I can get pictures?"

"Sure. I see a bench where we can rest." Stuart shaded his eyes against the sun. "My feet are still sore from wearing those water bottle sandals."

"I'm sorry. We shouldn't even be out here."

They hurried to the bench and Stuart sat with his legs outstretched,

Sue pulled the cell from her pocket. "You take it easy and I'll be right back."

"Remember, we're in the desert. It's important for you to watch for scorpions and snakes."

She'd only taken a few steps when a large yellow-striped lizard scampered across her path and vanished into the wild scrub ahead. After releasing a squeal, she felt a little silly when Stuart came limping her way.

"Are you okay, sweetheart?"

Her face heated. "Some kind of big reptile startled me. Go sit down, hon, I'm fine." She snapped a few more pictures of purple coneflowers, Dusty Millers, and some unknown plants that Stuart could identify for her.

He was smiling and rubbing his feet when she returned to the bench. "You looked so happy out there among the flowers."

Sue looked into his dark brown eyes. "I never knew the desert could hold so much beauty."

"The Lord puts a bit of beauty in everything He makes." His face took on a boyish grin as he patted the seat of the shaded bench. "Come sit beside me."

She took a seat next to him and raised her sunglasses to the top of her head.

The blue wings of a scrub jay fluttered when he

landed in the mesquite tree beside them. He clacked his mandibles and gave the couple a loud scolding.

She pointed to the noisy bird. "He seems to think we're invading his turf."

"I think he's jealous. That ol' bird can find his own girl." Stuart's arms pulled her closer.

The tender touch caressing her cheek caused her to tremble. "I love you, Stuart." Her head rested on his shoulder. Why didn't the man kiss her already?

As if hearing the subliminal message, Stuart lovingly raised her chin, and lowered his lips.

She held the back of his head and eagerly returned the kiss.

Pulling away slightly, Stuart looked down. "The fear of remarrying plus our age difference bothered me, so I backed off from this relationship."

"Me too." Sue nodded and grabbed his hand. "I was uneasy with Brian and really had to pray about that. But when you and I were together, it felt right and comfortable."

Stuart released a deep breath and smiled. "I'm so glad. There was a lot of soul searching and prayer on my end too." He reached in his breast pocket and presented a small velvet box.

With shaking hands, he opened it and revealed a princess cut solitaire ring.

Sue gasped. "It's beautiful." She reached out and took the box, gazing at the ring

"Suzie-Q North, I love you with every ounce of my being." He nervously cleared his throat. "Will you marry me?"

Her eyes flooded with tears as she handed the box back.

His kind face conveyed a spark of disbelief and then flashed to shock and hurt.

"Oh, Stuart, it would be an honor. I can't live without you." She placed her left hand in his. "Would you put it on me?"

He grinned, nodded, and gently slipped the ring on her finger. Then lifting her hand, he kissed it.

Sue wrapped her arms around his neck and their lips met to seal their promise.

The scrub jay returned, clapped his beak, and loudly squawked.

"We seem to be drawing attention again." Sue lowered her sunglasses. "It's been a hard week for you. Maybe it's time to go home and rest."

As they strolled back to the car, a troubled frown settled on Stuart's face. "Tomorrow's Thursday, right? Max and I have last minute things to tie up at the flower shop before the new owners take possession next week. The next couple of days are going to be busy, so I'll call you."

"My Friday is booked anyway. I'm giving a presentation at the Flour Power Baking Expo in Tucson again this year. I won't be home until late."

"That means we won't see each other until I pick you up Saturday for the ranch dinner." He squeezed her hand. "How will I get through the next two days without you?"

Early Saturday morning, Sue answered her front door. Stuart met her with open arms and gently rocked her back and forth.

She kissed his tanned cheek. "I missed you so much, Stuart. It was the longest forty-eight hours I've ever endured."

"Two days without you is too much." Stuart gave her one last enthusiastic smooch. "I hate to break this up, darlin', but we should've left for the ranch ten minutes ago."

"Everything I'm supposed to take is on the counter. Would you carry it to the car? I'll be there in a minute."

A short time later, Sue held his hand and hummed along while the car radio played "I'm Just a Sinner Saved by Grace." When the song ended, she shared her thoughts. "Just think, honey, after all the unhappy years we both endured, God brought us together and is showing us what real love is like."

"That time was filled with a lot of shame, embarrassment, anger, and discouragement." He shook his head. "Maybe we should write a book."

"No one would ever believe it. Besides, I'd rather count our blessings." She looked out the side window. "Today's party came up pretty quick. Rikki and Carol wouldn't give me a reason for it."

"Do they really need a reason? Knowing those two, it's because this is the first Saturday in September. Think of it as the perfect time to make our own announcement, Suzie."

"You're right. I'm not having any second thoughts. Let's go for it." She heard the name 'North' on the radio and turned up the volume. "The news is on."

". . . fingerprints were on record. Incarcerated for armed robbery, North was released from a Florida prison after serving twenty-five years. Since then, he appeared to be a model citizen working as a ranch hand at the Maverick Ranch for Children. An off-duty cop captured North late last night at a convenience store in Armadillo Flats, Arizona. He was charged with two counts of kidnapping. Now for the weather . . ."

"Now I *do* feel like celebrating." He stepped on the

gas and soon they were at the ranch, carrying in their potato salad and several dozen chocolate-mallow cupcakes.

"Poppy!" The kids quickly swarmed Stuart, giving him hugs.

Surprise filled Sue's heart when she saw Carol sitting beside her parents in the living room. It must be a special party. "Hi, Max and Sylvia. It's good to see you. Love the roses in your cheeks, Syl."

"Feel better too." Sylvia's blue eyes glowed with excitement as she watched the children dance around Stuart.

Sue snapped a picture of her soon-to-be in-laws. "Oh, Millie has the baby here." Sue sat in a chair next to Millie and took more photos. "Gracie has sure grown a lot in the past couple of weeks."

"She's gained three pounds." Millie beamed as she gazed at her daughter.

Lark played quietly with her doll on the floor between Lou and Millie's feet. Sue bent to pat the little girl's dark hair. "I see you have your party dress on. It's very pretty. May I take your picture?"

Climbing onto Lou's lap, Lark held up her doll and smiled from ear to ear. Lou rested his chin on the top of her head.

"So, do either of you know what Rikki's big surprise is?"

Rikki laughed. "Since Mom has interrogated everyone in the room, we're going to let Millie and Lou make their announcement."

Lou stood with Lark in his arms. "We wanted to let all of you know that Team Blythe is growing again. Baby Grace is going to have a brother and sister in a few months."

Instant silence. Confused eyes darted here and there.

Deep breaths followed.

"You didn't say a word to me, Louis Elliot." Gabby stood. Her shocked expression changed to one of awareness. "You're adopting Lark, aren't you?"

Lark nodded emphatically, then hid her face in Lou's chest.

"Who's her brother?" Carol asked.

The patter of bare feet sounded on the hardwood floor as JJ ran into the room, arms wide open. "It's me-e-e!"

"Poppy needs a hug from his new grandkids." Stuart's knees popped when he knelt down.

JJ ran and Lark skipped into his embrace.

Wiping his eyes with a handkerchief, Stuart got to his feet and blew his nose.

Ethan sent the children outside. "Colt and Becky, take care of the boys. Kathy and Sharla keep an eye on the girls." He turned to the adults. "They don't need to hear some of this. Sheriff Rowe called with news today. Carson North, or as we know him, Flapjack, is in custody, so we won't have to worry about him anymore. They confiscated his laptop and discovered he's been cyber stalking Sue and Rikki for a long time. That's how he found out about Maverick Ranch."

"That creeps me out." Rikki rubbed her arms and her voice quivered. "We trusted him around all these children."

Sue's hand touched her cheek. "My lawyer thought Carson still had to be in prison. All she knew at the time was he tried to contest Grady's will."

"Since he couldn't legally do that, kidnapping Stu became his backup plan." Ethan stood in front of the window. "North outlined his strategy in great detail on his computer. I imagine he'll be spending the rest of his life behind bars."

"The ransom note North left in the truck used the term, we." Frank bit his lower lip. "I wonder if Campton was involved in the kidnapping too?"

Ethan shook his head. "There's no evidence to connect the two events. It appears North worked alone. Rowe explained how Brian had too many gambling debts he couldn't repay. The mob put out a contract on him."

Mob? Sue felt the blood drain from her face. Thoughts of what could've been, crept into her mind. How fortunate she'd been to break away from him before getting more deeply involved. God had been protecting her from the beginning. Even in Vermont.

Her mouth went dry. She escaped to the kitchen for a drink of water, and Stuart quickly joined her. She sat her glass on the counter and fell into his arms. "If Grady's selfishness hadn't sickened me like it did, I wouldn't have recognized the red flags with Brian."

"Grady meant evil against you, but God used your memory as a wall of protection." Stuart held her close. "I'm glad He used my jaw and ribs to be the hedge between you and Brian."

Sue giggled and took his hand. "Come on, it's time for us to lighten the atmosphere and share our plans."

Arm-in-arm they strolled to the living room. Stuart cleared his throat. "If I can have your undivided attention." He waited for the room to quiet. "I'll make this brief since we're all hungry. It's been forty-eight hours since I asked Sue to become my wife. Yes, folks, it finally happened, she wore me down. I couldn't be happier."

A squeal came from Carol. "That means you're going to be my Aunt Sooze."

"How wonderful!" Ethan went to the living room doorway. "Everyone in the room has been praying for this union, Uncle Stu."

Standing beside him, Ines tugged on his shirt. "The

food's getting cold."

"Thanks, Ines." Ethan put an arm on the cook's shoulder. "Frank, as our resident preacher, would you offer a prayer?"

"I'd be happy to." He bowed his head. "Thank You Heavenly Father, for the food and bringing each of us through the seasons of change. We've seen recovery from a stroke, several marriages, relocations, a death, the birth of a new child, and now the adoption of Lark and JJ. We're thankful for Stuart and Sue who were brought together by Your perfect orchestration and for keeping our family safe through a fire and kidnapping. Your love never ceases and every morning Your mercies are new. In Jesus' name we pray, amen."

The children stood in line at the buffet, filled their plates, then headed for the porch. The adults followed suit, then sat at the table.

Conversations buzzed all around Sue as she sat at the table between Stuart and Rikki. Her gaze settled a moment on each individual who had become dear to her heart, lingering a bit longer on Stuart's face. Then a lull settled over the room.

Rikki caught Sue's attention. "Until Frank's prayer, I didn't realize how much has happened to the family in the last couple of years."

"Thank goodness God had a plan all along. I'm grateful He brought me to Arizona." Sue grasped Stuart's hand and held it in the air. "Now, this handsome man and I are going to be married, and I'll become a part of this new family."

At that moment, JJ appeared by the buffet table with icing smeared on his face. With a huge grin, the small boy snatched one of Ines's chocolate chip cookies. "And I'm gettin' a new family too!"

"Yes, you are!" Sue chuckled as he grabbed another

cookie and climbed on Lou's lap.

Scooting his chair closer, Stuart draped an arm around Sue. Her head fit perfectly in the hollow between his shoulder and neck. Convinced God intended Stuart to be her sweetheart through the rest of her life, peace settled within her mended heart.

Book Club Discussion Questions

In what way did Grady hurt Sue the most? Why did she continue to stay with a man who was guilty of verbal, emotional, and physical abuse? What would you advise a friend to do who is in an abusive relationship that would keep them safe from ongoing harm?

What lessons did Sue and Stuart learn from their first marriages? How did the experiences continue to hurt them? How did they help?

Sue and Stuart were very compatible, so why didn't they want to fall in love? Have you ever struggled with a relationship where there was total compatibility with another person, but no spark? Or where you weren't compatible at all, but you fell for that person? Do you believe a relationship can work in the long term, when there's very little in common?

Sue was adamant about not wanting another relationship. Why did she relent to go out with Brian? Why did she continue to date him? What advice could you give a friend who decides to date for the wrong reasons?

Sue's loveless marriage to Grady left her emotionally exhausted. When she moved to Arizona, why did her friends encourage her to go out? Stuart wanted her to date for a different reason. What was it? Why did it bother him when she went out with Brian?

Some men, like Stuart, are natural nurturers. Why was

he so hesitant to hug the orphaned children at the ranch? Do you feel there's a Christian way to overcome this issue?

Sue refused Brian's proposal. Was her rejection because of racism as he suggested? If it had been, is there a way we can overcome racism in our own relationships, or keep it from developing?

Brian underestimated Sue and made many mistakes in their relationship. What was his biggest error? Why?

Stuart wrestled with his growing attraction to Sue. What happened to make him realize he couldn't live without her?

Sue and Stuart's families didn't object to them getting married in spite of the difference in their ages. Have you known couples whose ages are separated by 10 or even 20 years? What do you think can help keep a marriage strong, despite the age difference?

Author Note

Dear Reader,

The Call of Indian Summer is a story of second loves and second chances.

Our goal for Sue and Stuart's mature romance is to show that sometimes love has nothing to do with age. In this story, we watch the progression of their relationship as they battle a shared attraction. How could this be God's plan when society often frowns on May/December marriages? Their inner turmoil draws them closer to the Lord, which is where He wanted them to be, joined in faith.

People caught up in poor choices are often able to make their lives meaningful in spite of past mistakes. Stuart learns firsthand that being a Christian doesn't keep us from the consequences of an act of rebellion, nor does it mean we're failures. God meets us where we are, forgives when we ask, and guides us to a better path.

Throughout the story, Sue discovers by looking up we find faith, by looking forward we feel hope, and by loving, we give of ourselves and receive love in return.

We thank you for taking the journey with us through the Seasons of Change series. Our readers have willingly traveled from Powder Ridge, Vermont to Apache Pointe, Arizona, as well as island hopping on a Caribbean cruise. We hope you enjoy this final visit with the Drake family.

Writing the Seasons of Change series has been an absorbing journey. It has seemed less like authoring and more like re-routing thoughts and experiences through our fingers and keyboard.

The two of us have had a close friendship since

1989. Through sharing and praying, we discovered our goals as Christian wives and mothers were the same.

Our first adventure in the literary field was our church newsletter. From there we dabbled with a children's mystery, *The Bones of Mr. Jones*, which we squirreled away on floppy disks. Our next project was to create a storyline for a cozy mystery, *Reflections of a Stanger*. We were asked to become directors of the senior adult ministry of our church. This grew to three churches being involved. We used our writing abilities to create themed programs complete with song parodies, poems, and unique bulletin inserts. Several years later, we agreed to take on the Northern Indiana district directorship.

After retiring from the district position, we returned to sharpening our writing skills. This included attending writers' conferences, seminars, and joining a local writers' group.

As co-authors, we spend long hours on the phone together. This is when our minds morph into fictional scenes inhabited by a myriad of characters. Some nice, others not so nice.

Our characters deal with major changes as each of the stories progress. While writing this series, we found our personal lives altered as well. When we signed the contract with Mountain Brook Ink, Debbie never guessed that her husband wouldn't live to see the first book release. Her life turned upside down. A month later, her daughter moved several states away to take a new job. The Lord continues to draw Deb into a deeper relationship as she learns to lean on Him. (He can do that for you too.)

On a happier note, while writing *The Call of Indian Summer*, Linda became a grandmother for the seventh time. Her grandchildren range in age from twenty-two years down to one year. She daily gives God all the praise and glory for her loving husband and growing family.

We love to hear from our readers and are open to speaking at women's organizations, libraries, church groups, women's retreats, and banquets. Feel free to contact us at:

www.facebook.com/groups/Thebooknookoflindaanddeb
dulworthandhanna.wordpress.com
Amazon.com/author/lindahanna
Amazon.com/author/deborahdulworth

Linda and Debbie

9 781943 959662